The Fall of Billy Hitchings

Kirkus MacGowan

Diapers, Bookmarks, and Pipe Dreams
www.kirkusmacgowan.info

To my wife.
For believing in me enough to allow me to pound
away on the keyboard for hours at a time.

To my son.
For being my best friend and forcing me to be a good
example.

To my daughter.
For dancing just to make me smile.

The Fall of Billy Hitchings

Chapter 1

John

"Hey, Kelly. I'm on a job right now so I can't talk long." John sat in the backseat of the Trailblazer watching the dilapidated buildings pass by.

Shawn poked his head around the Malaysian diplomat and made kissing noises. He spoke in a high-pitch voice, "Ooh, John. Come back to bed, baby."

John put his hand over the cell phone. "Real funny. She already hates you guys. Keep it up."

"Who was that?" Kelly's muffled voice said from beneath his hand.

John pulled the phone back to his ear. "It's just Shawn. He's giddy because of the paycheck we're getting for this transport run."

Kalid, the diplomat, tapped away on his laptop, ignoring the banter around him.

"You want me to take a left up here, Shawn?" The driver pointed to the approaching road.

"Yeah. It'll take us through the old factory district. Probably save us like ten minutes."

"Anyway." John brought his attention back to Kelly. "What's going on?"

"Oh, nothing. We're on a lunch break. I thought I'd call to see how you're getting along without me."

"I'm fine. Just trying to keep busy until you're done down there."

"You know, I might not come home after Kentucky. If we're assigned another job, I'll have to go there next."

"I know. Just wishful thinking."

A sharp turn slid Kalid's computer onto John's lap. John slid it back. The man nodded his thanks and continued typing.

"You're not doing anything dangerous are you, John? I hate not knowing." Kelly's tone held the same nervous edge it always had when he was on a job.

"Nah. It's just a quick transfer." He and his three partners worked for Elite Bodyguarding. He'd worked with Shawn in the past, but the two in the front were new. Their job was to transport Kalid Abadi to the airport. More of a political nicety than a real job. "We should be done in like an hour. You want me to call then?"

She didn't respond for a moment. "John?"

"Yeah?" *I hate it when she says my name like that.* When his name came out like a question, she was about to say something he wouldn't like.

"I want you to quit. You have enough money. Why don't you just work with Joel full-time? You know Brenda would love that."

"Oh, come on, sweetheart." Brenda, his boss at Pearl Publishing, asked him at least once a week to sign a full-time contract. "You know me better than that. What would be the fun in working behind a desk all the time? A little danger is good for the soul."

"Not mine." She sighed into the phone. "Shouldn't you listen to your fiancée?"

"I always listen to you, Kelly. That's why I took this transport job. It's a safe one."

"Are you sure?"

Shawn made the kissing sounds again.

"Look, I really need to go. Can we talk about this later?"

"Holy shit. That guy's gonna hit us."

John raised his head in time to see a semi speed through a red light and slam into their Trailblazer, flipping them end over end. They slid to a stop upside down, a hundred feet further down the road.

The impact left John's ears ringing. He looked for the other passengers. Shawn was no longer in the backseat; the impact threw him from the vehicle. *Should have worn his seatbelt*, John thought as he found his own. The button clicked and he fell free, hands catching most of his weight as he crashed into the ceiling. The Malaysian diplomat crashed next to him a moment later. The two up front hung from their seatbelts, unmoving. John's cell sat next to him on the ceiling of the SUV, looking no worse for wear. He slid it into the front pocket of his jeans. *Kelly must be freaking out.*

The sound of Kalid's moaning and car doors closing came to John through the dissipating ring in his head.

"Kalid." The man made no response, too busy righting himself. He wouldn't be able to hear either. "Kalid!" John's ears popped. The squat old man jumped. "Are you able to move?"

"I believe my lower leg is broken. I am in very much pain." Kalid rubbed his shin.

"We need to—"

Gunfire interrupted John. Bullets pelted the blazer. He grabbed Kalid by his suit collar and jerked him toward the side closest to a building, away from the gunshots. He gave one last yank to remove Kalid's legs from the shattered vehicle when pain exploded in his side. A man in desert camo stood between the front end of the SUV and the rear of the semi, pointing a shotgun. John drew his Glock, focusing the sight between the shooter's eyes. He squeezed the trigger before the man pumped another round into John's ribcage. He collapsed into a heap.

A few inches higher and the slug would have missed John's body armor, piercing his ribcage and heart. Multiple ribs had to be broken. He gritted his teeth and shoved the Glock back into his ankle holster, freeing both hands. The shotgun must have been for Kalid. The shooter's friends still pelted the blazer with their AK47s.

The building behind them was an old paper mill with rusty steel walls, surrounded by barbed wire. John pulled

Kalid toward the door, keeping the blazer between them and the assailants.

John gave the heavy door a shove with his shoulder and it swung open. They were almost into the mill when a single round from an AK pierced John's thigh. He grunted and gave a final tug, falling into the room with Kalid on top of him. He rolled the diplomat onto the floor next to him and stood, using his good leg. He closed the door and latched the long locking mechanism easily into place. "At least one damn thing went right today."

Praying his cell phone still worked, John pulled it out and dialed Rachel.

"What did you say, John?" Kalid's eyes darted around the room. "I cannot hear. Will those men reach us in here? Were they after me? What is going on?"

John held up a hand. "Calm down, Kalid. Hold off on the questions until I get us out of this."

The man laughed. He actually had the nerve to laugh.

"Get us out of this? Are you kidding? What kind of bodyguard agency do you work for? Those men plowed over your vehicle like a child's toy, and all three of your partners are probably dead. Tell me, Mr. Reeves, how do you plan on getting us out of this?"

John dialed Rachel again, losing his signal for the third time.

Kalid shook his head. "And now your cheap phone doesn't even work. If we survive, everybody will know what a poor job your company does." He tried to stand again, but fell, clutching at his leg.

"It's not my company." John slid the phone back into his shirt pocket, barely containing the urge to throw it at the diplomat. "And shut the hell up. Would ya? It's hard enough to think without your sniveling. Now get up. We need to make it to higher ground."

"Why?"

John sighed and shook his head. "This is the last question I'll answer. The first reason is so I can get a better signal on my 'cheap' phone. The second is that if we don't, those men will come in and cut us down with their automatic weapons. So unless you want your wife to have Swiss cheese instead of a husband, get your ass up."

John hobbled to where Kalid lie clutching his leg and helped him up. They climbed the metal stairwell together, taking turns supporting the weight of the other.

They made it to the top of the stairs, crossed over a grated walkway, and entered a second room overlooking an open area with rusted machinery lining the floor.

John leaned against the wall for support and removed his body armor and t-shirt. He twisted the t-shirt into a tourniquet for his thigh. Blood soaked through before he finished tying the knot. He pulled the body armor back over his head.

"Are you okay, John?" Kalid's voice cracked. His eyes darted back and forth between John's eyes and the blood drenched pants.

"You want the truth? Or the political version?"

"The truth. Please."

"Have you ever heard the saying, 'we're up shit creek without a paddle'?" *Not to mention my fiancée is going to kill me… if I survive that is.* John tugged on his blood soaked pant leg to reveal a Glock. "Take the Glock. I can't bend that leg to get at it anyway."

"What will you use?" Kalid unlatched the ankle holster and hefted the weapon.

"What's with you and the questions?" John smiled and pulled up his other pant leg, uncovering another holstered Glock. "I like to be prepared."

Khalid turned the Glock in his hands. "How do I turn on the safety?"

"It's a Glock. No safety. The manufacturer must expect the owner to not pull the trigger unless they intend to."

The factory entrance rattled with gunfire and burst open. John held his finger to his lips, hoping the Malaysian man understood what it meant.

Kalid nodded.

They tottered to a doorway leading toward the rear of the factory. A round of bullets clanged against the metal grate under their feet. John dove on top of Kalid, which sent them both tumbling to the grated floor through the doorway. John pulled himself up and slid the thick metal door closed behind them, locking it into place.

"That's not going to hold long, Kalid. We need to move, and now." John pulled out his cell and hit redial.

Rachel answered. "Why do you keep calling and hanging up? I'm watching a movie with Katy."

"Hey, Rach. Good to hear your voice, too. Ah, can you tell your daughter you'll watch the movie later? I'm in a bit of a pinch."

She squeaked. "Oh, God. Hold on, John. I'll be right back."

Hurry up he wanted to yell. Saying he was in a pinch was code to tell her to drop whatever she's doing and get to her computer.

"Okay. Tell me what you need." Rachel's words came between heavy breaths, all business.

John and Kalid came to the end of the grated section and started down another stairway. He prayed he wouldn't lose his signal. He prayed a lot today.

"We're on the south eastern corner of Division and 92nd in an abandoned paper mill. We need a way out of here. Any way except the front door, that is." Through a break in the gunfire, he heard Rachel's fingers tapping at her keyboard.

"Okay, I have the schematics. Where are you located within the factory?"

"We entered on the north side, climbed one flight of stairs. I think we headed east for about thirty feet. We just passed the main floor of the factory. Now we're on this —"

She jumped in. "Can you see a stairway from where you're at?"

"We're on it."

"Okay. When you reach the bottom, take a right. On your right-hand side, there will be an elevator. Get there."

The tourniquet had worked its way loose. Blood ran from his thigh down his leg and into his shoe, each step squishing as if he walked on soft mud. Kalid leaned against the wall, his face turning paler by the minute.

"We're going to make it, Kalid. Hang in there."

"Who's on the phone?" the graying man asked.

"Rachel. Our savior."

John pulled Kalid's arm over his shoulder and staggered his way to the old freight elevator. They lifted the gate together and limped in. More shots rang out behind them. The men following were to the sliding door.

"Made it." John pulled on the gate handle.

Multiple footfalls pounded down the hallway. Kalid pressed the up button before the gate closed.

"Get to the third level," Rachel said. "There will be an exit leading to a fire escape. There are only three levels, so hopefully your dopey butt can find it."

That was a good sign. If Rachel thought it was a good time to joke, they probably had a chance. The elevator squealed into motion toward the third level.

"Sorry I pressed the button, I was a little anxious." Kalid smiled. "Wait. Do you hear that?"

John couldn't hear anything except for the grate of the elevator moving.

"Hear what?"

"I think I hear sirens."

"Good." John squeezed his eyes shut and pulled tight the tourniquet. He moaned. "Looks like it's our lucky day. Somebody must have seen our trashed vehicle and called the police. Damn Shawn for having us take the back way."

Bullets clanged off the metal elevator floor. John and Kalid fell back against the rear wall.

"Let's just hope nobody else brought a shotgun," John said.

Kalid's wide eyes never left the floor.

"Oh shit," John heard from Rachel.

He pulled the phone tight against his ear. "What do you mean, oh shit?"

"John, there was a fire on the third level. That's why the factory closed."

John looked to Kalid. "Hit the emergency stop button when we reach the top. "To Rachel he said, "Keep working, girl. There's always another way."

"I'm working on it. Just give me a sec."

"We don't have a sec, Rach."

"Got it. When you reach the third level you have to climb through the emergency hatch."

This is going to be fun with a bullet in the thigh.

Kalid hit the emergency stop button. A buzzer screamed. Bullets bounced off the bottom of the elevator. Lucky they used AK's and not something with more kick.

"Get down on all fours right here." John pointed to the middle of the elevator floor.

Kalid's brows popped up, but he nodded and did as instructed.

John used his good leg to stand on the man's back. He reached to the latch at the top of the elevator and pushed it open. He stepped back to the floor and clasped his hands together.

"Get up there." John nodded to the open hatch.

Kalid stepped into John's hands and pulled himself through the hatch. A moment later, he held his hand out through the hatch toward John.

"I'm an old man," Kalid said. "Take it easy on me."

John thought the man spryer than his fifty-something body let on. Standing on one leg, John jumped as high as he could manage. He caught Kalid's hand with one of his own and the lip of the hatch with the other. Waves of pain radiated from his broken ribs as he pulled himself through. There was enough light to see Rachel was right about the destroyed third level.

"Where to, sweetheart?" Knowing Rachel was on the other end of the phone always gave him some measure of composure. If anybody could get him out of this shit-hole he'd been dragged into, it was Rachel.

"You should see an air intake vent. It's large enough for you to crawl through. You better hurry. The third level is all but destroyed, but the stairwell might still be open."

In front of them was a vent three feet in diameter. Kalid jumped when John fired two rounds to open it. He gestured for Kalid to climb in and followed close behind.

"Tell me when you're in." Rachel's voice echoed in the elevator shaft.

"We're in."

"The duct should lead to another intake vent on the second floor. Take your first left."

John opened his mouth to tell Kalid to take a left when the vent shuttered and Kalid fell through the bottom. John's section gave way next. The air fled from his lungs when he landed. His broken ribs growled in protest. He crawled from the vent, now on the floor. Kalid sat against the wall, his forehead in his hands.

The sirens grew louder.

"What was that noise?" Rachel said.

"Oh, nothing big. Just me and the Malaysian diplomat falling through the ceiling."

"How far did you go before you fell?" John heard Rachel's frantic pounding at the keyboard.

"We were about to take the left turn you told us about."

"Good."

"What do you mean good?" John slid beside Kalid.

"You should be in a storage facility. From the schematics, it looks like the only way into the room, besides the entrance you just made, was through the third level. The ceiling collapsed in front of the door. There's no way for them to get to you without taking the elevator."

He hoped she was right. The room was almost black. The only light emanated from cracks around the door and John's phone.

"Just be careful and stay there, John. The police should be there within seconds. I contacted them the moment you called."

Good girl. "Thanks, sweetheart. I better hang up. I had Kelly on the phone when this whole thing started."

John retied the tourniquet, stemming the blood flow for the time being.

"Looks like we're going to sit tight for a few minutes," John said to Kalid. "And I better call the fiancée back."

The diplomat looked at him. "Sit tight? Here?"

"What did I tell you about the questions?"

Chapter 2

Billy

"Would you like that Billy sized?"

More like fat sized, Billy thought. Employees at Billy Borks Burger Palace were required to ask each customer if they wanted their meals Billy Sized, meaning larger portions. He enjoyed working the drive-through. Customers at the front counter tended to ask him if he was Billy Sized too because of his 6'5" frame.

Billy Borks hired him when he was sixteen and just over six foot tall. That was the last time Billy saw the owner. The old man, Billy Borks himself, passed away weeks later from a heart attack. *Probably Billy sized his meals too often*. After three years of growth, and having the customers ask him the same stupid questions every day, his patience wore thin.

Quitting sounded better every shift but Billy always found a reason to stay. Beer money, a new computer, or date money, if he could find someone to go out with him.

Without the annoying comments, the customer finished her order and pulled through. Billy spun the lock into place on the window and turned off the cubicle light. The girls laughed when he called it a cubicle. *Anything to make a girl smile*. Tuesday nights were slow, so he'd completed his closing work early. He grabbed his backpack from the coatroom and made his way to the back door, hand poised over the computer to clock out.

"Billy Hitchings," he heard behind him. His manager.

Billy's eyes went to the back door. *I wonder if I could make it out of here and pretend I didn't hear him.*

"Billy Hitchings?" the manager's nasally voice said again.

He turned away from his escape. "What's up, Bryan? I was just about to clock out."

"Remind me. What was your side-work tonight?"

"I had to sweep and mop the thirties. Why?"

"Table thirty-two had bubble-gum stuck to the bottom. You should know by now that it's your responsibility to check under the edge of the tables as well."

"Fine. I'll go pull the gum off the table." Billy started toward the front of the restaurant.

"No need." Bryan held a piece of blue gum in his fingers. "I've taken care of it for you."

Eww.

"Just remember this during your next shift. You will be required to have two side-work responsibilities."

What the heck happened to the guy to make him such a weenie? It was just Billy Borks, not the White House.

He clocked out and left through the back door. Bryan tapped his toe with his hands clasped behind his back watching, as if he expected Billy to steal something on his way out.

The lock on his Huffy clicked open with his key. He pulled the bike from the rack and climbed on, looking forward to the cool breeze. The thoughts about leaving his job lingered; he counted on the cool night air to ease his tension. *How much customer service can one person handle in a lifetime?*

The managers treated him well. They allowed days off when he requested most of the time. Bryan was the only one who bothered him, and only then, because he was the most anal-retentive person in the world. Most employees were close to Billy's age, which made for good fun. Cringing, he thought about Crazy Jenny. Doing without her pinched face and pug nose would do wonders for his soul. Smiling Sam made up for Jenny's psychotic episodes. He was the only one who could climb under her skin and stop her from being rude.

When Eric still worked at Billy Borks, he and Eric assigned nicknames to each new employee, helping them remember who was who. The names stuck. They were straightforward for the most part. Crazy Jenny was literally crazy, and Smiling Sam was always doing just that, smiling.

Many of his friends left Myrtle Beach to pursue a degree, and those who stayed attended the local community college. He could apply, but there were too many reasons not to. Taking care of Grams was his highest priority. She wouldn't make it without him. When his parents passed away five years before, she'd taken him in. He owed it to her to stay. The hip she broke when he was thirteen still ached when the weather was just right. If he moved out and she broke it again, he would feel horrible and come back anyway.

As he took a deep breath, salty ocean air filled his lungs. *Breathe in and hold six seconds, breathe out and hold two.*

At age fourteen without any aunts or uncles and his mother's parents having already passed, Grandma Mable had been his only option. She'd stayed home with him when his parents, and her husband, left for Wisconsin. She hated flying and had been recovering from her broken hip the year before. Now, here he was, living with Grandma Mable in the small home his Grandpa built forty years ago.

He pulled his bike into the garage and locked the door. The smell of lavender and roses threatened to overwhelm him when he opened the screen door to the kitchen. Abe must have stopped over.

Once a week, Abe Reyes came by and gave Grams a rose. "My intentions are as honest as can be, young man. I simply wish to share nature's beauty with another," he would say.

The thought of a cool shower cleared his mind. Removing the smell of grease and raw meat would ease his frayed nerves. At least he didn't work with Eric at The Waterbar, a higher-end establishment than the Burger

Palace. Their specialty was seafood. Reminding Eric to bathe before stopping over became a regular practice.

"Who's there?" Grams called from the living room.

"It's just me. What are you doing up so late?"

"What?"

He stepped into the living room. She sat in her brown leather recliner, knitting yet another blanket, doily, or sweater.

"Hey, Grams. What are you doing up so late?"

"Hey, kiddo. I'm listening to the scanner. A house fire over yonder on 5th has the whole neighborhood worked up. I wanted to make sure everyone was okay." She looked up from her work. "Did you get a haircut?"

"No."

"Well you should, it's not right that a boy has hair that long."

"It's not even long enough for a pony-tail." His grandpa had been a military man until the day he died. She was used to a buzz cut. "So is everybody okay?"

"Oh sure, sure." She waved her hand. "Everybody is fine, though they can't find their kitten."

"They said that on the scanner?"

"Oh, no. I called Janice. It's her neighbor's house on fire."

It amazed Billy how many people his grandma knew. But, she had lived in Myrtle Beach most of her life, and she was seventy-seven years old.

"You shouldn't be calling Janice so late. It's past midnight." Billy used his best fake stern voice.

"Is it? Oh dear, it is late, isn't it? I just get so into my creativity that I lose track of time. I think it's okay though. Janice didn't seem to mind. She and Earle were outside watching everything happen. By the way, I made some sweet tea for you. It's in the fridge if you would like some."

That was another fact Billy hadn't known about old people: they slept less the older they became. A friend at work said something about a chemical old people's bodies don't produce very well.

"I'm heading down to sleep. See you in the morning." He waved, turning toward the basement.

"I'm fixing to head off to bed soon, too." She lowered her head back to her work. "Did you eat some supper? You're looking a little scrawny these days."

He yelled back through doorway. "Yes, I ate supper. And I'm not scrawny, I'm lanky."

"What?"

"Good night, Grams." He promised himself to save enough money to buy the hearing aid she said she didn't need.

"Night, Kiddo. Love you," she called.

"Love you, too."

The dark wooden steps creaked as he descended the stairs to his room in the basement. He tossed his backpack next to the R2D2 trash can in the corner. The unmade bed begged him to succumb to his sleepiness. A cool shower called his name.

He peeled off his gaudy, cow-covered work shirt and tossed it onto a pile of dirty clothes. He poured the contents of his backpack onto the floor and placed his cell phone and nametag side by side on the corner of his computer desk where he'd be sure to find them for his next shift.

Releasing a heavy sigh, he collapsed into the recliner in front of his computer. Taking a shower sounded glorius, but now all he wanted was to crash from exhaustion. Working twelve hours at Billy Borks tired his spirit and mind out as much as his body. Leaving that place and chasing his dreams sounded better than ever.

Thoughts of leaving Billy Borks invaded his mind every night before he flipped on the computer. Once his fingers touched the keyboard, however, he'd be lost to the world. What could he do that would be more productive? He had no homework, no girlfriend to spend his time wooing, and Eric, his one real friend, closed a bar shift.

He pressed the power button on his computer, situated the keyboard on his lap, and was lost within seconds.

***

Billy's eyes jerked open. He stood in the middle of a humming city street, steam rose from the manholes, rain splashed on the pavement around him. Cars streamed by, some honking, some with drivers holding up their middle fingers. Headlights bore down from the left. He launched himself away from the oncoming traffic and collided with a trashcan, its contents poured onto the rain-slicked sidewalk.

He rolled to his back and peeled the empty ketchup packets and cigarette butts from his soaked Superman t-shirt. The glowing lights of the building in front of him soared hundreds of feet toward the rain-filled sky. He scrambled to his feet, staring.

He lowered his eyes and spun in a slow circle, admiring the city's grandeur. The bark of a hotdog vendor and the mixed aroma of onions and horseradish made his stomach growl. Everything looked familiar, as if he should remember where he was, but his thoughts would not form. Squinting toward the sky, he hoped to see the stars, but the rain, smog, and brilliant city lights polluted his view.

Hairs stood up on the back of his neck. Someone was following him. People pushed by, covering their heads with umbrellas or newspapers, shoulders hunched as if it would help. It looked like an ordinary night, but his pursuers were there, closing in. A sense of empowerment washed over him. He felt as if he could hurt them if he wanted to, but he couldn't remember how.

Turning away from the over-turned trashcan, he found the closest side street—85th according to the sign —and ran. He was supposed to be somewhere. His feet slapped the wet pavement, and clouds of breath poured from his chest.

The rich scent of soil stopped him. So many trees: red oak, American elm, silver linden, they took the place of the soaring skyscrapers that had surrounded him minutes ago. Farther away from the city he ran, down the paved sidewalks and under the illuminated street lamps.

Whoever, or whatever, followed him was still there, bearing down. They want what he has, but it is not theirs to take. Their urgency was as clear as if it were his own. Faster he ran, head swiveling as he tried to catch a glimpse of his pursuers. They were just out of sight. Something urged his eyes toward the cloudy sky. A memory tried to impose, something vital on the edge of consciousness. The thought faded.

The weight on his back swayed in rhythm with his footfalls. The backpack, it was important, its contents the answer to his elusive memory. He slid to a stop on the wet grass next to a field surrounded by park benches, a cement stage to the side. He slid the straps from his shoulders and gently placed the backpack on the muddy grass. He gave the zipper a soft tug. The bag fell open, the contents almost visible. Tilting his head back, he threw his arms in the air and began singing Figaro with a deep, passionate voice; the beautiful Italian words reverberated throughout the park.

***

"You never mentioned singing opera in your other dreams."

"Go ahead and laugh." Billy waved his hand. "I did."

The aging Dr. Flanagan sat back in his chair. He ran his hands over his thick gray hair. Suze, a friend of Grams's, suggested he see a psychiatrist to help with his insomnia. Intense and realistic dreams dominated what little sleep he had, and they had been increasing in frequency every week.

"I'm sorry, Billy." Flanagan smiled. "That wasn't very professional. I just know how much you hate opera. You complain at least once a week about your grandmother playing it."

It was Billy's turn to smile. Grams played it every chance she had.

"I'm guessing it had something to do with my alarm clock playing Pavarotti that morning."

"You set your alarm clock to opera?"

"Can you think of a better way to get me out of bed?"

Dr. Flanagan wasn't the stereotypical counselor type Billy saw in movies. His frame was slim, he didn't wear glasses, and he was nice. No suits or dark brown sweaters either. He was likely to wear khaki shorts and a purple vest, like today, as anything else.

Flanagan looked to his wristwatch. "We have only a few minutes left, but let's talk about what the dreams might mean. Have you given it any thought?"

"I did, but I can't figure anything out. I'm not good with symbolism." Every week, Dr. Flanagan asked him about the dreams. They were supposed to be symbolic of other things in his life.

"Let's start at the beginning, the part with the cars trying to run you down. Do you feel as if someone is out to get you? That someone is forcing their way into your path trying to stop you from accomplishing something?"

"Not really." Billy tapped his chin with his finger. The doctor waited for a response. "I guess I feel like Bryan gets on my case too much. He's my manager at Billy Borks. He singles me out, like he has some vendetta against me."

"Okay, good. Now, let's discuss the large buildings and trees. The way you described them, it sounded as if they loomed over you, kept you under their watchful eye. Can you think of something, or somebody, you feel looms over you? Maybe you feel they hold you back, keep you away from something?"

"Well, there's Grams, but—"

"I know this cannot be easy Billy, but you need to dig deep here. Every time we discuss one of your dreams, it could be the next step in your recovery. Let go, let your emotions free. You will not be in trouble here, Billy."

Most of the time Dr. Flanagan was cool, but sometimes psychology excited him too much. Billy half expected him to jump up and dance a jig.

"I sometimes wonder what my life would be like if my parents survived the plane crash. Like if we would still live in Maine, or… maybe I would have more friends. Not that I need more than what I have, but… I just wonder. You know?"

"We should keep that in mind for your next visit, your relationships with others. What about the singing at the end? Do you have any ideas?"

"None." Though it was the fifth time he'd had this particular dream, the singing was new.

Dr. Flanagan appeared perplexed, eyes squinted, and lips pursed. He ran his hands through his hair again. "Is there something you think needs to be said? Or something you want to say but feel like nobody will hear?"

"I don't think so. Usually when I want to say something, I say it. Maybe not when it comes to girls, but most of the time. Bryan yells at me for it, tells me to have more tact."

Flanagan glanced at his wristwatch again, a gaudy, golden-yellow thing. "Looks like it's time to go, Billy. Great session today." He rose, offering his hand. They shook, but Dr. Flanagan didn't let go. Instead, he leaned forward and spoke in a quiet voice. "I want you to think hard about that last part Billy. I think it's important." He smiled. "Take care."

The fifteen-minute bike ride home gave him time to think after his appointments. There were subtle changes in each dream, hidden until he wrote the dream down the next morning as Dr. Flanagan suggested.

Hundreds of blogs are dedicated to insomniacs, Insomni-bloggers being the best he'd found. People from all over the world left comments about their issues, their night terrors, and a myriad of reasons causing them to go without sleep. He hurried home to see if anybody responded to his post.

The insomnia had come and gone for years for Billy. But six months ago, it made a vigorous return. Bryan, his boss at Billy Borks, was on the verge of tossing him. If it weren't a fast-food restaurant, Bryan would have fired him weeks ago. The turnover rate was too high as it was. Coming in hours late, not minutes, pressed his luck. Even Bryan had standards.

A white Cadillac turned in front of him. Billy yanked on the handlebars and swerved, missing the back bumper by inches. He jumped the curb and raised his hand to flip them the bird, but there was the possibility it was one of Grams' many friends so he decided against the vulgar gesture.

The Strip, or The Grand Strand, is the main road following the beach, surrounded by colorful hotels and restaurants. Riding a bike down The Strip during Spring Break could be dangerous with the drunken college kids driving, but he preferred the route during the summer. Even if the old people in their white caddies only look for people on their bikes after they've hit them. The glimpses of the Atlantic between the hotels and restaurants soothed him, as did the fresh air tinged with salt.

He breathed in through his nose until his lungs were full, then counted to six. With a slow exhale, he released the air until his lungs were empty, and then counted to two. Three more times he repeated the relaxation exercise Dr. Flanagan taught him. The exercise didn't help with his insomnia, but it did relax him.

The humid summer heat pressed in on him, causing his blue jeans to stick to his legs. It wasn't the lack of sleep or the heat causing anxiety now; it was the anger at knowing he'd have to spend yet another day at his crappy job.

John

"What can I get ya, Johnny?"

"Three red-headed sluts, if you would, Teddy. I've had a rough couple of weeks." John pulled out his wallet.

"Three shots? Is Kelly in town?"

"Nah. She's still in Kentucky." He pointed to the table where his friend had the time of his life. Ashley bounced up and down on his lap laughing, while Joel wore a hefty grin. *Who wouldn't smile with Ashley on their lap?* "She's just a friend." Kind of a friend, anyway. She worked at the pastry shop across from their work and they bought lunch from her at least twice a week.

"Three red-headed sluts, coming up."

John leaned on the bar. The seven or eight pints of Guinness, or maybe it was nine, catching up to him. Forgetting about the three friends he lost in the Malaysian diplomat debacle three weeks earlier proved harder than he planned. The bartender slid three dark red shots across the bar. John handed him a twenty and headed toward his lucky friend.

"Three red-headed sluts, just the way you like 'em, Joel." John passed the drinks around the table.

"Why do you have to tease about the red hair?"

Ashley slammed her shot and then tussled Joel's moppy head of hair. "I think it's cute." She smiled flirtatiously.

"Cute? Guys don't want cute. It should be manly, or strong or something."

"Well, I think it's cute." Ashley kissed Joel on the cheek, leaving a dark smudge of lipstick before abandoning his lap for John's.

"Oh, that's not fair. Just because he's the one buying." Joel crossed his arms and jutted out his lower lip.

Ashley slid her arm around John's neck, her face so close that her eyelashes tickled his face.

"Not just because he's the one buying, because he's hot too." She wrapped her other arm around his neck.

Joel rolled his eyes. "I get cute hair and he gets hot. I can feel my ego shrinking by the second. What about Kelly?" Joel raised his eyebrows in a questioning glare.

John opened his mouth to answer but Ashley spoke first. "Kelly is in Kentucky. Isn't she, John?"

"She is." John slammed his own shot and grunted. "Besides, you know Kelly. She expects me to have a good time when I go out with my friends."

Ashley leaned in; her soft lips brushed his ear. "So do I."

Blood rushed to his face. He hoped they thought it was the alcohol's doing.

"In that case," Joel waved to a passing waitress, "let's have a good time then. If you would just quit your second job like Kelly wants, you wouldn't need to drink so much." The waitress stopped by their table. "Can I get six red-headed sluts please?"

"Six?" John's brows shot up. "Here we go, then." He turned and delivered Ashley a tight-lipped kiss on the mouth. It surprised them both. He hadn't meant to, it just seemed like the right thing to do.

They split the six shots three ways, and Joel ordered another round. Joel celebrated his raise, but John was the one that should be celebrating. A beautiful twenty-something woman sat on his lap, whispering bad things in his ear. Or good things depending on how one looked at it.

Ashley lifted herself from John's lap and straightened her shirt.

"Where you going, Ash?" Joel's words were slurred.

"The ladies room. Wanna come?"

Joel sat with his mouth hanging open until she laughed and glided toward the restrooms. He shook his head, coming out of his daze. "How do women do that?"

"Do what?" John held one of the dark red shots in each hand.

"Turn your insides to mush with so few words."

"I hear ya man, really do."

Joel scooted his chair closer to the table and leaned forward. "How's the leg feeling?"

John tossed back one of the shots and grumbled. "I've been shot before."

"I was serious when I said you should work for Brenda full time. Get away from being a bodyguard for a while. You won't get shot sitting at a desk."

"You know I can't do that. I need the action. It's who I am."

A pause.

"Protecting other people won't bring that kid back, John."

John's fist slammed down on the table. "Enough! I know it won't bring him back. If I can keep just one person from being hurt, it makes all the cuts, bruises, and bullet wounds worth it. Can't you understand that?"

"What I don't understand is why you have to do it over and over. You've saved like ten people in the last year. Shit, you saved me. I bet that guy never tries mugging somebody again."

John sighed and leaned back. "Not tonight, Joel. We're done talking about it."

"About what?" Ashley tossed herself onto John's lap.

John shook his head. Joel wouldn't say anything to anybody, he never did.

Joel smiled and pointed to the long scar running down his jaw. "About the time I got this."

"Now that is sexy." Ashley nuzzled her face closer to John's neck.

Two shots later, Joel stood, light-blue irises standing out against his bloodshot eyes and red cheeks. "Well lovebirds, I'm going to hit it. Teddy called a cab. Should be here by now."

"See you on Monday." John waved. Ashley worked her tongue on his earlobe.

Joel shook his head and laughed, heading toward the exit.

John closed his eyes, relishing Ashley's labor. "I think I should be going soon too. When that last round hits me, I probably won't be able to drive."

"Okay." Ashley leaned away from John. "You said you would give me a ride in your Charger some day anyway." She picked up her purse and stood beside him.

Impressive memory. It had to have been almost a month ago he told her he would give her a ride. She'd been serving him lunch at Webb's.

"I guess it couldn't hurt." He dropped a couple tens on the table and rose. Ashley wrapped her arm through his and pulled him toward the door. He only stumbled a couple times on their way to the back door; he should be okay to drive. The bar's floor shouldn't ripple anyway.

They stepped into the cool night air. The automatic locks clicked open on the Charger. Ashley climbed in the passenger seat.

"What are you doing, John?" he mumbled to himself. He shook his head. "It's okay. Ashley just needs a ride home, no big deal." He opened the door and climbed in, placing the keys in the ignition. "Where to?"

The words were still coming from his mouth when Ashley crawled over the gear shifter and onto his lap, legs straddling him, short white skirt raised dangerously high.

"You said you were going to give me a ride in your Charger, John. And that's what I expect."

***

John stared at the clock in the lower right corner of his computer monitor. Almost noon on Tuesday and

Kelly still hadn't called. Five days was the longest they'd gone without speaking in their three-year relationship, yet now they were on day eighteen.

"Reeves," a voice called from behind. "Reeves?" it called again. "John!"

He flinched and spun in his swivel chair. "Oh, hey. What's up, Joel?"

"You were zoning pretty good there, buddy. You need some coffee." His pudgy, red-haired friend pushed coffee like it was crack. "I can make more if you need some." He raised his eyebrows.

"Nah, I'm good. What's up?"

"Are you done with the Noonan project? I'd like to take a look at it this weekend."

Joel worked himself up when deadlines approached.

"No worries. I'll have it on your desk by five."

"Perfect." Joel turned toward his desk and quickly spun back. "Hey, zombie boy. Before you zone out again, are you going down to Charlie's tonight? It's dollar draft night."

"I'll have to let you know. I'm not feeling well."

He flirted with Ashley during their lunch outings, as did any man in Webb's. Her long muscular legs, lustrous brown hair, and alluring smile saw to that. The way that tight pastry shop outfit clung to her body was unfair.

Who invited her to Charlie's that night? Joel swore it wasn't him. Maybe she overheard their drinking plans during lunch.

The clock read, 12:03.

Ashley was a firecracker in bed, but his relationship with Kelly meant more than a one-night stand. *Then why did I do it?* He tore himself up since, searching for the answer. Kelly was just as ravishing, more so because of her carefree spirit. Drinking beer on the porch and playing cards was as fun to her as shopping to other women.

The morning after their rendezvous, he'd driven Ashley home and called Kelly. When her machine picked up, he left a vague message, not wanting her to learn about his infidelity from a machine. When she called, he told her everything. Where he went, whom he was with, and how the night ended.

She didn't sob, didn't cuss, or call him names. She didn't even sound upset. She just whispered, "Why?" The same question he wrestled with now. Well, he knew why he did it, why all men do it, but that wasn't what she meant. They'd been so happy. They were a thousand miles apart for work, but that was no excuse, and it had only been a few weeks.

He turned off his computer and packed his briefcase. No use staying at work if he wasn't accomplishing anything. The job at Pearl Publishing was only a part time gig; his boss Brenda gave him a lot of leeway.

Joel spun in his chair. "What's up, Johnny? Taking lunch? Hold on a second, I'll go with you."

"No lunch, Joel. I'm calling it a day." Joel was too good of a friend to leave hanging. He would call him later.

"Damn. You must be sick. Have you taken a sick day since you've been here?"

"No. I'll e-mail you the Noonan project." He walked toward the elevator.

"Call me about Charlie's," Joel yelled after him.

Not tonight, he thought. *I have more important things to attend to.*

As he was leaving the building, he glanced at Webb's His stomach rolled. *Stop dwelling on the problem. Focus only on the solution*, his dad would have said.

Pulling out his cell phone, he dialed Brenda Dobos. It rang twice then went to her voicemail.

"Hey, Brenda. This is John Reeves. I feel a little under the weather. I hope you don't mind, but I'm heading to the doctor. I'll get back to you when I know what's going on." Brenda wouldn't mind if one of her 150 employees took the day off. Working for a large publishing company had benefits.

The parking garage elevator opened. He stepped in and dialed Kelly.

"There isn't anything else that needs to be said," she said. "We are done, no matter the reason. Please stop calling me." It was the first time she'd answered since the morning he confessed to his tryst with Ashley.

"Wait, please just hold on."

She sighed.

At least she didn't hang up. "Okay, I know I made a mistake, the biggest mistake you can make in a relationship, but I don't want this to end. I understand you being upset—"

"You understand? If you understand how I feel, then you wouldn't have cheated. End of story. I'm hanging up."

"You're right, you're right. I couldn't possibly understand, and that's the problem. *I* don't even understand." *Keep talking.* He had to keep her on the phone. "You know I cheated on past girlfriends, but it never mattered before, not like this. I knew it was time to move on when I cheated, but this time is different. I didn't even want to cheat. When I did, I realized how much you mean to me."

Holding back sobs, her voice raised two octaves. "It's okay, John. We're done. We had a great time, but it's obvious things aren't right between us. I will always be your friend, but I need a break from you right now, a break from you being a bodyguard. You're not ready to settle down. That's not who you are, at least not yet."

He told her as much when they began dating, a warning to keep her at a distance. Later, he'd been the one suggesting a more serious relationship. "But—".

She cut him off. "I'm okay with that, it was just wishful thinking. I'm okay with moving on. I'm hanging up now, John. I'll call you when I've had time to think."

"Wait! Kelly!" This wasn't the way the conversation was supposed to go. His words were frantic, and it pissed him off. His father taught him to keep tighter control of his emotions. "I'll come down there. Wasn't it Moosehead...Morehead! I'll be in Morehead tomorrow."

"I'm not in Morehead anymore, and don't come looking for me. I told you, I'll call you when I'm ready."

Click.

Standing next to his Charger, the reflection in the driver-side window showed a man with messy, dark brown hair. Two days worth of stubble shadowed his face and dark rings circled his eyes. He looked as haggard as he felt. He raised his arm to throw his cell phone at the pavement and stopped, an idea formed. No way was he giving up that easy. He dialed another number.

"Hello. Tom Jarrett's office, how may I help you?"

Amfar

Amfar Ditpra graduated from the University of Michigan at the top of his class. Three months later, he's someone's delivery boy. Tom Jarrett might be the top American archaeologist, world-renowned anthropologist, and recent best-selling author, but Amfar questioned his decision to sign on with a man whose ego was as vast as the Himalayas.

His father used to lecture him about how questioning his place in the world would hold him back. "Your thoughts should center on the whole, not the individual," he would say. Gurdrik Ditpra practiced internal medicine at Sagar Dutta Hospital in India. His sole purpose, be the best in his field, regardless of what he said about teamwork and being part of a whole.

"What do you think is in the chest?" Kelly broke him out of his thoughts.

Kelly Pierce, a fellow archaeologist, looked at Amfar from under raised eyebrows. Kelly was a pleasant enough woman, but why would Jarrett send two employees with exemplary records on a trivial task?

"I am not sure. I really did not have a good look at what they removed from the cave. From what I've read of the area, it is probably something with the Cherokee tribes. Most likely pottery or cookware. "

They sped down the freeway toward South Carolina in Amfar's Prius, a graduation gift from his father. Jarrett's instructions were to drive to Myrtle Beach and deliver the mysterious chest to a friend where further studies would take place. Find a hotel, and await further instructions.

Kelly gazed through the pounding rain, her face pinched in concentration. "Jarrett's men laughed when they put the chest in the car, talking about a dinner set. Of course, they might not have been talking about the chest." She shrugged.

Jarrett had called Amfar to his hotel room at midnight and went on at great length about how important the trip was.

"Take a seat, Amfar." He had pointed to a flimsy chair in front of his desk.

Amfar planted himself in front of his boss, feeling like a child on display for breaking the rules.

"I know it's late, not to mention hot as a witch's tit, so I'll keep this short and sweet." Jarrett leaned forward on the desk. His overabundant arm hair glistened with sweat. "Tomorrow, you and Kelly will drive to Myrtle Beach and deliver our find to a friend of mine."

Not 'would you please,' or 'I would appreciate it if,' but 'you will.' Jarrett left no room for questions.

"Sure, Mr. Jarrett. What are we transporting if you do not mind me asking?"

The hairy man had leaned back against the wall, crossing his arms. "I do mind you asking. You don't need to know specifics." He paced back and forth behind his desk, eyes far off, focused on something that wasn't there. "Let's just say they have the potential to be an important find."

Jarrett walked around the desk and stepped behind Amfar. His raucous laugh filled the small office.

"Oh calm down, Ammy." Jarrett slapped him on the shoulder. "You look like someone just killed your puppy.

Just do as I say. Take Kelly with you, and everything will be fine. I trust you, and I need someone I can trust."

He hated the name Ammy. His mother could call him by any name she wished; she had raised him. Nevertheless, the man was his boss. Upsetting him could cost Amfar his job. Jarrett may be brash and rude, but he was a paragon in the field of archaeology.

Amfar had agreed and here they were. At least they weren't standing outside the caves handing out bottled water as they were the last two weeks. Mindless work was not what he had in mind when he applied to college. Quiet brooding was what he wanted now.

Kelly focused on the heavy rain. She hunched her shoulders and her short brown hair waved gently in the air-conditioned breeze. What could he say to put her at ease and subdue his guilt for being grumpy?

"What do you think of the weather?" *What an idiot*, he thought. *It's a downpour, and you ask her about the weather?* Americans began the majority of their conversations with a mention of the weather his father had said, but not when a deluge of water fell around them.

Eyebrows arched, she looked at him. A smile came to her face. "The weather is beautiful, Amfar."

Understanding females was beyond him. In the three weeks they worked together in Morehead, Kelly baffled him more than any woman he had ever met. When she stepped on a butterfly her first day, she'd sobbed. He had mentally prepared himself for the emotional roller coaster sure to come, but it never happened. The next day, she laughed and joked with the other employees. Maybe she'd had a lousy day.

They guessed at the contents of the mysterious chest in the trunk for the next hour. The weather comment, no matter how off it had been, did the job. Then there was the embarrassing call from her ex-fiancée, John. After which, she cried for a half hour while sharing details about their break-up.

"Enough about John." Kelly dried her eyes with a tissue. "What do you want to do while we wait for Jarrett's friend to finish with the chest?"

"To be honest, I haven't really thought about it." Concentrating his anger on Jarrett caused him to forget they would have at least a few days to themselves until the completion of the research.

"I want to soak up some rays. Maybe get rid of some of these tan lines from working in Kentucky." She wiped at a lingering tear under her eye. "Oh come on, Amfar. Did you at least bring a book?"

"Actually, I did. The one I bought from the bookstore next to our motel."

"The one by Sheriff Scott?"

Amfar nodded.

"Only you would bring a history book on vacation."

"At this point, anything is better than being in Morehead. I guess I am just happy to have a break from work." *And the embarrassing menial tasks Tom Jarrett finds for us.*

Chapter 3

Amfar

They arrived in Myrtle Beach a few hours after midnight. Amfar promised he'd wake Kelly when they were fifteen minutes away. The muscles in her shoulder twitched when he poked her. She sat up, eyes wide, and unlatched her seatbelt. She slid to the edge of her seat and began bouncing.

"I think there is a welcome center ahead. There should be a restroom."

She paused. "I don't have to pee, silly. I'm excited to be in Myrtle Beach." She resumed bouncing. "Hey, turn right at the next road" She pointed in the direction she wanted to go.

The sign indicated *Downtown Myrtle Beach* was in that direction.

"According to the GPS, we need to stay on this road for another twenty-two miles before turning."

"I know what the GPS says, but I say we go this way." She hit him with the rolled up map. "Come on, it'll be fun. We can drive down the Grand Strand."

"The Grand Strand?"

"You don't know what the Grand Strand is?" She rolled her eyes.

He shook his head.

"That's what they call the main drag through downtown where all the big hotels, bars, and restaurants are for the tourists."

He slowed and made the turn, though he wasn't sure why. One of his father's lessons was to take care around beautiful women, or else, he'd find himself participating in affairs logic said he should not.

She just wants to see downtown, he told himself. *This does not have anything to do with logic*. Maybe this was how it began. Once you volunteered for trivial favors, they moved on to bigger and possibly more expensive favors. He forced the negative thoughts from his head. He would not think of Kelly as petty. She was excited to be in a new and beautiful place, especially the beach, and wanted to see it all.

"I thought you said you have never been to Myrtle Beach?" He rubbed at his eyes with the back of his hand.

"I haven't." She leaned against the seat, smiling. "What I have been to is Spring Break, and this is a huge spring break location. Do you need some coffee?"

"No, thank you. I will be fine. What do you mean Spring Break? What does the beach have to do with Spring Break?"

Kelly giggled. "While you spent your vacations studying, regular students used Spring Break for what it was meant for, taking a break." She paused. "Not necessarily taking a break in the normal sense, but a break from the rigors of school, and life. Tons of college kids go on vacation to a big party beach like this one. They spend the week partying, hanging out on the beach, and drinking too much."

"But why?" He shook his head. "It is a whole week to forge ahead with class work. Why spend it tiring out their minds and bodies?"

They were on the Grand Strand now. Kelly elaborated on the Spring Break subject, the whole time staring wide-eyed at the massive hotels, bright lights, palm trees, and beach. Though the late night made seeing the beach difficult, shining lights from the hotels lit small areas of caramel colored sand.

"Yes, it tires out the mind, and definitely the body, but it's good for the spirit. It allows the students a release from thinking about anything except their next drink. And don't look at me that way."

The shock of hearing a co-worker speak about partying and drinking alcohol must have shown. Amfar focused on using a calm voice. "What way is that?"

"I know what you're thinking. You're surprised Kelly the 'goody-goody' would spend a week partying with thousands of other students at the beach. First of all," she held a finger in front of him, "I'm not as perfect as you may think." She sighed. "I actually didn't party much. I'd spend a lot of time on the beach, usually reading. I drank just enough to relax, and then drifted off to whatever world my book held for me. Friends teased, but when we came back, I had a better tan and a calmed mind."

Amfar pictured her on the beach reading a book with a bunch of college kids drinking and running around. She ignored them and pushed the small wooden umbrella out of the way to take a sip of her margarita.

"I understand better now." Amfar nodded his head slowly. "At least from your perspective, it sounds very... intriguing. Maybe we can spend some time reading on the beach while we sip margaritas."

"I never said anything about margaritas." She poked her head out of the window to gaze at another hotel, this one the shape of a giant "H."

The dark saved him. He would not have to explain why his face flushed when he realized he mentioned part of his daydream about her.

"Okay, let's stay in that big blue one back there, the Starglazer I think it was called." She pointed behind them.

"Big blue one? You want to stay on the beach?"

"Sure, it looks nice. The welcome sign said they have a sauna."

"Don't you think Mr. Jarrett will be upset if we stay in an upscale hotel?"

Kelly smiled. "They're only expensive in the spring. It's the end of summer. Prices are cheaper this time of year."

He moved to the United States six years before, yet learned more about American culture all the time. Maybe Kelly was right to tease him about being sheltered.

They turned around in a dirt parking lot in front of a restaurant with blue brick walls called The Breakfast Nook.

The name of the hotel Kelly picked was Starglazer. When asked what a starglazer was, Kelly shrugged and said it sounded like a donut.

Kelly ensured their rented rooms were side by side on the ground floor. She wanted to be able to walk to the beach from their back door. The rooms smelled of bleach and had few decorations. Kelly explained it was so the college kids had less to break or steal when they vacationed. A television sat in the living area, and another in the bedroom. The only rooms side by side on the ground floor held king-size beds. Amfar decided he would enjoy the mini work vacation, the bed included.

It was late, but he savored a long, hot shower. He toweled off, ready to try the king-size bed. The free cable intrigued him, but he passed on the television idea in favor of relaxing a few minutes before turning out the lights.

The phone ringing woke him up. He sat up and slapped the alarm clock to the floor. The phone rang again, bringing him most of the way out of his stupor.

"Dr. Amfar Ditpra," he mumbled into the phone.

"Do you always have to be so formal?"

"Hi, Kelly, you surprised me. You're lucky I didn't knock the alarm clock through the wall at you."

"Was that a joke, Amfar? Boy, you're coming along, aren't you? Anyway, I just called to say thanks for the wonderful road trip and for listening to me babble about my ex."

"No need to say thanks, I had fun as well. And you were not really babbling. You had some important things to discuss, and I just happened to be in the car with you.

John didn't know how lucky he was." He paused; he hadn't meant to say the last part.

"Regardless, thank you very much."

"I'm sorry, Kelly. I did not mean anything by that, I just meant that you are a great person... I mean a great employee, a good person to have... to work with—" His mind reeled. The words wouldn't form the way he wished.

"Now who's babbling?" Kelly chuckled.

Amfar tried to speak but sputtered instead.

"I'm just teasing, Ammy. Have a good night. I'll see you in the morning."

His heart pounded and sweat dampened his forehead. Why did he let a woman have this effect on him? Was he in grade school again? He made a promise to himself to be more attentive to his feelings. No need to let a childish crush get in the way of being professional.

A crush?

He hadn't realized it was a crush. He would ask for a transfer to another jobsite when he and Kelly finished in Myrtle Beach. Working with someone he might have feelings for was not a good idea. It would compromise his ability to produce results. Tonight's behavior called for an apology in the morning.

For the first time in years, he could not fall asleep. His mind swam with thoughts of Tom Jarrett, the road trip, the mystery in the trunk. Most of all, he thought about Kelly Pierce.

Billy

A paper cup bounced off the back of Billy's head. He picked it up and turned to find Crazy Jenny wearing a devious grin.

"Hey, butthead. Your friend that smells like the friendly neighborhood tuna is waiting for you up front. Bryan's pissed about him loitering."

She'd probably been the one complaining to Brian. *Why would Bryan hire someone so grumpy?*

Crazy Jenny stalked back to the drive-through window. Her goal in life was to be a constant thorn in Billy's side.

Billy rolled plastic ware into paper napkins, the last side-work for the night. "What do you think? Are you coming tonight?" He glanced at Smiling Sam standing at the grill. Eric's friend, Jessica from the *The Waterbar*, was having people over. The parties at her apartment were always fun, though her brother Ian and his roommate had a knack for inviting unruly friends.

Sam showed Billy his large white teeth in a partial smile and flipped greasy burgers without looking. He tossed the spatula on the counter and pulled a towel from his apron to wipe sweat from his face.

"Nah, man, I have to close tonight. Benny went home; it's just me. Plus, Bryan wants me to open tomorrow." Even when Sam worked the dreaded close-open shift, he maintained that smile on his face. He always smiled; he loved life. Since coming to America and gaining his citizenship, he put on more than a hundred pounds and showed no signs of stopping. At least he's happy.

Billy finished rolling the silverware and clocked out before meeting Eric in the dining room. Jenny was right; Eric smelled like fish.

They hurried back to Billy's house to clean up. They had a system worked out for party preparation when pressed for time, and tonight they were a half-hour behind schedule. Everybody would be drunk before Eric and Billy showed up.

Eric spent most of the time primping. Billy teased him whenever he had the chance. Even a perfectionist shouldn't take that long to groom one inch of hair. No matter how much he teased, in the end, Eric would get the girl. He may not keep her, but he was usually the first one to kiss her, hold her hand, or sometimes go farther.

Eric drove his whining blue Ford Taurus toward Jessica's apartment complex. Rust particles danced in the air as the wind rushed by Billy's window. Eric was protective of his car, even if it was worth little more than the bike Billy rode. Billy just hoped the rumbling exhaust hadn't woke up Grams when they left.

"Did Jessica get us any beer?" He looked at Eric hopefully.

Eric nodded. "Yeah, I told her we'd pay her back when we get there. Is Sam coming? She got him some too."

"No, he has to open tomorrow. Great, now I'm going to have to pay for his Corona. I always get stuck with that crap."

Eric parked in a side-lot. He was probably worried about keeping the rust bucket away from the kid nicknamed Bull. The nickname came from him charging a car like a bull. The car won the fight.

Empty beer cans littered the small yard and the crowd spilled onto the sidewalk. "Oh, good." Eric pointed to the edge of the house. "Jessica is right there, we don't have to search for her to get the beer." He ran toward Jessica on the outskirts of the crowd, where she chatted with Ian and some friends.

Billy acted cool; he didn't run. Instead, he sauntered toward them, forcing a relaxed smile on his face, and an arrogance to his gait. In a magazine written just for men, he'd read an article that said this is how he should act if he wanted people to think he was interesting. He thought he was interesting, but anything he could do to help the look was worth it.

He was only able to give Jessica a half-wave before Eric grabbed him, pulling him toward the apartment.

"What's going on? Is the beer inside?"

Eric held tight to Billy's jacket, pulling him through the tight crowd, bumping into people as they went. "She put it in the fridge. Sam is in the kitchen too. I thought you said he wasn't coming?"

"He said he wasn't. He must have skipped out on a shower. I just hope nobody, including Sam, took any of our beer. Some people out there look pretty wasted already; it wouldn't take much for them to sample ours."

They reached the apartment door, and Eric let go of Billy, pushing his way into the crowd. He turned and yelled over the din. "I'll meet you by the fridge!"

Billy gave him a thumbs up and worked his way in the direction of the kitchen.

The crowded, smoke-filled living room made it hard to breathe. So many people smoking in such an enclosed area didn't allow the smoke to dissipate. Billy kept his hands up so the girls, or guys, didn't think he copped a feel. Every now and then, a friend would poke their face through the crowd, yell an excited hello, and go back to another swig of whatever alcoholic beverage they drank.

A few feet from the kitchen, Billy heard Eric yelling. He nudged his way through a few more people, keeping an eye in the direction of his friend. He stopped when he saw Bull at the kitchen table, smiling up at Eric and sipping on a Corona. Eric shared a few more obscenities, reached down, and grabbed a brown paper bag from the table.

Bull lost the smile, a scowl replacing it. He slammed his bottle on the table, knocking over others. He rose, eyes never leaving Eric's face. Bull's friends at the table were right behind him. They caught his arms and held him in place. Billy couldn't hear what they said, but he didn't care. He just wanted to get out of there. Eric tucked the bag under his arm and started toward Billy.

"You psycho, what the hell did you do that for!" Billy yelled when Eric was close enough to hear him. Eric actually smiled. Smiled. Who smiled when a crazy like Bull had been two seconds from creaming him? If Bull were a cartoon, steam would have poured from his nostrils. "Why are you smiling?"

No answer. Eric grabbed Billy's shoulder, pulling him toward the front door. It took them almost ten minutes to work their way through the crowd and back outside.

Eric pulled Billy behind a butterfly bush. "He took Sam's beer. I had to do something. If I just stood there, he'd do it again next time. I don't care about the beer; I just don't want to be seen as a pushover or a wimp."

"You may not be a pushover, but you might be a plowover. If that guy decides he wants the Corona back, he'll bull rush you like he did that car. I'm fairly sure your gut won't hold up as well as the steel door."

"Don't you understand, Billy? If we let him push us around, he'll keep doing it. It won't be a one-time thing. You want people looking at us like we're gutless?" A smile came to his face. "Why are we talking about this right now? We have warm Corona to drink."

Their friendship was more important than letting some muscle-ridden jerk push them around. The kitchen squabble would be worth it in the long run even if Bull came after them... he hoped. Besides, he could run faster than Eric.

"You're right. Thanks for putting me in my place." Billy put his arm around Eric's shoulder, urging him back toward their friends. "Let's not hang around to find out how mad he is." They reached Jessica and her brother. Billy began to say hi again when he took a palm to the chest and stumbled back a few feet. Bull. He took a few more steps back.

"Hey, Ian. Some piece of shit just stole my beer." Bull looked much larger up close than he had seated at the kitchen table. As tall as Billy, but more stout.

"I thought you didn't bring any beer." Ian thumped Bull in the shoulder with a fist.

"I didn't, but you said I could have the beer in the fridge."

Eric put his hand on Bull's shoulder. "See? This is just a misunderstanding. I apologize for saying those things inside. I thought you took the beer without asking."

"No worries," Ian said at the same time Bull's two meaty fists thudded into Eric's chest, sitting him on the ground.

Billy pulled him up, aware that nobody smiled anymore. "What's your problem, man?" Billy had to hold Eric back.

Jessica squeezed between them. She looked like a child in front of Bull. "Listen to me, you moron." She poked Bull's chest. "This is my party, and I don't care if you're Ian's friend, you need to leave. Now." She pointed toward the parking lot.

Bull put his hand over her face and shoved. Her feet came up in the air before she landed on her back. Her head smashed the pavement with a resounding crack. Bull pushed Billy out of the way with an effortless shove to the chest, grabbed Eric by the shoulders, and shook.

Time slowed. Jessica pulled herself up from the ground, and Eric's head snapped back and forth as if he weighed no more than a child. Ian and everybody else stared. People close to them backed up.

Billy's anger rose, tightly controlled, but yearning to explode. He closed his eyes, the decision made. This guy pushed a girl to the pavement hard enough that Billy heard her head smack the cement. This was the right thing to do. *The right thing*, he repeated to himself.

His eyes opened. He concentrated on the right side of Bull's jaw, the striated muscle bulging beneath the skin as he shook Eric. Billy's right hand curled into a solid fist as he coiled his arm back, ready to release like a spring. Never having been in a fight, he hoped his long arms made up for the lack of muscle.

He threw his fist at the large man's face like a bullet, his body responded as if he'd fought for years. He could not miss. Billy's fist traveled through the air toward its target, inching closer. The fist flew right by Bull's jaw and plowed into Jessica's forehead. Time sped up, hitting him like a wave. Jessica's knees buckled as she crumpled to the ground for the second time that night.

Bull stopped shaking Eric and turned his ruthless stare toward Billy. His eyes revealed a sadistic intent. Billy now understood why people lost control of their bodily functions in high stress situations. He didn't do so himself, but he was close.

Chapter 4

Amfar

Amfar woke to John Lennon telling him to "Imagine All the People." Hearing Lennon's soft voice was a delightful way to wake up, another vacation pleasantry. At home or the hotel in Morehead, he set his alarm to an annoying honk.

Rolling from the massive bed, he slid his feet into his slippers. He shuffled to the window and pulled the flowery curtains aside. Sunshine glared from the Atlantic into the room. The intense beauty caught him off guard. Seagulls floated on the soft breeze, and the fresh air infused with salt blew through the window enhancing the morning's perfection.

Amfar pulled on his fish patterned black and green swimming trunks. He stepped to the veranda. The steel guardrail was the only obstacle between him and the seashore. The dazzling sun straddled the horizon. He squinted to take it all in. The roll of the crisp water on sand held a steady beat. The morning was cool, and the gentle breeze gave him goose bumps. Someday, he would own a house on the beach. If not on, then somewhere close. The few seconds watching the sun's rays dance on the water refreshed him more than any morning shower or cup of coffee.

Movement to his right drew his attention from one morning beauty to another. Kelly sipped from one of the hotel's coffee cups. She faced the water, eyes unmoving, much as he must have been moments before. She wore a gray and blue striped pajama top and pants. Her hair was wet as if she just climbed from the shower. She leaned back in an Adirondack chair, her bare feet resting on the railing. The look of pure contentment added to her beauty. Not in the way a runway model is beautiful. But the way the sun reflected on the water, the way the waves and easy breeze fit together. She was in her element, she looked right. He saw in her something deeper, something profound. It was as if she had let him into her inner sanctum, allowing him to see into the depths of her soul. The apologies he'd rehearsed before going to bed disappeared from his mind. Kelly slowly raised the steaming cup to her lips and sipped again. Never taking her eyes from the water, she waved him over. He climbed the sturdy railing to her side.

"Coffee is on the table just inside the door if you want some." Her voice was just above a whisper.

He poured himself a cup and sat next to her, surprised at the chairs remarkable comfort. They sat in their padded wood chairs, sipping coffee and listening to the waves lap at the shore. The sun climbed above the horizon. He couldn't help glancing at Kelly every few seconds. Maybe he would not have to stop working with her. After all, they were both adults. Regardless of how she felt for him, he could keep it professional.

The moment was so perfect an artist could not have painted it more so.

She finally smiled and looked to him. "What do you think?"

That you're the most beautiful part of this beach. He caught himself before the words escaped his lips. So much for the promise to be more aware of his emotions. "I was trying to figure out how this morning could be more perfect. Then I saw you over here freshly showered, sipping on coffee. I have to admit, I'm a bit jealous."

"I've had practice preparing for sunrise. This was always my favorite part of Spring Break. I was too tired to take a shower last night so I set my alarm early." She looked back toward the Atlantic.

The sun was well into the clear sky when she breathed a heavy sigh. "I guess it's time to come back to reality. What was the name of the lab again?"

"Jackson Incorporated. No more than a fifteen minute drive from here."

"Good. I want to drop off the chest before we go to breakfast, and get the work stuff out of the way so we can enjoy our stay."

"We're going to breakfast?" Amfar hoped Kelly hadn't heard the surprise in his voice.

"Didn't you see all the pancake shops around last night? I saw at least five giant signs in the shape of breakfast food. There was a Pancake Palace a few miles back the way we came. And there was that Breakfast Nook place we turned around in last night. We have all sorts of choices. No reason to limit ourselves to the continental."

His empty coffee cup wobbled when he set it on the table. He climbed back to his side of the veranda. He hated for the moment to end. Kelly was right, though, it was time to come back to reality. The paperwork needed to be prepared before driving to the lab; and he needed a few minutes for the fog of emotions covering his brain to dissipate.

Billy

Billy passed the joint to Eric, cautious not to drop the little they had left. Coughing, he released the pungent smoke from his lungs and leaned back on his hands on the picnic table, peering out over the obsidian ocean speckled with the reflection of the night stars. Did the stars and planets hold other life forms? Were there other places like Earth? Places other than here? Was sitting on the beach and smoking weed all there was to life? Not that he minded.

"I still can't believe you popped Jessica the other night," Eric said.

Neither smiled. It was a night they both wished to forget.

"I told you it was an accident. Should I have let him get away with shoving her down? My conscience wouldn't let me. I had to do something."

"And that you did." Eric took a quick puff.

"I'm just happy she's okay. I would feel horrible if I'd permanently scarred her or something. Why does it feel like every time I try to do the right thing, I get into more trouble? Just once, I want to make a difference and not have it blow up in my face." He grabbed the joint from Eric and took a hard, long hit. He thrust it back when his lungs filled.

"Kind of like the time in ninth grade when you tackled the guy breaking into your house? The one that was there to repair telephone lines?"

Billy glared at Eric and released the smoke. "Yeah, kind of like that. I'm hoping these dreams are a sign."

Eric took another pull and ground the joint into the picnic table. "So you really think these dreams mean something? I thought you said it was the sleeping meds turning you into a freak."

Billy gazed at the reflection of a thousand stars. Eric wouldn't have meant for the words to sound condescending.

"It's hard to say. I've always felt there was something more for me. Nothing spectacular, but like a wife or something. A real job, a nice house. I'm beginning to wonder if that guy is right, if these really are just delusions of grandeur." The latest theory on Insomni-bloggers said as much.

"Don't start that again." Eric's eyes followed Billy's to the ocean. "I know we can't see it now, but I've told you a hundred times, there is a reason for everything. If your dream is to get married, have seven kids, and wear a white collar, then do it. Too many people give up on their dreams; it's a plague. Look at Bryan." Bryan is Billy's forty-year-old manager at the Burger Palace. If you listened to the way he described it, every moment of his life was a living hell. "I bet he didn't plan on being the general manager at a fast food joint in Myrtle Beach when he was forty. Yet, here he is, absolutely miserable and taking it out on everyone who works for him."

"I work there too."

"That's not what I mean. Bryan accepted his fate." Eric waved his hands faster with every word, more worked up by the second. "You don't have to do that. Right now, the job is a means to an end. You think I like coming home every night smelling like old fish? I do my job because it's what I have to do right now. A means to an end."

"A means to an end," Billy agreed.

They sat staring at the dark water, listening to waves beat the shore like a drum, steady and constant, like the beating heart of the ocean itself. Moisture floated ashore, misting their skin with the salty breath of the Atlantic.

Billy broke the silence. "That last dream has me thinking. Sometimes I'm in the city, sometimes I'm not. Either way, I always end up in a field. Someone is following me, but I can't see them. I'm so scared, yet so alive. Did I tell you about the last one? Where I sang opera?"

Eric's laughs shook him so hard he fell from the table into the damp sand. "That's what you get for setting your alarm to opera." He forced his words out between gasps.

"That's the strange thing. The singing felt right."

"It felt right that you sang at the top of your lungs like Pavarotti?" Eric started with another round of laughter. Billy didn't join him. "So, what? You think your destiny is to become an opera star?"

"No," Billy said quietly. He looked into himself, remembering what it was like in his dream. "Not like an opera star. It was the first time I felt like I did the right thing. What I was supposed to do at that exact point in time. My destiny." When Eric didn't respond, he went on. "I didn't say I understand, just that it felt different."

Eric crawled back on the table, changing the subject to a new girl at his work that had caught his eye. Girls seemed to be the topic of their conversation as much as his dreams or lack of sleep. They might be big dreamers; Billy in the literal sense, but neither had a girlfriend, or even any real friends that were girls. It had been that way for as long as they'd known each other. What would life be like if he led the life he dreamt? Would he have a beautiful wife? Children?

His thoughts came back to the present, to him not even having a girlfriend. *How depressing.* "Thanks for the dope, man, I'm going to head home and put Grams to sleep."

"Good idea. Hey, I almost forgot. Did you get this weekend off? Brandon is throwing a party up north at his parent's cottage, and the new chick is coming."

Billy sighed. "No. Bryan thinks we'll be slammed since it's the last weekend before school starts back up. He said that even if I get someone to cover my shift, I can't take it off. Maybe next time."

"That's cool, man." A broad smile appeared on Eric's face. "Less competition. I'll be getting some booty this weekend while you flip burgers."

Billy punched him in the arm, and they both laughed again. They left the beach and climbed on their bikes, heading in opposite directions. At least Eric had a place of his own. He'd asked Billy to move in with him, to their own *bachelor pad*, he called it. He couldn't. Billy's relationship with Grams was symbiotic. Though he supported him monetarily, she needed him as much as he needed her.

Amfar

Kelly appeared more excited than the evening before. Her lips had a slight curve and her eyes followed the beach more than the grand buildings.

The closer they came to Jackson Incorporated, the more business-like Kelly's demeanor became. He could not help but picture her as he had that morning.

"Who do we talk to again?" Kelly's eyes continued following the beach.

"Mr. Garrett said her name is Dr. Lisa Gibbons."

"I still don't understand why Tom had us drive to Myrtle Beach. Not that I'm complaining, but there is a lab right in Atlanta. Would have saved us a trip and some of his money too."

"He said something about owing her a favor." Amfar smiled. "You know how he is about sharing information. It is like pulling teeth."

Kelly paused, looking at him. When she didn't look away, he felt blood rising to his face.

"What is it?"

"Do you realize what you just did, Amfar?"

He shook his head.

"You used an American idiom. I've never heard you do that. Good job." She clapped him on the shoulder.

Impressing her made him happy, yet he felt his face turn a darker shade of red. The promise to himself and his emotions wasn't working out so well. He stopped smiling. *Maybe she won't like it if I'm not smiling*, he thought. He brought another smile to his face. It felt forced, so he stopped again.

"Are you okay? I tell you that you had a major breakthrough in your ability to communicate with Americans, and you look at me as though I killed your puppy. What's on your mind?"

"Yes. I mean, yeah, I'm fine. Just a little tired from the long car ride yesterday. I am happy I made… what did you call it? A breakthrough? I don't know about it being a breakthrough, but it seemed like the right thing to say. And why do Americans always talk about killing puppies? Seems a bit morbid."

"It was the right thing to say." Kelly patted him on the shoulder. "Not the puppy thing, but trying to get anything out of Tom. Although, I have to say, it's probably easier for me than you. But we both know why that is."

Was she aware of the way she acted around Tom Jarrett and its affect on him? Did she really just admit she was enamored with the man? If not, what did she mean?

"Why is that?" He tried to hide his surprise.

Her eyebrows raised. "Oh come on, you can't be that oblivious, can you?" He didn't answer. "You have to see how Tom acts around women. He can't take his eyes off them. I think if I flashed him like one of the spring breakers, he'd give me his house."

His face flushed again. *Why is that happening so much lately?*

"Oh don't look at me like that," Kelly continued. "I would never do it. I was kidding. I just can't believe you never noticed his weakness for women."

"I did notice. It's just that… I guess I did not see it for what it was. I saw that you acted different around him, but I thought it was because you… were attracted to him."

Kelly laughed hysterically, rocking back and forth in her seat and holding her stomach. How embarrassing. How could he have been so wrong about her? Her laughing paused, and she looked at Amfar. She began laughing again.

"How was I supposed to know?" *How can I be a doctor and such an idiot?* "Every time you speak with him you get a lilt in your voice, and bat your eyelashes."

"You notice when I bat my lashes? Interesting. Turn right up here." She pointed to a red brick building. It didn't match the other buildings in the area. Though the building was in the business district, most could still fit in anywhere on the beach. The brick stood out against the soft pastel colors and the stucco of the others.

Amfar pulled into the lot, parking close to the entrance.

Kelly sat smiling. "Okay, my primary goal for this trip has just changed. Oh, I will be relaxing for sure, but now I need to teach you about women."

He was about to tell her he knew enough about women, but she didn't give him the chance.

"I'm not saying you don't know about women. I'm just saying I'm going to teach you the little things. Noticing the difference in my eyelash batting, as you called it, was good. But you need to learn the reason behind those things. Not just that they happen. Deal?"

"Deal," he growled under his breath.

They left the chest in the car and stepped into the tall red brick building. The slight scent of pine needles permeated the cool air. The room was so cold they both let out a shiver as they walked to the front desk. An enormous woman with thick glasses slid to the window in her chair, greeting them with a wide smile. They were to take a seat in the waiting area while she contacted Ms. Gibbons.

***

Plush couches and cushioned gray chairs filled the waiting area. Plastic plants adorned every corner. Amfar lowered himself onto one of the chairs when an attractive woman wearing a lab coat entered from the nearest door. Her nametag read, Dr. Gibbons. Glasses with abnormally thick lenses sat suspended on the tip of her nose. She had dense chestnut hair pulled back into a ponytail, and she wore a beautiful smile.

He never totally lowered himself to his seat, but didn't stand up, either. He could not help but stare. She was undoubtedly beautiful, and although she wore a lab coat, a toned and muscular body underneath said she was an athlete. The glasses made her blue eyes pop out of her face like a pug. They sat too far down on her nose, pinching it to a point. Amfar concentrated on her symmetrical, sparkling white teeth.

Kelly smacked him on the side of the head, and he dropped the rest of the way onto his seat. "Stop staring like a four year old in a candy store." She grimaced.

He raised himself from the chair and lifted his hand to shake the one Dr. Gibbons proffered.

"Sorry about that, Dr. Gibbons." Kelly rolled her eyes. "We didn't get in until really late last night. He must have car lag."

"Dr. Amfar Ditpra." He let go of her hand, sad to release her lush skin. "It's a pleasure to meet you, Dr. Gibbons. Where do you like your chest?"

"Excuse me?"

Amfar's face was on fire. "Forgive me. I mean, where would you like the chest?" He would never hear the end of this one.

"Please, call me Lisa. We prefer to treat everyone like family here at Jackson Incorporated." The line sounded practiced, but she delivered it well.

"What he means is that we have everything locked in a chest outside." Kelly stifled a chuckle at his blunder. "Would you like us to bring it in?"

"That won't be necessary, Dr. Pierce. John and Pete will be happy to carry it for you." On cue, two young men, also wearing lab coats, stepped out behind Dr. Gibbons. "Dr. Pierce, Dr. Ditpra, this is Pete, and this is John." She pointed to each assistant in turn.

"If you don't mind, I would like to accompany them. I would like to take particular care." Mr. Jarrett trusted Jackson Incorporated, but Amfar wasn't sure how much he trusted a couple of kids to handle the artifacts.

"Of course, Dr. Ditpra. You are the archaeologists. I wouldn't pretend to know how to take care of the items nearly as well. After all, we're just lab geeks here at Jackson Incorporated."

"I'm sorry. I didn't mean to offend," he offered.

She held up her hand. "No offense taken." She smiled. "I'm very protective of my clients and their goods. I wouldn't expect anything different."

Amfar accompanied Pete and John to the car and unlocked it while he listened to the young men discuss their plans for Spring Break. He cautioned them about the importance of the chest and its contents. They took their time, gentler than Jarrett's men had been loading it.

They led him down a short hall toward the back of the brick building and into an elevator.

"Could you push the button for floor six, Dr. Ditpra?" One of them nodded toward the lit buttons. He thought it was Pete. Amfar pushed the glowing six.

The elevator dinged. They stepped out, and the young men led the way to an office a few feet away. Inside, a large walnut table sat in the center of a room with no chairs.

"This is the drop off area, Dr. Ditpra. We have one like this on each floor in the office area. Anything we might need can be passed through there." He pointed to a steel door, the size of a small television, built into the wall.

Pete and John placed the chest on the table. Amfar's shoulders tightened, he was about to see what is so important to Jarrett. They slid on the thin gloves hanging from the wall just inside the steel door. One punched a code into the keypad on the chest. It hissed open. They removed a layer of waxy white paper. On one side was a stack of items wrapped with the waxy paper, some as small as a golf ball, others thicker and cylindrical. On the other sat a plate the color of indigo. He wanted to reach out and touch it, but it was not his place. Underneath the first plate were two more, one yellow, one red, the colors rich and lustrous. A soft ringing sound reverberated from within the plates when touched. They did not look, or sound like any dinner set Amfar had ever seen.

He leaned over the chest as they brought each plate out one at a time. A glob of red landed close to one of the plates on the thick white paper. Pete and John looked at Amfar. One pointed to his face. He brought his fingers to his nose and they came away covered in blood.

"Oh dear. I am so sorry. Please forgive me." He pulled out his handkerchief and pressed it to his nose.

"It's okay, Dr. Ditpra. Happens all the time."

On the way back to the main floor, they apologized about the bloody nose. They explained that each floor had its moisture levels regulated with care. Most employees carried around moisturizing nose spray.

Kelly was in Dr. Gibbons' corner office finishing the paper work and giggling when he walked in. The giggling stopped when they saw the bloody kerchief.

"What happened? Are you okay?" Kelly stood.

"Let me guess. Bloody nose from the dry air?" Dr. Gibbons put in.

"Yes, the air must be very dry. I am fine, thank you both. Please do not stand on my account, Kelly. Is there any more paperwork to be taken care of?"

"Everything is set. Surprisingly, there was little to do. Lisa had it all ready for us."

"Yes, well I like to make things as easy as possible for our clients. Is there anything else I can get for you?" The cell phone on her desk rang; the ring-tone was John Lennon singing, "Imagine All the People." Dr. Gibbons picked up the phone and put her hand over the receiver. "I'm sorry, do you mind?" She gestured toward the hall.

"Not at all." Kelly stood and followed Amfar into the hall.

"I'll meet you in the waiting area in just a moment. This shouldn't take long."

"That was funny," Amfar said under his breath as they entered the waiting area.

"What are you mumbling about?"

"Did you hear her ring-tone?"

"'Imagine All the People?' Yeah, love that song. Why?"

"It has played on the radio for my alarm the last two mornings. Now she has it for her ring-tone. Just an odd set of coincidences."

Kelly paused by the front door. "Do you ever stop over-analyzing?"

"What do you mean?"

Dr. Gibbons stepped from her office. "Sorry about that. It was Tom Jarrett. Could you wait just a moment?"

They nodded.

"Tom wanted you to hold onto some of the items a little longer. Apparently, we're not able to offer the services he hoped. We'll keep the bones with the carvings, but he wants you to hold onto the plates and the manuscript until further notice."

Amfar looked to Kelly. He wondered if his excitement at finding what was inside the chest showed on his face as much as it did hers. A smile covered her face, even touched her eyes.

Amfar spoke for both of them. "That would be fine, Dr. Gibbons. We would very much enjoy looking after the plates for Mr. Jarrett."

A moment later, Pete stepped from the elevator with a padded cardboard box just large enough to fit the three plates inside with a leather tube on top.

"Here you go, Dr. Ditpra." Pete handed him the box. "Each is wrapped individually, and the box is heavy duty. Though I wouldn't test it. Sorry again about the nosebleed. I should have warned you. Have a good one." He waved.

Kelly still smiled at Amfar. He understood what it was that drew her to archaeology now. If she was this excited about looking at dinner utensils, he could only imagine how she would respond to a real find, like the bones with carvings on them Dr. Gibbons just mentioned.

Amfar looked back to Dr. Gibbons one last time to get a look at her perfect smile. He almost ran into the glass doors on the way out. Kelly caught the door and held it for him.

"That was easy enough," Kelly said when they were outside. "It's not even ten, and we have the day's work done. What should we do now? We could stop at the welcome center and grab some coupons, maybe find a list of all Myrtle Beach has to offer. Or do you think we should just skip everything, head back to the hotel, and take out the plates? What did she mean by plates anyway? Were they really dinner plates?"

"I'm surprised you can even talk right now." A small laugh escaped Amfar. "The way you looked at me in there, I thought you were going to kiss me." He tripped over a stone. The box landed on the roof of his car and he caught himself with both hands. His eyes squeezed shut, blood rushed to his face again. Some words are best not said to a colleague.

A hand gently touched his shoulder. His eyes opened. Kelly's face was inches from his own. She smiled a mischievous smile, pushed up on her tiptoes, and kissed him on the cheek. She giggled and ran to her side of the car.

He shook his head, pretending the last thirty seconds had not happened. "We can stop at the welcome center if you like. I would also like to get some food. For some reason my stomach feels queasy." He didn't want her to know of his embarrassment. "I'm sure it is queasy only because of the blood from my nose. Not that blood makes me queasy, just that it happened in the... ah... I would like to finish reading Sheriff Scott's book. I haven't had much of a chance to read it since we left Morehead." His face must be as red as the dark bricks of Jackson Incorporated.

Kelly opened her door. "You and your intellectual reading. We're on vacation, and you buy a book written by the Morehead Sheriff." She pretended nothing happened too. Maybe she just had a different view of how colleagues should act around each other.

John

John tried Jarrett's number a dozen times. Maybe his phone didn't have a signal when he worked in the cave.

He dialed again.

The phone rang ten times before going to voicemail. If Jarrett didn't have a signal, it shouldn't have rung at all but gone straight to the message.

So why isn't he answering?

The thick plastic rear window of the Wrangler bulged from the pressure of the three suitcases squeezed into the back seat. Preparing for any eventuality was important, but maybe three suitcases were too many. John slid the top one out and lugged it toward his bedroom. Buying whatever he needed while in Myrtle Beach would be easier than bringing too much. The to-do list scrolled through his mind as he shuffled toward his room.

The suitcase went next to the matching bagel-style pet beds. His two Labradors visited the local kennel. Finding a place for his dogs to stay took longer than he thought. Kennel owners were leery of clients not knowing how long they'd be gone. The two weeks he had saved up would make for a nice vacation as long as he was on a road trip.

His cell rang, the caller ID was the same area code as Jarrett's number.

"Hello, this is Nancy Karnes, Tom Jarrett's office assistant. I've listened to your three messages, and I wondered if there was something I could help you with. Mr. Jarrett is very busy."

Tom Jarrett's screaming voice in the background threatened to drown out Nancy's words. John met Jarrett once at an annual summer outing soon after Kelly was hired. He didn't like the guy when they met, and he sure didn't like an idiot that would yell at his employees.

"Hey, Nancy. Can I get the information I asked for in the messages?"

"Mr. Jarrett doesn't divulge his employee's information, regardless of relationship. Especially when said employee has a cell phone."

"I understand that, Nancy, but—"

"But, I explained to him your extenuating circumstances and that your need to contact Kelly was very important." A short pause. She whispered, "She's in Myrtle Beach, sweetheart; she left a week ago. We had a nice talk before she left."

Why women felt the need to gab about their relationships, and to any woman who would listen, he would never know. Nancy was from a different mold than Mr. Jarrett. She must bring a nice balance to the power hungry, arrogant man.

"Thank you so much, Nancy. Last time I spoke with her, she mentioned a road trip but Myrtle Beach is a good ten or twelve hours from Morehead."

Her voice returned to normal. "She's been a bit overwhelmed the past few weeks, and Mr. Jarrett thought it wise to give her a break. There were some things we needed delivered, so he sent her and Dr. Ditpra to do so."

Jarrett's yelling in the background grew in intensity. "Is that John Reeves?" Jarrett yelled close enough for John to hear through the phone.

Nancy's voice grew muffled. "It is, Mr. Jarrett. I told him—"

"You tell him to keep his personal business to himself. If he wants to call his girlfriend, he can do it on his own time."

"Yes, Mr. Jarrett."

The yelling continued but more subdued than before.

"Sorry about that, John. I should go."

"Be well. And Nancy?"

"Yes?"

"Thank you."

Chapter 5

Billy

"This sucks." Billy pushed the cheap mop through the ketchup, spreading the last remnants of the red goo across the floor more than picking it up. "Eric is probably drinking another gin and tonic, the first of many, and I'm stuck working a slow-ass lunch shift. Bryan should know we won't be slammed. We're never slammed. Even on Valentine's Day when we have ten people on and he sends half of them home within a half hour of opening."

Sam smiled despite the sweat dripping from his nose, each drop sizzling on the grill.

"What can I say, Billy? Eric asked for the weekend off. If you didn't have all that crazy dream shit going on, maybe you would have planned ahead too. The gears rocked in Eric's head the moment he came in here yapping about the new girl at the Waterbar." Sam let out a hearty laugh and went back to scraping grease with his spatula. "Besides, it's not like it would have mattered. Eric always gets the girl; it's that goofy grin of his."

"You're right, but no need to point out how single I am," Billy mumbled to himself.

Spilling the giant can of ketchup was a crappy end to a crappy day. He wasn't often jealous of Eric, but today he would give anything to trade places.

The mop squished when Billy pushed down the lever on the mop bucket. He went over the spill a few more times. Upsetting Bryan didn't take much. Billy sloshed the mop back into the bucket and rolled it back to the cleaning room, shooting Sam a quick wave on the way by. Today was front counter duty.

A Saturday lunch shift at Billy Borks meant it would be slower than normal. No high school kids on lunch break or drunken spring breakers to bother them. Bryan was wrong again. Today would be nothing more than a boring day in a greasy restaurant. Billy wished he were outside enjoying the sun, playing catch with some friends, or playing garbage man at one of Grams's barbeques. Instead, he wore a fake smile and pretended to like rude customers.

A couple walked in, but he didn't notice them right away through his daydreaming.

"Hey, turd. Pay attention!" Crazy Jenny rolled her eyes and went back to her book while she sat in the drive-through window.

Billy turned to the couple. The male customer's brows sat high on his forehead. The girl smiled and flipped through a coupon book from the welcome center. A sure sign of tourists.

"Hey there, you two. Great weather today, huh?"

The man still gaped at Jenny.

"Wake up." The girl used her hand to lift his lower jaw, and close his mouth. "This nice young man…" She squinted at Billy's nametag. He held it up for her. "This nice young man, Billy, just asked about the weather. In America, it's a greeting we usually respond to."

The man crossed his arms and tapped his toe. The woman smiled. Though she was at least ten years older than Billy, she wore a gorgeous smile and showed off great legs in her slender khaki shorts. Normally he preferred women his own age, or at least close, but he'd make an exception for her.

Neither responded to his question about the weather. How long did he have to stand there like an idiot with a smile on his face until they decided to order?

The man pulled his eyes away from Crazy Jenny to Billy. "Are the women always so rude in Myrtle Beach?"

Billy needed a moment to understand the man's words. He'd heard a similar accent before but wasn't sure where. Rude sounded a lot like "root."

"Nah, it's mostly just Jenny." Billy nodded toward his nemesis seated in the drive-through cubicle. "She's like that." He leaned forward conspiratorially. "That's why the manager puts her in the window. People can't see how grumpy she is."

The woman laughed, but the dark-skinned man looked confused. A sharp elbow to the man's ribs from his woman friend brought a smile to his face.

The two weren't dating but were more than friends. Billy prided himself with his ability to read people. It embarrassed him to admit Jenny fooled him. When she came in for her final interview at Billy Borks, she acted so bubbly that Billy made a bet with Eric that he'd make out with her before the end of her first month.

Jenny's first day, Bryan assigned Billy to train her on the computer system for the drive-through. Reaching behind the computer to show her the emergency reset button, his elbow brushed the side of her breast. She landed a quick jab to his kidney. The muscles in his legs turned to jelly, and he fell to the dirty floor, smacking his head on the edge of the counter. For over an hour, he explained to Bryan that it was an accident and Jenny overreacted. Bryan went into his sexual harassment tirade and gave him the week off. The worst part was explaining to friends how a girl gave him a black eye.

Lost in his thoughts, he realized the man spoke to him.

"Sorry. What was that?"

"I was simply commenting on your previous statement about how great the weather was. I agree with you, very much so. I thought the sea salt mixed with the humidity would be bothersome, but it is rather refreshing." He directed the next comment to the woman at his side. "And thank you very much for the lesson on American greeting standards, but if you would kindly refrain from offering the information unless asked, that would be wonderful."

The girl's cheeks reddened but the beautiful smile never left her face as she turned to Billy. "Well, Billy. I think the grilled chicken sandwich—"

Bryan stalked around the fry machine to Billy's side, nose to nose. The memory of his altercation with Jenny reminded him about the personal space talk. Bryan didn't follow his own rules.

"Okay, Billy Hitchings. I don't know if you grew up in a barn, or on the street, or wherever. But around here, when we spill something, we don't do a half-ass job. We clean it until it is clean." Bryan gave him a firm poke to the chest.

These things happened in movies, not to him. His cranky, 'too young to look as old as he does' manager just poked him in the chest. The bulging eyes and flying spittle reminded Billy of the people on talk shows. Only they usually argued about who the daddy was. Jenny stared wide-eyed from her seat in the drive-through, her book falling to the floor.

"Don't give me that innocent look, you shit!"

Did he really just call me a shit?

"Did you even look at the floor back there? You're supposed to mop when you spill, it's code. You know that. You didn't even put any salt down. Do you want us to have a lawsuit when someone falls on their ass? Do you want us to go out of business so you can go back to your grandma's house and play some more damned games?"

This psycho ripped him a new one right in front of guests. Maybe Eric was right about him going crazy.

Billy turned to the couple. "I'm sorry about this, I—"

"You listen to me when I'm talking to you, punk." Bryan poked him in the chest again.

"Calm down, Bryan. What happened?"

"Shut up! I'm so sick of your shit. How can you be so lazy?" His lips pulled back in a snarl.

The couple backed away from the counter. The dark-skinned man raised his hands. "There is no reason you gentlemen cannot take this to the back. There are no children around, but I do not appreciate this manner of behavior in front of a lady."

Sweat beaded on Billy's forehead. The few seconds since Bryan's freak show began felt like an eternity. Billy's hands shook, and he ground his teeth to keep from saying anything he'd regret. Crazy Jenny was at the top of his most likely to freak out list, not his anal-retentive boss.

Bryan stopped with his tirade to look at the dark-skinned man. "You keep your nose out And if you don't like it, get the hell out! We don't need your business anyway." He waved toward the door with both hands.

Sweat rolled between Billy's shoulder blades. *It wasn't this hot a few minutes ago.* He wanted to yell back, but the guy was his boss. The couple standing there watching made the whole thing worse. Frustration grew like a burning ember in his chest.

Amfar

The manager yelled at him. Amfar was a guest in this establishment and had been ready to spend money, which he sure was not going to do now. *Time to leave.* He turned to say as much to Kelly when the light over their head burst, showering sparks and glass down around them. They jumped away from the exploding bulb.

Kelly tucked her arm into his. "What the hell was that?" She looked back and forth between the crazy manager and the glass on the floor. "We need to go." She gave his arm a tug toward the door, picking glass from her hair with her free hand.

Grown men do not usually show such emotion, let alone in a public place. The only time Amfar had seen something similar, he was a child. When a man working a fruit stand in the market accused Amfar of stealing, his father reacted in a comparable fashion.

"Did you hear that?" He asked the question without taking his eyes away from the two men.

Billy yelled back at Bryan, their faces darkening by the second. The General Manager frothed like a rabid dog.

"Hear what?" Kelly tugged at his arm again.

Amfar lowered his voice and allowed Kelly to pull him closer to the door. "It sounded like he growled right before the light exploded over our heads."

"Who? I didn't hear anything. Let's get out of here."

The pulling on his arm grew more insistent. A light bulb near the back of the restaurant burst into flame and a greasy ceiling tile crashed to the floor behind them.

"Are we having an earthquake?" Fear replaced Kelly's easy smile. Her eyes drew wide as she searched for more falling tiles or exploding bulbs.

The scientist in him wanted to stay. He felt intrigued and a little guilty. Both times when a bulb burst, he thought the boy growled, a deep and menacing snarl.

Amfar absorbed a tremendous amount of detail. More bulbs exploded, corresponding with the strange noise coming from one of the two men. He could not be sure which. With every poke in the chest, the boy's skin grew a darker shade of red.

The two fighting didn't seem to notice anything going on around them. The girl working the drive-through went from wide-eyed shock to grinning, and losing it again when the first light burst. She ignored the two cars waiting in line outside her window, slowly working her way toward the rear of the restaurant. She had the right idea.

Kelly let go of his arm and started toward the door. "I'm going to the car."

Before she took two steps, the growl became a low rumble. Amfar felt the vibration in his stomach like a booming parade band. The sound came from the boy.

Impossible, the human vocal cords cannot make such a noise.

The room began to shake and vibrate, more tiles fell, and light fixtures swayed. The rude girl ran at full speed toward the back of the restaurant. The manager stopped yelling mid-sentence. His eyes searched around him as he finally noticed something was wrong. The kid no longer yelled, but still made the strange noise. A sound like a deep growl, or mewling mixed with a freight train. Amfar had never heard anything like it.

Kelly grabbed the handle to the exit. The large glass door burst inward, sending her flying into Amfar who had been halfway across the restaurant. Shards of glass pierced Amfar's skin as he slid across the floor with Kelly on top. Glass and chunks of concrete shattered and whirled around them. The rumble turned into a roar, as if they were in the heart of a tornado. An intense pressure, as if gravity had doubled, pressed around them. His eardrums were about to burst. He managed to turn himself over and cover Kelly's body with his own.

Sure of his impending death, Amfar's inquisitive mind searched for answers. *A bomb? A tornado? What could cause the building wall to implode?*

The roar stopped, but not the cacophony of sounds tearing at Amfar's ears. His eyes opened and looked to Kelly beneath him. White powder from the obliterated drywall and cement covered her body as she lay motionless. Lacerations covered her face and neck. Blood trailed through the powder on her skin. He felt her neck for a pulse. A heartbeat. And it was strong.

He reached to his shirt pocket, delighted to find his cell phone still in place. He tried to dial 911. His hands shook so much he kept dialing a six.

Amfar lifted his head. Billy hadn't moved. *How is that possible?* Amfar stared in wonder; the boy was unscathed. Billy turned with deliberate care in a half circle and stopped, tears formed in his eyes, and a look of utter horror lit his face. His mouth worked, but no words formed. Billy barely stayed on his feet as he sprinted toward the back of the restaurant where the rude girl had moments before.

Amfar's eyes went to where Billy stood before running away. The manager's lifeless body dangled a few feet in the air, impaled by the handles of the ice cream machine. Blood and ice cream poured from the holes in his chest.

His eyes passed from the innards of the restaurant toward where his car should have been. Part of the frame was the only thing left. It was pushed down into the cement as if it had melted.

The wall between Amfar and his parked car didn't exist. Part of the roof was gone as well. The wall wasn't gone really but pushed into the restaurant much farther than it should be. The violent tremors had tossed everything else around. Pieces of the ceiling and wall still fell to the floor every few seconds.

The chaotic scene doubled. He shook his head. Big mistake. Another excruciating explosion took place inside his head, blurring his vision. He cupped his hands over his ears as if covering them would stop the pain. Blood poured from his ears and down his hands. The restaurant whirled in one quick circle and the world went black.

Chapter 6

John

John glanced at the overflowing black bag in the passenger seat of his Wrangler. His eyes went back to the road whipping by as he laughed about his over-preparedness striking again. Sticking from the top were maps, caffeine pills, and his Glock. He said a silent thank you to his dad. People said John was paranoid, but they could say whatever they want. Ed Reeves taught him how to survive, and that's what he planned to do. Besides, having the gun on the seat next to him had saved him from being carjacked twice; once in downtown Chicago, and again in Laguna Beach. The only place he didn't take the Glock was on airplanes; he preferred to keep his feet on the ground anyway.

The Wrangler's top was down and the humid night air blew through his hair. Absorbing some rays on his vacation sounded better than ever. Brenda didn't know it was a vacation, not yet anyway. She thought he'd return to work on Monday. A phone call in the morning to tell her about his trip to Myrtle Beach might cost him his job, but it was just a way to make extra money anyway, maybe meet a few friends. No big loss.

The long drive wore on his eyes as he looked to the clock showing it was three in the morning. The GPS told him he was fifteen minutes from downtown. He could tell by the tang of salt in the air. Every time he visited the beach, he reminded himself that one day he'd buy an ocean-side home. Not yet though, he couldn't justify spending the millions for what he wanted. Vacations would do, for now.

He made a quick stop at a Fast-Mart and bought a bottle of Tums. The closer he came to facing Kelly, the more his stomach churned. His mind had been clear when he left New York. He came to Myrtle Beach to fix their relationship. Now he second-guessed himself. He blamed his flagging self-esteem on the late hour and cranked up the Grand Strand's Country station. Nothing like listening to a country boy sing about his broken-down truck to pump up the spirits.

Minutes later, he pulled into his vacation spot for the week, one of twelve tiki-themed cottages on the beach. Part of a group named Lisa's Getaway. Not a very creative name—cottages had that luxury when they were ocean-side. They were always the same, no matter the time of year. Much like Rachel was in high school when their relationship wasn't platonic. Even now, she looked as good in a pair of sweats as she had in her prom dress. Like the cottages, he could depend on Rachel to be there when he needed her, reliable to a fault and never changing.

Enjoying his time on the beach was worth the few thousand dollars a week to stay at Lisa's. Rachel made the reservations for him and let the owner know he would arrive late.

Rachel McCall called herself an office assistant, but he preferred to call her friend. They spent every day together as children in Michigan and were high school sweethearts with big plans. Those plans changed when her dad died in a car accident six months after graduation. Two weeks later, Rachel and her brother moved to Seattle with their mother. Rachel lived there now with her husband Elliot.

John paid her three thousand dollars a month, a steep amount to pay a secretary, but not a friend. The money made her available all times of the day, or night. *And worth every penny.* Her savvy computer skills saved him plenty of times while he worked for Elite Bodyguarding.

He turned the Jeep off and jogged over to the cottage with a sign in the window that read 'Front Office'. Lisa, the owner, told Rachel if the lights were out, John was to knock loudly because she'd be sleeping. He knocked and tried the knob. It wouldn't turn. He knocked a few more times and was about to call the number on the door. A woman with tanned leathery skin opened the door, a cloud of smoke around her head. She wore a see-through white blouse unbuttoned almost to her navel and canary colored spandex pants.

"Are you John?" her voice rasped around the cigarette dangling from her lips. An ash fell to the floor.

"I'm John Reeves. Thank you for your hospitality, Mrs. Lancaster, especially on such short notice."

She closed the door in his face, and he heard movement inside. A few seconds later, she opened the door again and came out with an enormous ring of keys in her hand. She smiled and started toward the cottages.

"No problem, John. I'm always willing to accommodate. You treat me good, then I treat you good. You know?"

"Sounds like a good philosophy, Mrs. Lancaster."

"Please, just Lisa. Sorry about the grumpy look back there." She yanked up her spandex. "I just need to establish who is in charge when someone comes to my door at three in the morning. You know? Even though I figured it was you, I still needed to make sure, you know, for my safety and all."

She winked at him as another ash fell to the sand.

Lisa went on. "Anyway, here is your cottage. Number seven; best one we got. That girl, Rachel, said you wanted the best, so here it is. Check out time is normally at 11:00 AM, but she said you didn't know how long you're staying. She booked you through the week. No housekeeping, so keep it clean if you would. Give me a call up at the front office if you need any more towels, sheets or anything. The number is on the phone." She walked him to the front step of the cottage facing the beach. "Anything else I can get you?"

"No, ma'am, you've done enough, thanks again." He offered the best smile he could at three in the morning.

"No problem, John," she called over her shoulder as she scurried back in the direction of the front office. "Oh yeah. There is plenty of coffee up at the office if you'd like some tomorrow. Keep it warm all day."

***

The sun was well up in the sky by the time John woke just after noon. The road trip made him more tired than he realized. He changed his wrinkled, slept in clothes, washed his face, and walked to the front office. Lisa sat behind the front desk next to a two-gallon carafe of boiling hot coffee. Lisa was true to her word.

"That's a lot of coffee, Mrs. Lancaster." She watched him over the top of a *Woman's Day* magazine, one eyebrow raised. "I mean Lisa. People actually drink that much java around here?"

She smiled at his correction. "Sure do, John. Usually two or three of those carafes a day. Most everybody here is long-term, and they come up here to play cards when they can. You know?"

People come to the beach to sit inside and play cards? He filled his mug and headed out the door with a quick wave to Lisa.

Rachel hadn't called yet to let him know where Kelly and Amfar stayed. Breakfast was the first thing on his schedule for the day, even if it was after noon. There were certainly enough specialty breakfast restaurants around. He hoped Rachel called back soon with some information, otherwise he'd need to start searching the old-fashioned way. He smiled at the thought of driving around the beach in his Jeep. *Sounds like fun.*

There was a cozy restaurant a quarter mile from Lisa's Getaway, a sign out front in the shape of a giant donut. Either the air-conditioner didn't work, or it wasn't on. The temperature was almost as hot inside as out. John was the only customer in the place. An old man with a paper hat covering his hair stepped from behind the counter and laughed at the look John must have made.

"Howdy, young man. Don't tell me you're afraid of a little sweat, are ya? The old lady likes to keep it warm. Says there's no reason to make people think they left the beach just because they walk into a restaurant. Personally, I just do whatever she says. Makes things easier on me. The name's Buster. Take a seat." He gestured toward the dining area.

John sat at the bar. The diner looked to belong in the forties, with the swivel stools in front and the checkered tiles on the floor and wall.

"Anyway, you ain't here to get my life story are you? What can I get you to drink, son?" He stepped behind the counter and grabbed a pot of coffee.

John turned over the coffee cup in front of him, and slid it closer to the old man. At this rate, he'd be floating around South Carolina; a full mug still sat in his Jeep. Buster tossed a menu on the counter next to him and walked to the television in the corner of the kitchen. He crossed his arms and watched the daily news.

John was pouring a second creamer into his cup when he noticed the ripples on the surface of his coffee. The television screen shuttered for a moment, blipped out once, then came back on.

"What was that?" John's eyes darted around the restaurant for any signs of danger.

"No idea, haven't never seen that happen before. Felt like the room shook for a few seconds too. You think we had an earthquake?"

"Anything is possible I guess, but in South Carolina? Have you ever had one here before?"

Buster seemed to be deep in thought for a moment with his fingers brushing the stubble on his chin. "I don't think there's been an earthquake since the first year I moved here, not measurable anyway."

"How long have you lived here?" John calmed, and took a drink of his coffee.

"Going on forty plus."

John laughed, but the old man continued rubbing his chin while looking out the front window.

"I'd like a number five if you wouldn't mind. Eggs over-easy."

Buster turned to the griddle behind him and went to work with practiced movements. He glanced up to the television while cooking and never missed a beat.

John picked up the local newspaper from the counter and began reading to keep his mind off Kelly.

Billy

Billy turned his head side to side, scanning the horror surrounding him. He closed his eyes and held them tight. Maybe this time when he opened them he would wake from his nightmare. A moment later, he opened his eyes. Destruction encircled him. The window where Jenny sat a few minutes before was gone. The parking lot and swampy area was all that stood between him and Lizards next door.

Jenny was gone too. He hoped she had made it out okay. Had he seen her run away? What the hell had been wrong with Bryan? Why would he freak out like that? Bryan had been right in front of him.

Slowly, he ran his hands over his body checking for blood, or broken bones. Nothing. His clothes looked the same as they had before the explosion. Not a mark on him.

The anger had been so intense it was palpable. He could have reached out and caressed his emotion. He'd never been so furious. Once Bryan began freaking out, it was as if a switch flipped inside. Bryan's yelling needed to stop, and it had.

There were no flames or soot; it was as if the wall had fallen in on them, swift and deadly. He turned in a circle. In front of him hung Bryan, eyes open wide with terror etched into his face, motionless. Ice cream machine handles protruded from his chest.

Billy froze. Then he ran, jumping over and slipping on empty fry containers and chunks of broken drywall. Movement to his right made him slide to a stop. Sam sat under the bathroom sink, covered in blood and still smiling.

"What happened, man?" Sam's voice cracked, and his breath came in huffs. "Wow! That was crazy. First, I see Bryan cussing you out. Next thing I know, I'm standing on the mashed potato mixer."

A gurgling sound accompanied Sam's every breath. The handle of a spatula stuck out from between his ribs, blood frothing around the handle when he breathed in.

Sam followed Billy's eyes to the wound. "Oh that. Yeah, you would think it hurt but it's not that bad really. Just a little funky. Look at you though, man. You look great. Did you hide in the cooler or something?"

"You'll be fine, Sam. The police are on the way. Just stay calm. You never saw me."

"Sure thing, Billy."

Sam slumped a little and looked toward the floor. Billy had never seen anyone in shock before.

He grabbed his coat and ran through the back door to the bike stand. Four attempts later, he unlocked the chain from his bike.

The emotions were powerful; his anger had begged for release. Similar to the way he felt in his dream. The dream. He paused. The emotions hadn't felt similar; they felt exactly the same.

In every dream, he felt something growing or building inside him when he came to the trees. The point of release never came though. He'd wake just before. *What a fool.* The dreams were supposed to mean he'd fulfill some great destiny, some feat only he could accomplish. Instead, the dream had been a premonition for someone blowing up the restaurant.

He flew on his bike toward Grams's house as fast as his legs could take him. Sirens blared from behind. The police would arrive to Billy Borks within minutes with the station less than a mile away. The firefighters would take longer; they would help Sam. Guilt flooded through him at leaving Sam behind. *There was nothing I could have done.*

He pulled into the garage. Through the screen door, he saw Grams dancing in the kitchen. A laugh escaped his lips. Only minutes ago, he'd stood in an exploding restaurant, and here was his spry little grandma bouncing around the kitchen without a care in the world. She must be making spaghetti. Spaghetti reminded her of her late husband so she danced for him whenever she made some. The dancing stopped when he stepped into the kitchen.

"Hey there, kiddo, you're home early."

"Um, yeah, they said that they, ah..."

"Oh, who cares? Now you're home with your Grams. Come give me a hug." She pursed her lips, closed her eyes, and pushed her arms out as far as they would go.

He gave her a quick hug and a kiss on the cheek.

"Thanks, Billy. You always warm your grandma's heart. Dinner will be ready in about twenty minutes if you would like some."

"Thanks, Grams. I'm going to lay down for a bit. I'll try to make it up for some of your great spaghetti."

"See that you do, kiddo." She pinched the skin on his stomach. "You need to thicken up a little, put some meat on your bones. Women like a man with a little meat on their bones." She smiled up at him once more and went back to bounding around the kitchen.

Each step toward the basement sounded like thunder. He tore off his work clothes, checking again for any injuries. Not a scratch on his body or clothes. Not even a speck of dust.

Impossible.

The building flying apart wasn't his fault. He'd just wanted Bryan to shut up, and shut up he did.

If it's not my fault, why do I feel so guilty?

The bathroom mirror showed him the same unbelievable truth. He was unscathed. Then the jackhammers started. The sound hammering in his head made the restaurant explosion seem like a mosquito flitting by. Each pounding of his heart made his eyes cross.

His eyes opened. *I don't remember closing them.* The tile on his bathroom floor pressed against his cheek. *Did I fall?* Something dark on the floor slithered away from him. Something that didn't belong there. Something as shiny as the tiles, reflecting the dull light from the bulb on the ceiling. Blood. His blood. It soaked through his underwear and crawled across his body. He was dying. *Please… no more pain.*

Chapter 7

Amfar

Did *someone just talk to me? Where am I?* Amfar moved his mouth, but no words came from his dry throat. Pain assaulted his ears, burning as if filled with molten lead. Every heartbeat cracked his skull further. He threw his hands to his head and squeezed.

The restaurant… Kelly! He sat up and opened his eyes; the sudden rush of adrenaline dulled the pain. The fluorescent light stung his eyes, and the bite of strong chemicals filled his nose. The tag on his wrist read, *The Grand Strand Regional Hospital.* Next to that, his name. *Kelly should be here, too.* He found the nurse call button on his lap and pressed it repeatedly.

"Can I help you?" the sweet sounding voice asked from the speaker on the call light.

"This is Dr. Amfar Ditpra. I would like to speak to my nurse as soon as possible please."

"Sure thing, Dr. Ditpra. Liz will be with you in a moment. Is everything okay?"

"I believe so. I wish to know about my friend." His voice cracked when he said friend. The strength of his emotions felt out of place. Kelly had to be fine, but the thought of her in the hospital made him sick.

"Sorry, sweetheart. I'm not sure who your friend is, but as long as you're okay, Liz can help you."

A moment later, Liz showed up with a smirk. Either that or a smile. Hard to tell with the corner of her mouth pulled down from the small scar on her jaw line.

"Hey there, sweetheart. Have a good nap?"

"I appreciate your hospitality. Please answer some questions about my friend, Kelly Pierce. She should have arrived about the same time I did. Is she okay?"

"Why don't you sit back, Dr. Ditpra, and I'll tell you all about Kelly. I don't think you're ready to sit up just yet."

Eager to hear about Kelly, he sat back too quickly causing the buzz in his ears to ring louder. He closed his eyes and ground his teeth together to dull the pain.

"Ms. Pierce is just fine. She has a nasty gash on her head and a few cuts and bruises. She's under some heavy anesthesia now, though." The nurse walked to the door and paused. She looked back to Amfar. "I probably shouldn't have told you so much, but you look like a lost kitten. There's nothing to worry about, Doctor Carmichael is prepared for any eventuality."

Amfar popped back up in bed and threw off his sheets. Liz hurried to his side, put her hand on his chest, and eased him back down.

"Now just wait a moment, Dr. Ditpra. You seem the type of man to appreciate candor, and that is what I'm trying to show you. But you need to listen to me or that candor ends now." She applied gentle pressure until he stopped struggling to sit up.

"Please continue," he mumbled. Her stern look disappeared, and a smirk took its place.

"Like I said, she is on some heavy sedatives and responding well to the anti-inflammatory meds. I can't tell you much more than that because your name isn't on her release forms. Enough about Ms. Pierce. How are you feeling?"

"I'm a bit tired, and my ears feel horrible. Otherwise, I feel okay."

"That's understandable, your ear drums burst before the EMS arrived. You lost quite a bit of blood. You had them worried. Other than the burst eardrums and the lacerations, your injuries were minor. Your MRI showed no swelling or abnormalities. Doctor Carmichael believes you passed out from shock but should have awakened sooner. He wants to keep you under our supervision for at least another week.

"What do you mean I should have awoken sooner? How long have I been unconscious?"

"Two days. It's Monday afternoon. And you are rather chipper for just waking up from such a long nap."

"May I see Kelly? She is my... co-worker. I really need to ensure she is okay." *Two days? Please let her be okay. She doesn't deserve this.*

"Soon, Dr. Ditpra. Take my word for it, she's fine. For now, we need to monitor your progress and ensure your continued improvement. Now that you're awake, we need you to undergo a few more tests. And I'm sure the doctor would like to ask you some questions." She lowered her voice. "Also, there were police officers here yesterday, asking for you and Ms. Pierce. They were here about the explosion and wanted to interview you as part of the investigation. Dr. Carmichael and I wouldn't let them near you though."

"Thank you for looking over me Liz. It is deeply appreciated. So this Dr. Carmichael is my doctor as well?"

She checked his vitals while she spoke. "Sorry about that. With you so eager to get out of bed, I skipped procedure for a moment. Your doctor is Dr. Carmichael, too. A great guy, very good at his job." She pulled a loose curl back over her ear and looked away from the vitals into his eyes. "This is really none of my business, but I'm too direct for my own good. You really like her, don't you?"

"No, I mean yes...I mean of course I like her. She is my co-worker and friend. And no, this isn't any of your business." He didn't mean to snap at her.

"If you say so, sweetheart." Her eyes turned back to his vitals. She lifted his file from the wall holder, made a couple notes, and put it back. "Okay, Dr. Ditpra, Dr. Carmichael will be with you soon. You might as well get comfortable; you'll be here a couple more days at least."

She started toward the door and paused. She spoke over her shoulder. "You know, Dr. Ditpra, if either of you had been killed in the explosion, she never would have known how you felt." She walked the rest of the way from the room.

Amfar felt like a horse kicked him in the chest. He hadn't thought of Kelly as more than a friend. Well, maybe he had a few times, but it was something that could never work out, they were too different. Besides, if John Reeves was any indication of what she wanted in a partner, he didn't stand a chance.

John

"Is there anything I can get for you Mr. Reeves?" That was the forty-fifth time the nurse asked him if he needed something. Maybe not the forty-fifth, but it felt like it. He guessed it was the nurse's polite way of telling him he needed some fresh air. The chair in Kelly's room had been his home for most of the last forty-eight hours.

"I'm fine. Thanks, Jimmy."

He hadn't shaved since leaving New York on Friday, and dark rings formed under his eyes. The nurses pulled a cot out for him at night to stay with Kelly. The two times he'd left, he drove by the restaurant where the explosion took place. *Who names a restaurant Billy Borks anyway?* He felt sorry for the owner if his real last name was Borks.

Jimmy waved and left John alone. Jimmy made him nervous. He looked like a fourteen-year-old kid, yet he held Kelly's life in his hands. According to Dr. Carmichael, Kelly and Amfar are stabilized and barring any unforeseen complications, they'd be fine.

Carmichael's only concern was that Kelly's injuries didn't coincide with the length of time she'd been unconscious. The worst of her injuries was the swelling in her frontal lobe. The only real bruising was on the back of her head where it smacked the floor. She had two black eyes, cuts covering her face and hands, and one curved gash from her hairline to just above her eyebrow that took twenty-two stitches. Her injuries seemed substantial to him.

He pictured her showing off her battle scar, and laughed. She was so laid back; sometimes he'd created arguments just to rile her up.

"Mr. Reeves?" A nurse poked her head around the corner. He thought her name was Liz.

"Yes?"

"I thought you might want to know, Mr. Ditpra is awake. Dr. Carmichael is in with him now, but you are welcome to see him when the doctor is done."

"Okay, thanks."

Amfar was awake, a good sign, although his injuries weren't as severe as Kelly's. At least somebody who had been at the restaurant might be able to shed some light on what happened. Sam had been next to useless. He was a cook and in the back during the explosion. The only thing he'd seen was a spatula impaling him. The kid had to be in shock the way he always smiled.

John headed down to the cafeteria and ate a bland lunch. Upon his return, Amfar's door stood open. He knocked once and peeked in to find Amfar propped up on a stack of pillows reading the newspaper.

"Come in, Mr. Reeves. Have you seen Kelly?"

What an odd question to ask. Of course, he'd seen Kelly. Why would he visit her co-worker before the woman he loved?

"Ah, yeah. Sure have, Amfar. She's doing well. How are you feeling?"

"I am doing well, thank you. Other than the pounding headache that is. Dr. Carmichael suspects I will be out soon, which is quite the miracle I hear. He said they want to keep me here for at least two more weeks for observation, but I believe Mr. Jarrett gave them a call." Amfar let out a small laugh.

"You don't have to call me Mr. Reeves, Amfar. We had this conversation last time we met."

"Yes we did. I apologize, John. I didn't wish to assume our friendship was something as casual as using first names without asking." He rolled the newspaper into a tight coil.

John knew a few people from India. While they shared common cultural differences, all seemed to respect proprieties. Until you get to know them that is. Then they threw proprieties out the window like everyone else.

"John, I wondered if you could give me a few more details on Kelly's condition. The nurses say she is shaken up but doing well." Amfar's hands squeezed the coiled newspaper and twisted back and forth.

"She has cuts all over, just like you. Her biggest problem is the gash down her forehead. They had to put stitches in. No internal damage, and her CT scans all looked normal other than the minor swelling on the first day. I'm sure she'll be complaining about the stitches as soon as she wakes up." John let out an uncomfortable laugh.

Amfar looked in the direction of Kelly's room. "No, she won't complain. She won't let that get to her any more than she lets anything else." He continued looking in her direction as if he could see her through the wall.

They must have grown closer. John had used the last comment to gauge Amfar's reaction, and been surprised. Amfar had feelings for Kelly, more than just friendly feelings. *Poor guy.* He was one of the nicest people John knew, and he had a heck of a head on his shoulders, but he wasn't Kelly's kind of man. She needed somebody outgoing, strong willed, somebody who... he'd named off the qualities Kelly said she loved about him. Yet he wasn't what she needed. *Maybe she does need somebody more like Amfar.*

Leaving New York, he felt his chances with Kelly were at least marginal. In the few days he'd been in Myrtle

Beach, he couldn't think of more than a handful of reasons why they should stay together.

Kelly Pierce will never be my wife, he thought. He wanted to say they weren't right together, that he didn't love her, or she him, but they were great together. Just because he wished something were true wasn't going to make it so. He'd have to be content being no more than friends with the woman he loved.

***

John was lost in deep thoughts about Kelly when Amfar said something to him.

"I'm sorry, what was that?" He thought Amfar was goofy for staring through the wall at Kelly, and now he'd done the same thing.

"I asked if you had spoken with Mr. Jarrett. I haven't had the chance. I need to know about some items we had in our possession at the restaurant when it exploded, or imploded I guess."

"I spoke to him for a moment. He called to ask how you two were."

Amfar's eyebrows lifted.

John laughed, a good hearty laugh, one that made him forget about how crazy things were, if only for a moment. "I'm sure he called to see whether he needed to contact a lawyer. He doesn't seem the type to care about much more than his image and his check book."

"I figured as much." Amfar nodded. "I still can't hear very well. The two times I tried to use the phone, everybody sounded too muffled to understand."

"You want me to tell him something?"

"There were some things we found at the cave inside the trunk of my car. I need to know if they were found. If so, they need to find their way to the right hands. I hate to say this, but those hands belong to Mr. Jarrett. If he doesn't get them back, we can expect problems."

John sat down in the orange chair next to Amfar and slid closer.

"What happened, Amfar? I know there was an explosion, but what caused it? Why weren't your injuries worse? And why are the police acting so hush-hush? Every time I ask for information they act like I'm trying to pull teeth."

Amfar leaned further back against the pillows and took a deep breath. "Maybe you should have been a scientist John. You certainly ask questions like one."

When John didn't respond, he continued.

"To be honest, I'm not really sure what happened. I hate to jump to conclusions, but I remember some strange happenings. Why the police are not talking, I'm not sure, but the explosion itself doesn't make sense.

"We were standing in line at Billy Borks when a young man and his manager began arguing. In front of guests of all things. The argument became heated." He paused, eyes going out of focus. "I do not understand what happened next. I know what I saw, but when I put everything together in my head, it doesn't add up." His face went slack. Looking into John's eyes he said, "When the argument peaked, light bulbs began popping, the room shook, and I swear a strange noise came from the boy."

"Strange noise?" John's brows furrowed.

"It is hard to explain. At first, it sounded like he growled at the older man. Then the sound changed. It resonated from within him, almost like a hum, and that was when the wall blew in on top of us. It doesn't make sense, but I think somehow the boy made the explosion happen, or signaled someone to detonate the explosion. I just don't know. Moments before, he'd seemed so calm, even commented on the weather. How could he change so much and so fast?"

"You think a kid caused the explosion?"

Amfar sighed. "That is what I have been trying to figure out from the second I opened my eyes. My logic says yes. If I listen to my heart, which I try not to do as a scientist, it says there is no way he could do something like this. I only talked to him for a few seconds, but I do not believe it was within him to do something so horrible, at least not intentionally."

Questions swirled through John's mind. From what he gleaned from the news and speaking with the police officers, the information Amfar gave about the wall imploding made sense. He needed to contact Tom Jarrett, find out just what Amfar had in his car. The police didn't mention a car. "What about your car?" John said. "Were the things you mentioned explosive materials?"

Amfar shook his head.

"Is there a reason for someone wanting to hurt you, Amfar? Or Kelly? Like someone upset about the cave you two worked in. Kelly said something about the locals not being too happy."

"There was no reason, John. At least none that make sense." Amfar shrank into the bed and spoke quietly. "In the trunk were three disks and a leather tube containing a manuscript, though I'm sure the manuscript was destroyed. The disks looked like dinner plates, and that is all they may have been, but Mr. Jarrett will be livid if we lost even that little."

John needed to see things for himself. He'd been finishing his breakfast and chatting with Buster when Rachel called and told him Amfar and Kelly were in the hospital. Police tape surrounded Billy Borks when he drove by on his way to the hospital. As long as the investigation was still open, the restaurant wouldn't be undisturbed.

John said his goodbyes to Amfar and checked on Kelly again before leaving. He left instructions with Kelly's nurse to call him if the situation changed. Jimmy looked relieved that he was going. John really needed a shower and a shave.

Chapter 8

Billy

Billy's eyes opened. Though blurry, he saw Grams in front of him, knitting. Knowing she was there was a comfort. Her chair was different; she should be rocking. The wall wasn't the usual pastel pink. They weren't at her house.

Where am I?

Beeping echoed and penetrated the otherwise silent room. The scent of old urine and a chemical he couldn't place assaulted his nose. The bed was smaller, thick pillows propped his head up.

The hospital.

The memory of Billy Borks crashed back into place. Pain radiated from his temples to the nape of his neck. He sat up. Grams's knitting needle flew to the ceiling and her glasses fell to her lap.

"My God! Billy?" She jumped up, and her hands fluttered as if she wanted to find a part of him to hug.

The terror from the explosion still filled his mind, but seeing Grams jump so high brought a wealth of emotions down upon him. He laughed.

"Real funny, Billy Boy. Here I am worrying you're gonna die on me, and what do you do when you wake up? You sit up like a beaver popping its head out of a hole like on that kid's game."

He didn't remind her the game she spoke about was her favorite when out for pizza.

"What's going on, young man? What happened? Are you okay? Why were you bleeding?"

"I love you, Grams." He moved the pillows until comfortable.

Grams breathed deeply, a smile coming to her face. "Well, I love you too, kiddo. You gave me quite a scare. I thought you would leave me in this world all by my lonesome." A tear sat on the brim of Grams's eye.

"I don't know what happened." Billy slowly shook his head. His eyes went over the hospital equipment surrounding his bed. "But we'll figure it out together. I'm not going anywhere. How did I get here?"

She nodded to herself and picked up her glasses and knitting pen, going back to work on whatever the pink fuzzy thing was on her lap. "We have all the time in the world, then. I yelled to the basement to see if you'd seen the cable bill. Instead of an answer, I heard a clunk. You were lying in a puddle of blood on your bathroom floor. So I called the ambulance. Do you remember anything?"

Billy explained everything with as much detail as he could muster, from complaining to Sam about Eric out having fun to the intense argument with Bryan. The words caught in his throat when he told her the explosion killed Bryan.

She pushed herself out of the recliner, placing her work on the seat behind her. Stepping to his side, she listened as he told her the rest.

"I've always been honest with you." He fought to keep his emotions in check. "Even when I didn't want to. This is one of those times. Will you sit back down?"

She patted him on the shoulder and kissed his forehead before she turned back to the lime-green recliner. "I'm all ears, Billy boy. You know I love you." Back to the knitting she went.

"Grams," he began slowly, "I think I might have caused Bryan's death."

She shook her head. "I heard about that poor man, Billy, but you need to remember this right now, and remember it well." She pointed at him with her knitting needle. "His death was not your fault, you hear me?" She raised her eyebrows in an intense glower.

"But I was so mad, mad in a way I've never been. And there was this noise coming from inside me. I can't describe it."

"Coming from inside you? You mean like your stomach growled?"

"Kind of, but not really. It doesn't make sense. The more anger I felt, the louder the sound became. At least to me. Nobody else seemed to notice. Something inside me begged for release. At the exact moment of the explosion, I felt a release. I think whatever was inside me pulled the wall in toward us. I wanted Bryan to stop yelling, and he did."

Her eyes were on him now, expression unchanged.

"I know it sounds crazy," he went on. "But it's the way I felt. You tell me to listen to my gut, and I'm telling you, I had something to do with that explosion. I don't want it to be true, but I'm the only one without a single scratch. How is that possible when every window on the West side of the building flew in on us, and I stood in the middle of it all?"

"I should've told the nurse when you woke. You bonked your head harder than I thought." She put her hands on the arms of the chair, struggling to push herself up.

He just nodded and agreed. She wouldn't believe him. Not yet. He wouldn't believe himself either. "Can we wait on the nurse, Grams?"

She nodded and thumped back into her seat.

"What about Sam? Is he okay? What about the police?"

"I don't know anything about the police, or the explosion. I didn't even know anything happened to your work until I drove by on the way to the hospital. Are you sure you were there when it happened? And who's Sam? Is he the nice young man that knows so much about grilling?"

Billy nodded.

"I don't know anything about him either. You think he's here?"

Pain inundated Billy's skull. He squeezed his temples. "Maybe it's time we get the nurse in here."

They called the nurse in, who in turn called the doctor. Billy spent the next three hours undergoing tests. They found no physical symptoms from the explosion; no lacerations, no bumps, no bruises, except the one he received hitting his head on the sink when he passed out. Even his ears looked fine, though blood poured from them when Grams found him. They were concerned about the blood loss, but he wouldn't need a transfusion. The tests showed no wounds or internal injuries that could have caused that amount of blood loss. They kept him for observation nonetheless.

When the doctor left, Eric walked in, arms held wide and a smile from ear to ear.

"Hey, brother. What's this I hear about you blowing up Billy Borks?"

Billy didn't respond.

Eric's smile withered. "I was just kidding, man. They told me you were okay. Are you... okay I mean?"

"I'm fine. Thanks for coming. Things are a little crazy right now, but I'm good."

"Good to hear. Man, did you miss a great party. You should see the things Kristin does when she gets alcohol in her. She did this dance that... " He stopped and glanced at Grams. "Um... she's a great dancer. Anyway, I'm glad to see you feel better. Sam is already out of here. How much longer until you get out?"

"Not sure. The Doc said he wants to keep me under observation a few days. Sam is already out? So he was here then. Is he okay?"

"He must be." Eric ran his hand through his hairspray stiffened hair. "They let him walk out of here. Couldn't be too much wrong with him." Eric glanced to Grams again. "Well I better get going. Kristin is supposed to meet me at the apartment in a half hour. I want to clean up before she gets there. I just wanted to make sure my drinking... er, my pal was okay."

"Good luck getting that place clean." Billy gave an exaggerated roll of his eyes. "I hope you have a shovel."

"Real funny, Hitchings. Catch you later." He turned to leave.

"Hang on a second. I need to get out of this bed. You feel like walking me to the bathroom down the hall?"

Eric waved his arm. "Come on then, girly boy. You need me to unzip your pants too?" He cringed and quickly looked to Grams. She still knitted, or at least, she pretended she didn't hear.

Getting out of bed felt good. They said their goodbyes and Billy did his business in the restroom. He washed his hands and stepped into the hallway. A nurse walked by pushing a bed with an Indian man, he looked like the same dark-skinned man in line at Billy Borks when it exploded. The man had been awake after the explosion. Their eyes had met before Billy ran.

He stayed a few paces behind and followed until the nurse turned into room 207.

Billy made his way back to his room and into bed.

Maybe the man remembered something. *Did he hear the sound coming from inside me?* At least the man didn't look like he was hurt too bad.

Billy needed to find out if the man knew anything, but Grams would be furious if he left bed again. "Isn't tonight the night you usually play chess with Abe?" He put on his best smile.

"Sure is. I'm fixing to call him and cancel. My Billy needs me today." She smiled at him from her chair.

"When are you going home?" He hoped it didn't sound rude.

"Oh, I don't know. My hip is a little tight from sitting in this chair." She wiggled back and forth. "I left my meds at home, so I'll have to get them some time."

A soap opera played an emotional roller coaster on the television. The local news and soap opera channels were the only two options. They sat there from the show's opening to the closing credits. Billy's mind reeled as he tried to find a reason for Grams to leave.

She stood and stepped toward the door.

"Where are you going, Grams?"

"Why're you so nosy?" she shot back at him. "I'm going to the crapper. Do I need permission to go to the bathroom now?" She started down the hall away from him.

Her hip must really hurt for her to be so snippy.

When she went to the 'crapper', it meant she'd be busy for at least a half hour. He hurried out of bed and to room 207 when he heard a deep voice coming from the dark-skinned man's room. Billy squatted, pretending to fix his hospital issue sock.

The two men discussed the explosion. The dark-skinned man, Amfar the other man had called him, told the same story Billy told Grams. He heard the scraping of a chair across the floor and the voices became harder to hear.

Billy shook. Sweat beaded on his forehead. His lungs felt like he breathed water. Amfar heard the noise too; it hadn't been Billy's imagination. Maybe Billy Borks held the answers.

John

John pulled his Wrangler into the parking lot. *Hard to believe this used to be Billy Borks.* He parked on the side with no glass on the pavement, next to where the frame of Amfar's Prius melted into the pavement. The windows had blown through to the other side.

The evening heat overwhelmed him. John thanked God for convertibles and tossed his jacket in the back.

He peered into the restaurant, a window into what must have been hell for the people inside at the time. The fact only one person lost their life was a miracle. The pressure must have been unimaginable to blow the wall in like that. No wonder Amfar's eardrums burst.

Electric cables and steel rods hung from the roof, their ends bent toward the rubble inside. To prevent further explosions, the city turned off the power and gas. He could walk up to the grill, or the soda machine, from outside without issue.

Before he reached the police tape surrounding the restaurant, he stopped, his mouth going wide. He snapped his mouth shut when he realized how he must look. There were no scorch marks on the building, or in the parking lot. He was no explosives expert, but there couldn't have been an explosion of this magnitude without leaving some type of residue. Maybe there was chemical residue.

The wind slammed one of the remaining doors into the back wall. He hopped back a few feet. He shook his head. *Calm down, John,* he told himself. The door would be a safer entrance than the blast opening.

The back of the restaurant looked like any other building. Enough light streamed through the opening in the side of the building that he wouldn't need a flashlight.

The front is where Amfar stood when the explosion took place. He stepped around the back wall into the short hallway leading toward the front. Two feet in front of him stood a boy who looked as shocked as he must. John's hand shot to his side, searching for the Glock that wasn't there. Still in the Jeep.

"Whoa, hey! Calm down, man. You scared the crap out of me." The kid held his hands up.

"That makes two of us." The kid wasn't any threat; he couldn't be more than seventeen years old, though he was quite tall and lanky. A white plastic band wrapped around the kid's wrist, much like the one Kelly and Amfar wore. "What are you doing in here? It could be dangerous."

The kid tried to stand taller, pulling his shoulders back. "I could ask you the same thing."

"Look kid, I don't think—" Snick. An arrow stuck in the wall between them, shaft vibrating. They both eyed the arrow. They dropped to the floor as another arrow snapped into the wall right next to the first.

The kid huddled against the wall with knees wrapped in his arms, whole body shaking. John scooted next to the kid, cursing himself for leaving the Glock in the Wrangler. It sat on his passenger's seat the whole way from New York. A lot of good it did him now.

"Hey, kid. What's your name?"

"Billy Hitchings."

"I see you were at the Grand Strand Medical Center." John nodded to the plastic strip on Billy's wrist. "Are you healthy enough to run?"

Billy nodded.

"Okay, Billy. My name is John. I'll get us out of here but I need you to listen."

Only two arrows were stuck in the wall above them. That could mean the shooter moved to a better position.

"My Jeep is on the west side of the restaurant, the side where the wall is missing. We're going to keep our heads low and head to the Jeep through where the wall used to be. If... I mean when, when we get to the Jeep, we'll be fine. Listen carefully, though. I need your help. I need you to watch to the left and right. Let me know if you see anything or anybody. Can you do that?" John hoped occupying the kid's mind would allow his body to respond quicker.

Billy nodded quickly. "Wait, who's shooting at us?" Billy hunched his shoulders. His hands shook, the fear obvious on his face.

"Does it really matter? No more questions. On three. Ready?" He didn't wait for the boy to respond. "One... two...three!"

John darted toward the front of the restaurant staying in a crouch. Billy breathed hard behind him, eyes flicking back and forth. *Good, he knows how to listen.* They hid behind metal shelves bolted to the cement floor.

They moved to the end of the shelving. The front counter was another ten feet away. The arrows had come from the north. Nothing would be between them during those ten feet.

"Stay as close as you can. When we get to that counter," John pointed, "get down on your belly and stay there until I tell you to move again."

John searched the cluttered floor around him and found what he needed, a metal cylinder used to hold fountain pop cups. He tested the weight and pitched it in the direction they'd just come from. It clanged noisily on the tile floor. No sooner than the cylinder hit did an arrow zip into view from somewhere north of his Jeep. They had a chance they'd get out without this arrow-toting maniac skewering them like a wild pig.

John grabbed Billy and pulled him forward. Billy dove to his belly as John told him. There was barely enough room behind the end of the front counter.

"We're almost there, kid. The Jeep is only fifty feet away. We're mostly covered on our way out, but I want you on my left side." John would be closer to the shooter, blocking Billy from any arrows if things went bad. "When we get there, I'll open the door, and you jump in. Just keep your head down. Okay?"

Not waiting for an answer, he lifted Billy by the back of his shirt. Judging from the arrows trajectory, they should have a clear path to his Jeep. Once out of the restaurant, they would be in the open.

Running in a crouch, they reached the outside of the restaurant. Ducking beneath hanging wires and metal rods, they launched into a sprint. John pictured arrows piercing their skin or flying overhead.

They reached the Jeep, and John flung the door open. Billy leapt in when open far enough for him to fit. John dove in behind and slammed the door.

***

John drove from one end of the strip to the other, zigzagging across the city by way of the side streets. He needed answers but was preoccupied searching the rearview mirror for signs of a tail.

"It's clear. We're going to the place I'm staying; we can talk there." John turned to the teenager next to him.

Billy had regained some of his composure but still stared out the window. He'd sobbed for the first five minutes after making their getaway and spent the next five hyperventilating.

John pulled the Jeep into Lisa's Getaway and parked in the back of the parking lot. He dialed Rachel, but her machine answered.

"Hey, Rach. This is John. Could you call Lisa and tell her to go ahead and charge me for next week as well? There are some things I need to find out, and I'm not sure how long it will take. Thanks, Hun." He hung up his cell and put it back in its case at his belt.

Billy looked at the carrying case and a smile came to his face. "You know those things went out of style ten years ago, right?"

"That may be, but in my line of work you never know when you might need to grab your phone. The couple of seconds it takes to reach into my pocket could be all it takes to lose my life. And welcome back from La La Land." They climbed from the Jeep as John's eyes scanned every passing car.

Billy raised his eyebrows. "Really? What do you do?"

John winked. "I'm an assistant editor at a publishing firm."

Billy stopped for a few seconds and then hurried to catch up. John watched him start to say something as they walked toward the cottage. Instead, Billy closed his mouth and continued following.

Once inside, John gestured to the blue floral print couch under the front window. Billy shuffled to the couch and sat. John tossed his jacket onto the back of a kitchen chair and put his Glock on the table between him and Billy. Billy's eyes flicked to the gun and then back to John.

John leaned on the table, hands on either side of the weapon. "I don't appreciate being shot at, kid."

"I didn't have anything to do with it!" Billy leaned forward on the couch.

"Shut up!"

Billy leaned back, looking like a reprimanded puppy.

"Like I said," John continued, "I don't appreciate being shot at, whether by bullets, arrows, rocks, or whatever. The point is, I need some answers, and I'm not in the mood to prattle."

Billy nodded once.

"What did you say your name was?"

"Billy. Billy Hitchings." The words spluttered from his mouth.

"Good. You have the idea now." John leaned back against the kitchen counter and crossed his arms. "I know it wasn't your fault. I'm just trying to put things together. What were you doing at Billy Borks?"

"I work there, or at least I used to."

John waited in silence, so the boy went on.

"I worked there, and I wanted to see if I could find anything."

"Anything for what? Were you trying to loot the place? Score some free burgers? Come on, kid. You need to do better than that."

Billy rose and looked John in the eyes across the small living room. "John, I'm only going to tell you this because you probably saved my life tonight. But when I'm done, you're going to tell me what you were doing there. Deal?"

The kid has balls. I'm the one with the gun, and he's making deals. "Deal."

Billy nodded and paced the few feet between the couch and end table. "I was there the day of the explosion. I was in the middle of an argument when the wall blew in toward us. I didn't get touched, not one cut from the flying glass. I don't understand how that's possible. So that's why I was there." Billy flopped down onto the couch; rusty springs creaked in protest. He took in a large breath and let it out in a deep sigh. "I *think* I might have caused the explosion."

John lunged forward, hands clenched on each side of the gun. "What do you mean you caused it? You had better answer fast, son. My fiancée was hurt in that explosion."

"No, no, I don't mean I caused it on purpose. I'm not even sure if I did cause it. I think I caused it. I don't really know how to explain it. I didn't put a bomb in there, or cross any wires or anything like that, but I think something inside me might have caused it."

"Great! Should we tell the police some kid's belly ache caused the explosion?"

"That's not what I meant." Billy shook his head.

A deep sigh escaped John's chest, and he rubbed his eyes. The kitchen chair squealed on the linoleum as he slid it out and sat down.

"I'm sorry. This whole situation is frustrating. I told you I'd tell you what I was doing there. But when I'm done, you'll be a little more forthcoming."

Billy nodded and released a long breath when John turned and sat the pistol in the drawer behind him.

John clasped his hands and continued. "I came to Myrtle Beach to work things out with my fiancée. We had a falling out a few weeks back."

"What did you do?"

"That's none of your business, kid. Don't make me get the gun back out."

Billy put his hands up, and John smiled. The kid had a sense of humor.

"Why do you keep calling me kid?"

"Sorry about that. An old habit I picked up from my dad. Anyway, I get down here and I can't find her right away. I get a phone call telling me she's in the hospital. I get there, she's unconscious, and she's been that way most of the week. I think you can understand why I'm a little frustrated."

Billy nodded.

"Today, Amfar woke up. He was the first one who could tell me anything about what happened. He thinks it had something to do with some plates he had in his trunk, but I'm not so sure."

If Billy were a dog, his ears would have just stood on end. *He knows something. The plates?*

John continued. "It's more likely there was a gas leak, or maybe somebody planted a bomb on Amfar's car. Then, there's the police department. They treat me like a leper every time I talk to them."

"I wonder why?" Billy rubbed his hands back and forth on his legs. "Oh. I forgot!" He sat up and slid to the edge of the couch. "My grandma said they stopped by while I was in the hospital. I hope they don't get mad when they find out I'm not there."

"Why would they be mad?"

"I wasn't exactly discharged from the hospital. I just left."

"Wait a minute. You weren't supposed to leave the hospital?"

Billy shook his head.

"Then we need to get you back." John stood and lifted his jacket from the chair. "I won't let it be my fault if something happens to you. Let's go."

"But, what about the people shooting arrows at us?" Billy's eyes flicked to the curtain covered windows.

"It won't matter if you get shot by an arrow if you're already dead."

***

John wrote down Billy's phone number before escorting him back to the hospital. He stopped in for a quick hello to Amfar. Kelly's condition hadn't changed in the few hours he'd been gone.

Daylight faded as he left the hospital. The sun would be down within minutes. He needed to hurry. A tail is harder to see at night.

John climbed into the Jeep. His brain processed the day's information. *So many questions*, he thought. *Like, why arrows?* There were plenty of ways to kill people—or scare them. He took as much air into his lungs as he could stand and let it out slowly. Coming to Myrtle Beach was supposed to relax him, minus the part about confronting Kelly anyway.

His phone vibrated. A voicemail from Rachel. Tom Jarrett had called her number looking for a way to contact John. She remarked how rude the man was.

Jarrett must have some powerful friends, but why get Rachel's number when he could have easily found John's? *Unless he's showing me just how resourceful he is.*

The phone vibrated again, and the panel lit up. Tom Jarrett's name showed on the Caller ID.

John sighed and pressed the talk button. "Hello?" He had no desire to talk to the man.

"This John Reeves?"

"It is. What do you want, Jarrett? Kelly is still unconscious. Amfar only just woke up but can't talk on the phone because of the damage to his eardrums. And why call Rachel?"

"I'm not calling about them, John. Can I call you John?" He didn't wait for an answer. "This is the deal, John. I have the police working on what happened at Billy Borks as we speak, but there are some things I need help with. I believe you're the man to do that. That's why I called Rachel. To learn more about the man I'm asking for help."

He isn't the type to ask favors.

John laughed. "I'm sure Rachel had a lot to say. Anyway, I'm a little busy with Kelly at the moment. For curiosity's sake, what did you have in mind?"

"I hear you're a man that knows how to get things done. I need to find something—a few things actually—but I can't because I'm in Kentucky," he growled. "Listen, I know you don't contract out your services anymore, but this won't be anything like that. I just want you to head over to Billy Borks and have a look around."

"You're right. I don't do contracting anymore; I'm a bodyguard. You seem to know a lot of things that would be very hard for most people to find out."

"I'm not most people, John. I have a lot of friends and even more resources. If you find what I want you to find, you'll be rewarded."

His friends and resources must not be that good, or he would know that I don't need a reward; I have enough money for the both of us.

"What is it you want me to find, Mr. Jarrett?"

"I'm glad you're willing to see things my way. You need to find what was lost in the explosion. Amfar and Kelly were in possession of three plates, most likely in the trunk of Amfar's piece-of-shit car. They were in an airtight chest, specially made for transferring bones and other items."

"You want me to find you some plates?" John huffed in disbelief. "Were they family heirlooms? Unless they were titanium, they wouldn't have made it through the blast. Besides, wouldn't the police have already found them if there was anything to find?"

He ignored the questions. "Find those plates, John. I'll answer your questions then. In the meantime, you'll find I transferred five thousand dollars into your bank account. A deposit four times that amount will follow upon delivery of the three plates. One of the plates is indigo, one is maize, and the third is blood red. They are distinct. You will know them when you find them."

Jarrett hung up.

The guy was arrogant, but when you had twenty five thousand dollars to hand out for finding and delivering some plates, people tended to listen. John wouldn't let someone lead him around on a leash, at least not for long. He'd find those plates for himself. He didn't know why they were so special to Jarrett, and he didn't care. What he wanted to know was whether they survived the explosion. If so, how.

Chapter 9

Billy

Billy sat at the kitchen table. Eric lounged across from him and stuffed handfuls of Doritos into his mouth while they watched the storm approach. The wind picked up as thick dark clouds raced by. The first fat rain drops echoed on the chimney chute and slapped at the opened kitchen window.

"You really like her that much?" Billy held his hand out for a chip.

A peel of thunder shook the window frame. Eric flinched but kept his eyes focused on the incoming maelstrom. "I really do. Kind of scary, huh?" He put a chip in Billy's hand and nibbled on another.

Since the Billy Borks explosion a week earlier, Eric spent every minute with Kristin, the new girl from his work. Billy didn't want to point out that he'd done the same with so many other girls. Each time, Eric insisted the girl was different.

Eric finished munching the last Dorito and walked the empty bag to the trash. He stepped to the sink and washed his hands, paying extra attention to the cheese under his nails. He finished and turned to Billy.

"I know what you're thinking. I see it in your eyes. You think this is just another infatuation, like Camille."

Like every relationship you've been in, Billy thought.

"Think about this though," Eric continued. "Did I ask Camille to move in with me? Other than you, have I ever asked anybody to move in with me?"

Billy wanted to believe this time was different. Eric put himself through the same cycle of infatuation, break up, then depression, over and over. At least there was an easy cure. A few beers, a party, and the next day Eric's ex was a dim memory.

Eric smacked Billy on the back of the head as he walked back to the table. "Enough about me." He rubbed his still orange fingers on his khaki shorts. "How are you feeling? You exploded, and yet you were only in the hospital for two days. Then only because you passed out and cracked your skull on the cement. Is my drinking partner okay?"

Billy leaned forward whispering, "Be quiet, man. I told you, nobody can know I was there. If Grams found out it wasn't some cracked out story from hitting my head, she'd have me back at the hospital before you can say false teeth."

Eric's head cocked to the side.

"I don't mean to get on you about this, but I don't want to go to jail for something that wasn't my fault."

"You mean Bryan."

"Yes, I mean Bryan. I feel bad for the guy, but whatever happened was just some freak accident." Billy leaned back into the uncomfortable oak chair and inhaled a deep breath. "I really need you to listen, Eric. We've been friends a long time, and I need your help."

Eric leaned in. "What's up, Billy? You know I'm here for you."

Billy fought off the urge to hug his friend. Eric *was* there for him, no matter what came their way. He loved his friend as much as any man could love another.

"I'll tell you something I haven't told anybody about that day at Billy Borks." Billy looked over his shoulder to see Grams in the living room napping in her chair. He turned back to his friend. "Not even John. Well, I told John a little, but not what I'm going to tell you. I *did* have something to do with Bryan being killed, but it wasn't on purpose."

"What do you mean?" Eric's eyed were wide.

"There was something inside me—no that's not right. Something churned inside of me when the explosion happened. Not an object, but an—awareness, a feeling. I was angry. Bryan kept poking me in the chest. The one thought going through my head was that I wanted to be away from that place." Billy lunged forward and slapped the table with both hands. "I wanted Bryan to stop, and I wanted to be away. I repeated it over and over in my mind. I hoped it would happen, or saying the words would calm me down. That's when the feeling began welling up inside me. Not something alien, but part of my soul, part of me."

He hadn't realized he stood and told the story with his hands. Eric leaned back in his chair, scrutinizing Billy's every movement. He looked back to Grams again, ensuring his outburst hadn't woke her.

He turned back. Eric hadn't moved. His mouth hung open and he stared dumbly at Billy. "Why are you looking at me like that?"

Eric shook his head like he came out of a fog. "Like what?"

"I don't know. Like a kid watching a dog poop."

"Where do you come up with stuff like that?" Eric laughed and quickly covered his mouth, peaking over Billy's shoulder. "I didn't mean to look at you like…like… what you said. I imagined what you must have felt, and what you must feel now. I've never seen you so animated or passionate, even when you talk about women. Why do you think you had something to do with the building exploding though? You think somehow your words did it?"

Billy slumped back into the chair, making one of the legs pop out of place. "I just don't know. That's all I've thought about since it happened. The more I said those words, the faster I said them, the more the power grew. Right at the instant when I knew my chest would explode, the building did instead. The pressure, or power, just disappeared. Like it let go. I could be reading too much into it, but I don't think I am."

"If you don't even know what happened, what do you want help with?" Eric reached to the back of the chair and grabbed his jacket, placing it on his lap.

"Remember I told you about those two people waiting in line when it happened, and how I saw them at the hospital?"

Eric nodded.

"When that Indian guy talked to John, I heard him say something about having a chest in their trunk. I guess they are archaeologists. I think maybe whatever was in their trunk had something to do with the explosion, like it was tuned in to my anger."

The thick clouds and pounding rain slowed. Storms were like that in South Carolina—pitch-black sky and torrential downpours followed by sunny, ozone-filled aftermaths.

Eric lifted his jacket from his lap and stood. "This is a little crazy, Billy. You know I'm on your side, but it sounds like you're jumping to conclusions. Let's go." He gestured toward the door. "I have some nice green we can use to clear our minds."

Amfar

Amfar sat in the beige recliner watching the rainfall through the tinted hospital windows. His normal workday didn't allow him time to sit and enjoy something so simple as reading a book, relaxing, or watching nature's beauty.

The pain and ringing in his ears were only a whisper. He'd filled out his release forms two days before. The doctor explained that a combination of the sound and air pressure from the explosion caused Amfar's eardrums to burst. He said not to listen to loud music for a few weeks, but there shouldn't be any permanent damage.

The comfortable chair became his friend while he read Sheriff Scott's book cover to cover multiple times. The hospital's comforts were enjoyable for the most part, except the cafeteria. Minus the fried foods and pizza, there wasn't much of a selection. Most of his time he sat in one of the chairs in Kelly's room, waiting for her to wake. The most recent tests showed she remained in an extended REM sleep and should wake soon.

John Reeves visited multiple times a day. Amfar reassured him that he would be the first to know when she woke. The last time John came in, he had dark rings under his bloodshot eyes. Lack of sleep Amfar assumed. John's fiancée and girlfriend of three years lay unconscious in the hospital in a city neither of them lived and nobody knew why. Not to mention she had been in an explosion a few weeks before. Who could blame him for not sleeping?

The police department hadn't tried contacting Amfar, including the two police officers who spoke with his nurse. When Kelly woke, he would visit the department and ask for a look at the police report. He needed to know who the boy behind the counter was. The nametag said Billy, but Amfar needed more than a first name to get answers.

He'd tucked away his feelings for Kelly. Only when Amfar's world blew up did he realize how much she meant to him. Life and death situations can cause inaccurate views of one's feelings, but his affection for her blossomed before the explosion. Telling her how he felt was the best idea, but he had to wait. She and John only broke up a few weeks before, and there was the explosion at Billy Borks. If he believed in gods, he would say they conspired against him.

"Hey, Ammy."

Amfar's recliner almost spun in a complete circle before coming to a stop. Kelly smiled, but her eyes betrayed the depth of her fatigue.

The chair squeaked as he rose and walked to her side. He pulled her hand into his, careful to avoid the IV. "It's good to have you back, Ms. Pierce."

She squeezed his hand. "Are you really being that formal right now, or is that a sense of humor I detect?"

"Honestly? It's probably a combination of what little sense of humor I have and the tired expectation I've had since I woke up five days ago."

Kelly licked her lips and ran her free hand through her hair.

"Don't they have shampoo in this place?" She tried to sit up but only made it a few inches. Her eyes opened wider as she looked around the room. "Speaking of *this place*, where am I? Wait. Five days ago? Oh my God, Amfar."

Pulling one hand from hers, he held it out in a grand gesture.

"Mr. Jarrett said our hotel cost too much. We now have accommodations at The Grand Strand Regional Hospital."

Her eyes tried to take in the whole room at once.

He took her hand with both of his again. "Sorry. I'm so excited that you're awake I forgot you have no idea what happened."

"How long have I been here, Amfar?"

The plastic chair squealed across the linoleum as he slid it to her bed and took a seat. He told her everything. At first, he wasn't going to tell her his idea about the kid having anything to do with the explosion, but he didn't hold anything back. Kelly remembered the exact same things Amfar did, including the strange sound that came from the boy's direction.

"There is something else I need to tell you." He cast his eyes toward the floor. "It doesn't have anything to do with the things we have just discussed, but you will want to know."

She waited for him to continue.

He brought his eyes back to hers, hoping his emotions wouldn't betray him. "John Reeves is here."

Her face flushed, but whether from embarrassment or anger he didn't want to guess.

She closed her eyes and took deep breaths. "What does he want?"

"I'm not sure. We haven't had much time to speak. He came in a few days ago when I woke up. Since then, he has been coming and going every few hours." He paused. "I know I always say we should keep things at a strictly platonic level, but as you stated before, we are friends. I know you two are not currently courting, but I am certain he shows genuine concern for you."

Her eyes fluttered back open, and she smiled. Her face returned to its normal pallor. "Oh, Ammy. I know he's concerned. That was never the question. I still care for him deeply. I would even say I still love him, but that doesn't matter. A relationship isn't based on how much you love the other person. If that were true, we would still be together. When I can't trust him to keep his pants zipped around random women, then there is no basis for us to build that relationship."

"I… uh…" She'd just confessed to still loving John. Was he ever a fool. However, she also said their relationship wouldn't work. *Why do women speak in riddles?*

"I'm sorry." Kelly squeezed his hand. "You've been such a sweetheart. You spent all this time with me, and here I am handing out relationship advice."

He managed a small laugh. "It is okay, Kelly. I just thought you would like to know." He lowered his eyes to the floor.

"Get over here and give me a hug."

"Right now?" His eyes widened as he searched for an escape.

"Yes, right now. I need a hug from my friend."

He sat on the edge of the bed. She put one hand on his shoulder and the other on the back of his head, and pulled him close. The warmth of her breath on his ear gave him chills.

She whispered, "Thank you so much for being here for me, Amfar. I mean it. You really are a sweet guy. I'm glad it was you here with me."

Thoughts wouldn't form. He sat hugging her, enjoying the moment. She pulled his head back and kissed him on the forehead.

What does a kiss on the forehead mean? Isn't that something a woman does to her little brother? Or her child? He enjoyed the kiss, but now his mind swirled with questions.

"I'm glad it was me too, Kelly." An involuntary chortle escaped Amfar's mouth. "Now I'm going to press this red button to get your nurse in here. If they find out you've been awake for almost a half hour and I did not contact them, they will have my—"

"Hide," she finished for him.

Chapter 10

John

Jarrett's call prompted John to spend the next few days searching Billy Borks and the surrounding area. He explored the ruins in the early morning hours when the sun just crested the horizon or late in the evening by the light of the moon. No need to catch the attention of the local police force. Jarrett said they closed the investigation but no need to test them.

Twice he visited the police station, and they politely told him to leave. The case didn't involve him or one of his family members, and his fiancée didn't count. Their final report would read like any other explosion—gas left on, a burner going, or an unknown leak somewhere. The trip to the local fire department proved useless as well.

The dollar store flashlight dimmed enough to make working his way to the back difficult. Billy Borks was the same as the first night, minus the arrows. *Shouldn't this be cleaned up and made safe for the public?*

John made it to the back door and walked toward his Jeep in the Lizard's parking lot. Acid stirred in his stomach, fighting its way toward his throat. The clock in his Jeep read eleven o'clock. Time to check on Kelly.

The stomach acid flared when his thoughts centered on Kelly. Sleep remained elusive as well. The doctors had been so sure she'd wake up soon. Every day she didn't, his heart broke that much more.

The next growl from his stomach he attributed to lack of food. Nothing had sounded good since breakfast. A large neon sign flickered in front of him. Lizards. 'Not just another burger joint' according to the sign.

White powder from the shattered concrete covered his clothes. Easy to clean off in the restroom, no need to stoke the other customers' curiosity.

The glass doors pulled open with a tug. A businessman sat in the corner chatting on his phone, few people stood in line. *Slow night.* John's boots squeaked across the wet floor and left footprints from the entrance to the bathroom. A Lost and Found poster hung on the door beneath the men's restroom sign.

Do you know who owns this blanket, the sign read.

The picture showed a tattered blue blanket. More like a pile of strings. Some poor kid lost their best friend. The child must have loved the thing to get that much use out of it.

The bathroom door swung open with a shove. The mirror just inside the door showed the worsening rings under his eyes. Much longer without sleep, and he'd have to call in another favor from Rachel. Sleeping pills sounded better every day.

The water splashed white dust from his face into the sink. He leaned forward and stared at his morbid expression. His breath caught.

The copper handle slammed into the tile wall from the mighty shove he gave the bathroom door on his way back to the hallway. He pulled the door back closed as his eyes ran over the Lost and Found sign. Beneath the blue blanket was a pair of Adidas running shoes. Below those, three plates. The sign ripped in half as he tore it from the door. He struggled to keep himself from running as he made his way to the front of the restaurant.

John cut in front of a young couple in mid-order and slammed the poster on the counter in front of a stick-skinny girl wearing the Lizard's outfit.

"Do you still have these? I need to know. Now."

The young couple backed up, the teenage boy glared at him. John returned the glare. The boy's eyes went to the floor before he pulled his girlfriend behind him. John felt bad scaring the kid, but he'd spent three days searching for the damn plates, barely even slept.

Moments later, a man in his early twenties stepped to the service desk. Jeffrey the General Manager according to his nametag. "Is there something I can do for you, sir?"

"I asked your employee if you still had these." He pointed at the picture of the plates.

"Our lost and found is in my office. Can you prove the plates are yours?"

John imagined his fist breaking the dweeb's nose. He leaned forward and gripped the counter with both hands. "How the hell can I prove the plates are mine?" His knuckles turned white.

"Well, sir, I'm sorry. But according to our policy, I'm not allowed to take anything from the lost and—"

"Listen, you little shit. I don't care about your policy. I've spent the last three days climbing through all that crap over there," he pointed at Billy Borks, "slipping on grease and getting poked with the random pieces of metal. I even spent this morning walking through the swamp by your parking lot. I'm not in the mood to discuss policy." His chest heaved; he was way out of hand. John's father warned him about losing his temper. Good ole Ed Reeves couldn't take the chance of losing his; a police officer losing his temper could mean the difference between life and death.

Jeffrey's eyes were wide; he bit his lower lip. The situation wasn't exactly life and death, but John took a calming breath anyway. He remembered Tom Jarrett's description of the plates.

"I'm sorry, Jeffrey. The plates were my mother's, and I'd really like them back. Knocking on the edge creates a metallic sound rather than the sound glass would."

Jeffrey adjusted his bowtie, nodded, and turned toward the back of the restaurant without saying a word. A moment later, he returned with a plastic Winn Dixie bag and handed it to John. He thanked the manager and left Lizards, forgetting about food.

The feeling was surreal. He'd spent days searching for the plates. The longer they had been missing, the more he was convinced they had something to do with the explosion. Was Jarrett protecting himself from legal problems? Maybe that's why the restaurant was left as it was.

John thought about how the police treated him. Did Jarrett have the resources, and the balls, to pay off the police department? Jarrett had money, but his pockets weren't deep enough to buy off an entire police department. Were they?

Why not hold onto the plates for a few days, see what he could learn before handing them over to Mr. Power Hungry.

Amfar

Amfar pushed Kelly in a large wheelchair; bits of rust fell from the wheels as they squeaked through the hotel lobby. The man behind the front desk showed his teeth in a fake half-smile.

He wheeled Kelly to her room. Once inside, she climbed out of the chair and walked to the coffee maker. Amfar followed, arms held out behind her, ready to catch her if she fell.

"Are you sure this is okay, Kelly? Doctor Carmichael said you should take it easy the next two weeks."

She finished pouring water in the coffee maker and hit the brew switch.

"The coffee in that place probably did more damage than that stupid explosion." Kelly pretended to put a finger down her throat and vomit. "Did you try it?"

Amfar nodded. The coffee was horrible.

"Besides," she went on, "Doctor Carmichael said I should walk when I can. What better place than my home for the next week?" She stepped into the living area and sat on the couch. Amfar remained close behind. "I still can't believe Tom is letting us stay another week."

Amfar was tempted to tell her why Mr. Jarrett allowed them to stay. He lowered his arms when he saw she didn't plan to stand back up. When his arms lowered, she stood.

"What are you doing?" Amfar's arms popped back up behind her.

"Calm down, Ammy." She grabbed the remote from the end table and sat back down. "I'd like to watch the news, catch up with the world a little, see what big events I missed lying in that stinky room. Why do hospitals smell like that?"

"Probably the combination of bodily fluids and the chemical solutions used to clean them."

Kelly moved her hands to the sides of her head and fell back against the couch, eyes held tightly closed.

Amfar sat next to her. "Kelly? Are you okay?" He gave her hands a gentle tug.

Her eyes opened, and she laughed so hard she had difficulty breathing. "Oh, Ammy. We almost died, but we come back here to the hotel and you're the same as always. You take everything so literal."

When he saw she wasn't having an aneurism, or some other scary medical condition, he smiled and slid to the other end of the couch.

"Will you check on the coffee?" Kelly wiped the tears from her eyes and turned on the television.

Amfar shot Kelly a pretend dirty look and stepped into the miniature hotel kitchen. He pulled two coffee cups from the cupboard and tore open some sugar packets. He could hear the voice of the local news anchor Anna Brooks from channel nine. The fiery little woman was born and raised in Myrtle Beach. Amfar became a quick fan while in the hospital. Channel nine was one of two channels the hospital played. Cartoons and soap operas didn't hold much appeal.

"Amfar? Come in here a second. They're talking about Billy Borks."

Kelly turned up the volume, and he sat next to her again. He handed her a cup of coffee and held his own on his lap.

Anna reported from the parking lot in front of the husk of Billy Borks. Her voice held the stern tone today as it did when she reported upsetting news. Evidently, according to her broadcast, the police were not showing the journalists any favors either. They didn't return any of her twenty-two calls, and they threw her out of the police station twice.

"What do you think?" Kelly kept her eyes on the television.

"She has a point. The police have been somewhat quiet about the whole situation. One would think that with an explosion in their city, they would do everything in their power to learn what happened. Who knows? Maybe they have it all figured out and are waiting for the right time to capture the person or persons involved."

"Did you hear what she just said?" She turned the television up further. Anna compared the explosion to another seven years before blamed on a natural gas leak. The city tore the building down within a week, yet Billy Borks still stood, and was a danger to the public she pointed out. The police would not tell her when they planned to let the bulldozers in.

"It doesn't add up." Amfar steepled his hands and sat forward. "Do you think the investigation is ongoing? Mr. Jarrett said it was closed."

"When did you talk to Tom?"

"When he called about letting us stay another week after leaving the hospital. I guess it does seem strange they've kept the building standing for so long. Maybe if the investigation were still ongoing, but if it is closed, then why? And why will they not speak to the press?"

Kelly lowered the volume when they began discussing shark sightings off the coast.

"No wonder you're a scientist, Ammy. You ask more questions than a two-year-old."

Not sure what she meant, he assumed it was a compliment. Amfar went to the kitchen and poured the rest of his coffee down the drain. He prepared a second for Kelly, adding her two sugars.

"If there is anything you need," Amfar handed her the coffee, "Charlie at the front desk will help. He also has my cell number."

She took a sip and set the cup on the end table. "Where are you going? You have some big date you didn't tell me about?"

He put his hands in his pockets to keep from fidgeting. "Nothing like that. I am taking your advice and relaxing a little. I'm going for a drive to get a better look at the city and beach."

She paused a moment and then nodded, picking up her coffee. "Have fun."

He waved, but she just took another sip and kept her eyes on the news. The coffee's rich aroma made him thirsty, but he had other things to take care of.

John

John stretched back in his bed and stared at the ceiling. The sun peeked through the shades, casting light across the ceiling. The clock showed seven o'clock. Two hours and he'd confront Kelly.

John replayed the three cell messages in his head from the night before. The first was Amfar, the second Rachel, and the third the hospital. All three were the same —Kelly was awake and fine. *Sneaky Rachel*, he thought. Access to the hospital's records was the only way she could have called fifteen minutes before they had.

When John called Kelly's room after midnight the night before, Amfar answered. He told John that Kelly was asleep, and the nurses wouldn't let anybody in to see her. *Then why let Amfar?*

He climbed out of bed to make a pot of coffee. The lack of sleep wore on him. There would be enough time to look at the plates again, too. He didn't know what he was looking for or what he expected.

He held his cup over the warming plate where the carafe should be. Patience wasn't one of his virtues. The coffee overflowed onto his fingers. He growled at his stupidity and put the pot in place before too much was lost.

Cooling his fingers with cold water from the kitchen faucet, he held his coffee in the other hand and drank. The paltry two hours of sleep let his thoughts get in the way of safety. His father taught him better.

When John first spoke with Amfar at the hospital, the man had a staring contest with the wall. Right in Kelly's direction. There were questions John needed answered.

Amfar said they'd be back at the hotel around eight in the morning, and he should call around nine. *When did he volunteer to be her big brother?*

Three cups of coffee finally gave him enough ambition to shower and shave. He wore the brown t-shirt Kelly bought him on their trip to the Keys the year before; she said it made his eyes stand out. Leather Jesus sandals and khaki shorts completed his outfit for the humid day sure to come.

Getting ready took longer than expected. It was almost eight already, just enough time for him to stop at Buster's for his daily coffee and newspaper, maybe enough for breakfast. He'd need a full stomach when meeting Kelly. He didn't need it growling at an inopportune time. After their last conversation, he needed every advantage.

***

At nine, he said his goodbyes to Buster, flipped open his cell, and stepped outside. His body was already prepared for the heat from the lack of air-conditioning at the Breakfast Nook.

"Hey, Kelly. It's John. It's good to hear your voice. How are you feeling?" The questions poured from him; his nerves were worse than he thought. He climbed into the Wrangler and pulled onto the Grand Strand toward the Starglazer.

"Don't come here, John. Amfar told me you called last night. I'm fine. Please don't come."

"I know I deserve that, but please, just give me five minutes. That's all."

A pause.

"Fine. Room six. I'll give you ten minutes and a cup of coffee. Then, you'll leave."

He agreed and told her he'd see her in a few minutes. A growl came from his stomach even though he just filled it with eggs and hash browns. Maybe that's why it growled. Buster seemed to think the more grease the better.

Two pots of coffee could make his heart pound, but not as hard as it pounded now. This was his last chance. He'd tell her how he feels, say sorry one more time, and that would be that. Most likely, she'd just tell him to leave Myrtle Beach, but he wouldn't without giving their relationship one last try. Maybe she'd sense his sincerity.

The hotel looked expensive. John was surprised Tom Jarrett would spend so much money on somebody other than himself, especially lowly employees.

Room six was on the ground level and less than fifty feet from the front desk. He stood five full minutes in front of Kelly's door before knocking. The acid in his stomach made him wish he'd turned down the to-go coffee from Buster.

The door clicked open a few inches. He nudged it forward and saw Kelly walking toward the back room. He closed the door and followed her past the bedroom into the living area. She grabbed a pack of menthols from the end table and pointed to the window. Two coffee cups sat on a table outside.

"Did the doctor tell you those would help with your recovery?" He plopped down in the padded white chair.

She lit her cigarette and tossed the pack on the table. She must have been practicing her glower.

"I'm not here to discuss cigarettes." John smiled. "I'm sure you know that, but when did you start again?"

"Five minutes ago."

This was not going well. She arched her brows and looked as though she'd kill him.

"I get it. No small talk."

She gave him a mock smile that never touched her eyes.

"I'm sorry that I—"

"You already said you're sorry," Kelly interrupted.

"Give me a break, Kelly. I know I hurt you, but it wasn't intentional. I told you from the beginning I've always had trouble staying with one woman. It had nothing to do with you."

She ground her cigarette into the dolphin shaped ashtray on the table. "Is that supposed to make me feel better? Of course it had something to do with me. You screwed some girl while *we* were engaged. Do I know her? Was it someone you worked with?"

"It doesn't matter who it was." He picked up the coffee to give him a break from her scowl.

"It matters to me."

The coffee burned his tongue. He quickly put it back on the table. "It wasn't anybody you know. Just a girl I met from the pastry shop across the street from work."

"That's much better. I'm glad you destroyed our relationship because of some girl you didn't even know."

John didn't know what to say. Everything he said made things worse.

She closed her eyes and took a long, deep breath. When she opened them, she pointed toward the door. "Get out."

I shouldn't have tried this when her wounds are so fresh. He nodded and walked to the front of the hotel room. The door opened, and Kelly called from behind. He turned.

She was a silhouette in the doorway to the veranda, the reflected light from the ocean glowed behind her. "Be careful. The explosion wasn't an accident."

"What do you mean?"

Kelly took quick strides toward John and grabbed his shoulders. "I don't know what I mean. Just be careful." She placed her hands on the back of his head and pulled him to her. They kissed. The warmth of her tears fell on his face. She pushed him back and gave him a small smile, then pointed to the door.

Billy

"I know what I saw, Eric." Billy took a hit from Eric's cigarette while they lounged behind the Waterbar.

Eric grabbed the cigarette back.

"I'm sure you have no doubt what you think you saw. Think about it, what are the chances John would just happen to carry the plates out of Lizards right when you ride by?"

"I told you, I've been back to Billy Borks almost every night this week, and he was there three different times searching the place."

"How do you know he was searching?"

"He was picking shit up, throwing it around, eyes moving all over the place. How would you know if somebody looked for something?"

"Good point." Eric paused, eyes going to the pavement in front of him. His brows raised and he looked back up. "But you said all you saw was a white bag that looked like it could have the plates in it. Maybe he got some take-out. Lizards has great burgers. You know that."

Eric tossed his cigarette down the sewer grate, and put his rolled up apron in his armpit.

"Are you done with work?"

"I'm working a double today, but I'm on break. Why?"

Billy smiled.

Eric shook his head. "No. Whatever it is, no. I don't like that look, Billy. That's how you looked just before you gave Jessica a third eye."

"Come on. You said you'd help. It shouldn't take longer than fifteen minutes."

***

They climbed into Eric's car and pulled onto the Grand Strand.

"He's staying at Lisa's getaway down by the pier." Billy rubbed his sweaty palms on his blue jeans. "He's gone most of the day almost every day, so I'll go in and look for the plates. You stay outside and text me if you see him. If he shows up, I'll get my butt out of there. I'll have you back to work by three, promise. Oh, and doesn't your boss get mad when you do that?"

"Do what?" Eric asked.

"Leave a huge circle of rust in the parking lot every time you close your door."

Billy covered up just as Eric tried swatting him. Eric tried a couple more times, but Billy's long arms proved too much for him.

They pulled into Lisa's Getaway and around to the back. Billy gave Eric a quick description of John's Jeep and climbed out.

Billy acted as if he belonged there, as if he simply walked out to his own little cottage on the beach. He stepped along the red paving stones set into the sand to look like cobblestone. Last time he'd been to John's cottage it was in the evening, and he'd been freaking out. The place was quite nice. The cottage looked like it belonged on the beach, but not in the middle of seven or eight other cottages that looked the same. The twenty story pinkish hotel next door seemed out of place.

There were four cobblestones between him and John's cottage when his phone vibrated. He wiped the sweat from his forehead with the collar of his shirt and looked at the text. Eric asked if he knew how to pick a lock.

How could I be so stupid? Am I going to walk through the wall? Turning around appealed to him, but he was so close. He would at least try.

He stepped over the last cobblestones in two strides and slid his hand over the doorknob, frozen, not willing to turn the knob yet. He took a deep breath and gave it a twist. The door clicked open. *Strange. John doesn't seem the type to leave doors unlocked.*

Billy put the phone back in his pocket and pushed the door open the rest of the way.

The plastic bag John carried from Lizards the night before sat on the table, a few feet inside the door. He let out the breath he didn't realize he held and reached forward. Something was wrong. It was too light. He spread the bag open on the table. Empty.

"Hey there, Billy. Good to see you again," John's voice said behind him.

Billy's heart stopped, and he began to turn, head filled with explanations. Eric flew through the door and landed on top of him, sending them both crashing to the floor next to the kitchen table. John Reeves loomed in the doorway holding a gun, the same one that sat on his table during their conversation a few weeks earlier. John didn't aim it at either of them, but the way he stood, he looked ready to pounce.

"This isn't what it looks like, John." Billy rolled from beneath Eric and crab crawled backward.

"I'm pretty sure it is. Looks like a punk kid is breaking into my cottage while his punk friend is on lookout. What's the matter? Your grandma not giving you enough allowance? You thought you'd break in here and take my gun? Speak fast. I'm not having a good day."

Billy stood and wiped his hands on his t-shirt. "I was checking if you found the plates. I thought I saw you with them last night at Lizards. When you didn't call me last night, or today, I thought maybe you forgot about me."

John walked the rest of the way into the room and put the gun down in front of him the same as he had before. This time, however, he looked like hell. Dark circles ringed his eyes, and his shoulders slumped.

"How in the hell could I forget having arrows fly by my head? If this were the Wild West maybe, but these days that doesn't happen. Why did you follow me?"

"I know I said I wouldn't go back to Billy Borks, but I had to. I just drove by on my bike. I rode by last night, and I saw you come out of Lizards with that bag. What happened? You looked like you wanted to kill someone."

John shook his head. "Nothing that concerns you. I was there as a favor to a friend. Why did you break in to my cottage? Why didn't you just call?"

Eric sat on the couch, and Billy took a step forward.

"I wanted to, but I forgot to get your number. I know it was stupid, but you know how important this is to me, John. That night with the arrows scared me, but the explosion... that leaves me barely able to breath. I went back because I didn't care if they shot at me again. I need answers."

John's shoulders slumped further. "I believe you, but next time just call me, or leave a note. No breaking the law. And who is your friend over there?" He nodded toward Eric.

"I'm Eric. How did you know I was on lookout? And how did you get all the way to my car without me seeing you?"

John pointed to the couch for Billy to sit next to Eric and paced the few steps back and forth across the kitchen.

"Nice to meet you, Eric. John Reeves. If I told you all my secrets, they wouldn't be secrets, would they?" He winked.

Eric sank further into the couch.

"So, did you get any answers?" John leaned on the kitchen table. It listed dangerously to the side but John didn't seem to care.

"What do you mean?" Billy asked.

"You have the plates. Did you get your answers?"

Billy and Eric looked at each other; his face must have held the same confusion as Eric's.

"I don't have the plates, John. You do. You just said you got them from the restaurant."

"And I left them here, on the table, in the bag. They're no longer in the bag, so you must have them."

Billy and Eric shook their heads.

John's eyes opened wide, the muscles in his neck and hands tightened. His hand quickly went to the gun. He lifted it in front of him like the police did in cop shows. John put a finger to his lips and motioned for them to get down on the floor behind the table.

Billy saw his emotions reflected back at him from Eric. His friend's face took on a light pallor as he slid down to the floor.

Letting the gun lead the way, John walked from the kitchen area to the back of the cottage. Sweat dripped from Billy's nose onto Eric's pant leg. John came out moments later, no longer holding the gun out in front.

"You can get up. They're gone." John used a dishtowel to wipe the sweat from his head and sat at the kitchen table.

They hurried from under the table, eyes searching for hidden enemies.

"Who are *they*?" Billy ran through Dr. Flanagan's breathing exercise.

"Calm down, kid. I told you, they're gone. And I'm not sure who *they* are, but I have an idea."

Chapter 11

Amfar

Amfar found a car rental coupon in his hotel room. He phoned a cab for a ride to the agency and rented a Prius, the same year as the one that melted in the Billy Borks' parking lot. He was used to how it felt on the road, and it wouldn't hurt to save a few dollars on gas for Mr. Jarrett. The next stop was the Myrtle Beach City Police Department; he was to talk to a Sergeant Kirkwall.

When he arrived, the clerk told him to have a seat and that the Sergeant would see him shortly. Almost a half hour passed before Amfar checked to make sure the clerk hadn't forgotten about him. Her seat was empty. The sign on the window said she was out to lunch. He was about to ring the bell on the counter when a man stepped from a room beside Amfar.

"Sergeant Kirkwall?"

The Sergeant nodded and held out a briefcase. Amfar accepted it, and Kirkwall turned and stepped back into the room.

"Wait, what is this? What am I supposed to do with it?" Amfar took a step toward the room Kirkwall had come from.

The door slammed shut. Amfar waited for a moment. Kirkwall didn't return, so he shrugged and took the briefcase back to the Prius. He wasn't sure whether to look inside or call Mr. Jarrett. Considering Kirkwall's strange behavior, he opted to look in the case.

The clasps clicked open when Amfar pressed the keyhole on the edge. He opened the case slowly. His breath caught. The briefcase held the leather tube that had been stored in the chest with the three plates. *Impossible.*

The explosion should have destroyed the tube, and the manuscript within.

The case felt as smooth and unmarred as the day Dr. Gibbons gave it to him and Kelly to hold. He unwound the string from the tip and looked inside. The manuscript was still intact.

How did Mr. Jarrett know the ancient texts were with the police department? There was much more to this than his boss let on. Jarrett told him to bring the case back to Dr. Gibbons, but Amfar had another idea.

Amfar hurried back to the hotel, tempted to speed. The door to his room clicked shut. He hoped it was quiet enough for Kelly not to hear. Amfar hoped the bright lights in his scanner wouldn't hurt the ancient text. The file transferred to his hard drive in seconds. The scheduled time for his appointment with Dr. Gibbons came up fast.

Amfar's friend Park Huang studied Paleography at the University of London. He would jump at the prospect of getting his hands on a text like the one they found in Kentucky.

Jarrett wasn't telling Amfar everything.

Maybe the manuscript had something to do with the explosion. Either way, Jarrett, I will find out what you are hiding.

***

"Oh, sweetheart. I heard about the accident, are you okay?"

"Don't mind the wheelchair, Dr. Gibbons, I feel wonderful. It's really just a precaution." Kelly's face flushed at the attention.

"Well, you look great." Her lips parted to show off her perfect teeth.

Pete and John, the same lab assistants that helped them carry in the bones over a month earlier, stepped out of the elevator. They carried a chest similar to the one the bones had been stored it, only this one was made of a thick translucent glass or plastic.

"You look good, too, Amfar. No lasting effects?" Dr. Gibbons said.

He concentrated on the chest the young men carried. Her words broke his concentration, and he jumped.

"No," he managed to get out. "I feel fine. Thank you for asking." He lowered his head in a half nod, half bow. His face turned scarlet.

Did I really just bow to Dr. Gibbons?

Her face turned as red as his, a great time for an exit.

"Okay." Amfar dry washed his hands. "It looks like you two have things under control. I will wait outside." He turned and almost ran into Pete and John with the chest in their hands. He backed up to hold the door open.

Kelly had one hand over her eyes, and Dr. Gibbons concentrated on the chest. When the lab assistants were past, he stepped outside into the sunlight.

Maybe he *was* having long-term effects. His ears felt fine, but his brain didn't work the way it should. His father was right; women do make your brain foggy.

Kelly and Dr. Gibbons would take a few more minutes to fill out the paperwork and probably make many jokes at his expense. To take his mind off the two women, he called Park.

Park's voice was beyond flamboyant. He spoke with an exaggerated Southern drawl. "Ammy! How you doin' pardner? I figgered you'd be ridin' them horses and drinkin' whiskey."

"Hey there, Park. You never were any good at geography. I was in Kentucky, not Texas, and this isn't the Wild West anymore."

"They don't talk like that in Kentucky?"

"Not exactly. Wait a moment, isn't it like midnight over there?"

"Sure is, Ammy. Just got back from the pub."

The excess joviality made sense.

"Great, I call to tell you about my first find and you are drunk before I get the chance."

"You had a find? Congratulations, Ammy. That's great. So what's up? Why are you calling your old college roomy?"

"We found a manuscript I would like for you to take a look at."

"How old?"

"You tell me." Amfar heard the pop of a can opening. "I heard the boss say something about Aramaic when he yelled at the guys handling it."

A gurgle sound came from the phone.

Amfar checked his phone to make sure he was still connected. "Are you still there?"

His friend sounded more reserved. "I'm still here. You just caught me off guard. I had to take a drink. I'm not sure what I expected, but not that."

"Pretty exciting isn't it? After all of this schooling, we are finally able to use what we have learned."

"Speak for yourself; I have another year to go. Anyway, I have an exam in the morning so I should get some sleep. Send me a copy, and I'll take a look at it."

"Thank you, Park. And yes, you are still the best Paleographer I know."

"And don't you forget it!"

Billy

"Now he's back outside." Billy adjusted the binoculars and put them back to his eyes. "Looks like he's talking on the phone. He almost laid out the two guys carrying that chest inside."

"Did you see what they put in the chest?" Eric leaned forward and squinted, as if he could see what Billy looked at.

"Not really. These binoculars suck. They took a couple things out of Amfar's car, one was a dark brown tube, and the other was a bag."

"Could the plates have been in the bag?"

"Maybe... probably."

Billy sat in the passenger side of Eric's rust bucket parked fifty yards from Jackson Incorporated at the Ocean Front Inn, an inn for pets. John asked Billy to keep an eye on Amfar and Kelly.

John watched for a Sergeant Kirkwall at the police department. His friend Rachel dug deep and learned Sergeant Kirkwall was currently in charge of the Billy Borks' case. She sent John pictures and a bio so he'd know what to look for.

"I still don't understand why I couldn't have just done this on my own." Eric leaned back in his seat and crossed his arms. "It's not like you're really good at using binoculars or something." Eric complained from the moment John handed them their duties.

"Be quiet." Billy gestured for his friend to be quiet but kept the binoculars to his eyes.

"Oh? Now they have super hearing? Give me the binoculars a second. Maybe I'll see something you don't." Eric grabbed the binocular strap and yanked.

The eyecups smacked Billy so hard he'd probably have two black eyes.

"Stop, Eric. This isn't a game. These may be the people that shot at me and John with the arrows."

"They are not the people that shot at us, Billy," John's voice said from Eric's speaker phone. "Get that thought out of your head right now. One is my ex and the other is too big of a prude to know how to shoot a bow and arrow. However, I think they work for the man who hired the shooters."

Damn, John heard us arguing.

"Keep following until they go back to the hotel," John continued. "Call if they make any more stops. And you two better be sneakier than you were at my place."

Eric gave up pulling on the straps. Must be the prospect of being pierced with an arrow didn't sound like much fun.

Billy needed to change the subject. "Did you ever upgrade your phone?"

"Yeah, man." Eric picked it up from the dash. The phone was blood red with black dragon designs. "Last week. Got the fastest Internet you can get, unlimited any time minutes—"

"Good, get on that fast Internet. See what you can find about Jackson Incorporated." Billy didn't enjoy interrupting his friend, but the guy liked his phones almost as much as he liked his women. Given the chance, he'd spend the rest of the day chatting about all the amazing things it could do.

Eric deflated a little and flipped open the phone. "Man, this whole spy thing is kind of crappy. First I get yelled at for wanting to take my turn with the binoculars, and now I'm your internet bitch."

Billy sat the binoculars on his lap. "I'm sorry, Eric. This is serious business. I trust John, but he scares me, too. I want to do what he says. He knows more about what's going on than me. I need to keep an eye on him. I think the only reason he wanted me on the binoculars instead of you is that he knows he can trust me. You know, the whole arrow thing brought us closer together or something."

"When you're done talking about your boyfriend, let me know."

They laughed and Billy put the binoculars to his eyes again.

"Jackson Incorporated is all over the place." Eric's looked at his phone. "It looks like their main office here is an animal research center."

"I wonder if the people who send their pets to the Ocean Front Inn know." Billy chuckled.

"Good point. They also have a storage facility. The comments on two different sites mention the building must be larger than it looks because there's no way they could have that many separate labs in the building."

"How many?"

"At least seven."

They both looked at the building again, as if they would somehow see things differently now that they knew it had more square feet.

Eric went back to looking at the huge screen on his phone. "What was that guy's name these people work for? Was it Tom Jarrett?"

Billy dropped the binoculars again. "That's his name. What about him?"

"It's nothing big, but I did a search for Jackson Incorporated and archaeology to see if we'd get lucky. This Jarrett guy wrote a book a few years back and it mentions J.I. more than once. They were the financiers behind the dig that led him to writing it. According to Jarrett, they spent a lot of money promoting his book. I don't understand the connection."

Billy shook his head. "Neither do I, and maybe there isn't one. John said the Jarrett guy might have something to do with all this. That's why we're following Amfar and Kelly, in case they lead us to him or somebody that knows him. Looks like we found our place."

"Good, let's get out of here. I'm kind of freaked out being this close." Eric started the rumbling engine.

"A few minutes ago, you were all gung-ho about the spying thing. What's holding you back now?"

"The prospect of becoming a pin cushion."

Chapter 12

John

John snapped shut his cell phone. Talking on a phone for hours while sitting outside of a police station might cause suspicion.

Letting Billy and Eric help was a big risk. The more he thought about it, the worse he felt about his decision. They were just kids, but he needed their help. Kelly and Amfar were too close to have an accurate view of what was happening. Besides, who was he to tell Billy he couldn't help? They'd shot arrows at him too, and he had the balls to break into John's place.

A man stepped out of the police department toward the parking lot. John compared the picture of Kirkwall to the man leaving. *It's him.* John started his Jeep when Kirkwall climbed into his Mercedes. A Mercedes? Somebody made a few bucks on the side. Even a ten-year-old Mercedes should be out of his pay range.

John stayed a half-mile behind the black Mercedes, enough of a distance when Kirkwall didn't expect a tail. The information packet from Rachel said his home was on the southern end of the beach, near the zoo. They came up on Billy Borks when Kirkwall's brakes lit up, his right turn signal blinking.

"No way. Why would he go to Billy Borks right now?" John mumbled to himself.

The Mercedes passed the driveway to Billy's and pulled into Lizards. What were the chances? John pulled in and watched the tall cop climb from his car. His stomach hung over his belt an inch or so. *Pretty good shape for a cop.*

Kirkwall pulled open the door to Lizards and turned toward the bathroom. This was John's chance to act, what better place than the bathroom of some fast-food joint. Much better than the breaking and entering he'd contemplated.

John placed his cell in the glove box and slid the Glock into his ankle holster. He hurried toward Lizards. He pulled open the door and turned down the short hallway to his right.

The public restroom was the multi-person type. No locks. The smell of stale urine and bleach accosted him. Kirkwall sat in one of the two stalls. John picked up the steel trashcan and slid it under the door handle, making as little noise as possible. The can wouldn't hold if someone really wanted to get in, but he didn't plan to be in the bathroom long enough to see that happen.

John bent down and peered under the bathroom stall. Kirkwall's pants were around his feet, nine millimeter at his ankle covered by the gray slacks. John looked to the sink. He quietly pulled a few used paper towels from the trashcan and wiped the sink dry.

The plan would only work if Kirkwall weren't wearing a shoulder harness. John hadn't seen the telltale bump under his jacket. Using the edge of the stall and the paper towel dispenser for support, he pulled himself onto the sink. He leaned forward and pressed the barrel of his Glock onto the top of Kirkwall's balding pate. Kirkwall grew stiff and lifted his hands slowly out to the side.

"I know your piece is in your ankle holster," John spat. "Don't move, and don't look at me and we'll be fine. Got it?"

Kirkwall nodded.

John made his voice deeper than normal and a little gravelly in case he ever met Kirkwall outside of this bathroom. "Good. You understand." John pressed the gun harder onto the officer's head. "I have some questions, and I expect the truth. Don't think about lying because I'll know if you are."

The whole scene was a bit comedic, but John wasn't here to have fun. Someone had shot at him, and his life was somewhat important. He preferred to do things a little easier, a little more legal, but during his time as a bodyguard, he found it's better to get to the point. Scare a person into telling you the truth before they have the chance to calm themselves.

"Who is paying you to be hush-hush about Billy Borks?"

Kirkwall began to look up and John slapped him on the back of the head with his free hand.

"No. You don't get to do that. Answer the question."

"I don't know what you're talking about." Kirkwall sounded like he was out for coffee.

John pressed the gun down, hard. "Wrong answer, Mr. Mercedes. You won't be able to spend the money they gave you if your brains join the graffiti on this bathroom stall."

"Okay, okay." A single bead of sweat rolled down Kirkwall's forehead onto his nose. "I don't know the guy's name. I was at The Green Dragon when some guy approached me. Offered a wad of cash if I just played dumb on the one case. Probably a gas leak caused the explosion anyway, so I took the dough. What's the big deal? The place was a shit-hole."

Kirkwall began to look up again so John slapped him a second time, harder this time. Kirkwall straightened. Red colored his cheeks and forehead.

The slapping was a tactic John's dad said to use in situations like this. Most police officers, military types, or rich guys had an ego problem. You had to catch them off guard, embarrass them, and keep embarrassing them until you get what you want. He would say, "And if you catch them on the shitter, it doesn't matter what you ask, they'll be begging to tell you. No man wants to die taking a crap."

"That was strike two, Kirkwall. Try it again and you won't make it to strike three." He nodded.

"What was his name?"

"He never told us his name."

"Who sent him?"

"I told you, I don't know."

John smacked him on top of the head with the butt of the Glock. It wouldn't hurt that bad, but it would be worse than a slap to the face. Maybe not psychologically, but he wasn't about to give up on his bathroom technique.

"Okay." Kirkwall's voice cracked. "Just stop hitting me. I overheard him talking to some guy named Jarrett. That's all I heard."

"Last question. Have you seen anybody in town masquerading as a Native American?"

"Are you serious?" Kirkwall stifled a small laugh.

"Answer the damn question," John commanded.

"No. Why the hell would I?"

"None of your concern. I have a C4 explosive tied to your stall with a three-minute timer. If you open the door before you hear it beep, you'll be joining the other pieces of shit in the sewer."

John forced himself to walk out of the bathroom and to the parking lot. Kirkwall believed John would shoot him if he didn't give him what he wanted, so he bet he believed about the C4 as well. He'd stay in his stall for the full three minutes.

John called Billy on his way back to the cottage. He answered on the first ring. "Did you follow them like I asked?"

"Yeah. They didn't do anything special. They just went back to their hotel after Jackson Incorporated. Eric pretended to go for a walk on the beach and saw them drinking coffee together, just chatting."

Chatting? With Amfar? Maybe there was more going on than he thought. That would explain why it seemed so easy for her to end their relationship. Of course, him cheating on her probably didn't help.

"I need you and Eric to meet me at my cottage at eight."

The phone rasped as Billy sighed into the receiver.

"What's with the heavy sigh, Billy?"

"I know this is only the second day you've asked Eric to take off from work, but he's still whining about the last time. He's worried about making his rent."

"Fine. Whatever he makes on a normal Friday night, I'll double it. Now, meet me tomorrow at eight. Jarrett wants the plates for himself. Bad enough that he's willing to hire arrow-shooting hoodlums to come after us. We're not going to let that happen."

Amfar

Amfar sat at the desk in his hotel room with the balcony door open, allowing the salty sea air to roll in. Going over his finances took most of the morning. He woke up to seven messages from Johnny on his cell phone, the neighbor watching his house in Michigan. The urgency in the kid's voice grew with each message. A water pipe had burst.

His cell phone rang. He planned to apologize to Johnny and give him a bonus, but the number was international. "Dr. Amfar Ditpra."

"Yes. Could I please speak with the really anal retentive Indian that owns this cell phone?"

"Hey, Park. That was fast. I thought you had an exam this morning." He carried the phone with him to the balcony.

"The exam? Already aced it. I'm calling because I dropped the fax at Dr. Dawson's office. I figured he could take a look while I was in class. And yes, I know you said not to mention it to anybody, but you sounded like you were in a hurry, man. You know Dr. Dawson's the best. I'm glad I asked him, too, because he already figured some stuff out. I looked it over last night and had no clue. Some looked familiar, but it might as well have been gibberish."

Amfar dropped into his white Adirondack chair on the balcony. "What did you find out?" There were far too many questions jumping around in Amfar's head. Losing sleep had never been an issue, but in the past week, he'd had little.

"Dr. Dawson found out, not me. The only thing I learned is that being a Paleographer is hard when you're drunk. Anyway, he said the information on that document contained at least three types of communication."

"Communication? You mean languages?" Amfar choked back a laugh. His friend still drank as often as he had when they were roommates.

"Communication. One isn't a language at all. Well, not in the sense that you're talking about anyway. Some of the symbols on the manuscript are mathematical equations. And whoever you overheard, they were right about it being Aramaic."

Amfar leaned forward in his seat. "How did they combine equations with a language?"

Park sighed into the phone. "I'm not sure, to be honest. Dawson didn't have much time to tell me what he learned. He had lab until nine, then he was going out with his ex-wife. Told me not to bother him until tomorrow."

Dr. Dawson was Park's mentor and friend. He'd been the one that officially accepted Park into London University.

"What was the third one?"

"This one surprised me." Park let out a nervous laugh. "The last type of communication is ancient Cherokee. It's called a syllabary. The oldest Cherokee texts are only a few hundred years old, yet combined with Aramaic. I'm not sure what to think."

Amfar spoke aloud, more to himself than Park. "Three communications. No obvious relations between them. Two used centuries apart. All of this right there in

Morehead. I don't understand. Why use three separate languages? And why those three?"

"Not sure, Amfar. I hope Dawson can explain. If that wench would stay away from him, I'd be chatting with him right now."

Amfar assumed he was talking about Dr. Dawson's ex-wife.

Park continued. "There isn't anything I can do now. I guess I'll just give you a call tomorrow when Dawson wakes up."

"Thank you for what you did give me, Park. At least I have something to look into while we wait for your friend."

"Anytime, man. Have a good day, and don't lose any sleep over it. There isn't anybody in the world better than Dawson. He'll figure it all out."

"I'm sure he will. Thanks again, Park."

Amfar hung up and gazed at the waves slapping the shoreline. *What's so special about these plates, Jarrett? What are you hiding?*

Chapter 13

Billy

"What's the plan then?" Eric concentrated on the road.

"He wouldn't tell me." Billy shook his head. "He told me that we're to wear dark clothes and meet him at the Ocean Front Inn." They were ten minutes away, but he couldn't shake the clenching in his stomach.

"Why meet at the dog inn? You think John wants us to break into the Jackson place?"

The thought had crossed Billy's mind. It would accomplish his goal of gathering the three plates back, if they could even find them once inside. *Is my imagined destiny worth going to jail? And how far is John willing to go to learn why a building exploded around his fiancée?*

"I'm not sure, Eric. But you're probably on the right track. I don't remember seeing any cameras set up at the dog place, do you?"

Eric shook his head. "Shit, I didn't even think about that. This was all kinds of fun when I thought we were just playing around. But if there are cameras..."

"I think John is legit. I trust him." *Do I?* He wanted to. "There have to be people in the world like John. Those that want to do things because they are right, because they should be done."

"I don't know, man, it's just—" A loud cough stopped Eric mid-sentence. Eric sounded like Grams's brother Leroy used to when he coughed. He died from emphysema complications. Eric wasn't a seventy-year-old man with emphysema, though.

The car swerved over the centerline. Billy grabbed the wheel and straightened the rust bucket until between the lines again. He fought to keep them on the road but risked a glance to his friend. Eric held both hands over his mouth, coughing so hard his eyes looked about to pop out of his head. At least he still had enough sense to press gently on the break as Billy guided them to the side of the road.

When they came to a complete stop, he pushed the gear shifter into park. Eric still coughed, but it wasn't as horrific as before.

"What the heck is the matter with you? Can you breathe?" The adrenaline didn't give Billy much control over the way he spoke, so he sounded meaner than he planned.

Eric's hand came away from his face long enough to pat Billy gently on the shoulder. Billy still leaned across the car holding on to the wheel with both hands. Eric's gentle touch on his shoulder soothed his flow of adrenaline. Billy sat back in his seat, waiting for his friend's spasms to stop.

Eric scrunched his eyebrows together, pulled his hands from his mouth, and wiped them on his pants. He took a deep breath and released a drawn out wheeze.

"Wow. That sucked." Eric turned with a large grin for Billy.

Billy punched him in the shoulder. "What are you smiling about, man? Your crazy old-man coughs just about put us off the road. Are you okay?"

"I'm fine, but I'm not sure how much help I'll be tonight. Wouldn't do much good to wear black clothes if I heave loud enough to get the whole neighborhood's attention."

"But what are we going to do? About you, I mean. That didn't sound good. Do you have a lung infection or something?"

"I feel fine." Eric rubbed his chest. He barked a few more coughs and clutched at his chest, face crunched in pain.

Billy climbed from the beater and walked to the driver's side door, pulling it open. Eric looked confused.

"Get out, chump. I'm driving you to the hospital."

"No way, Billy. I told you I'm fine."

"Yeah, you look fine. Just get out, and I'll drive. You're still on your mom's insurance right?"

"I am, but I can't afford the fifty dollar co-pay."

"I'm sure John can loan it to you if something happens. Now out." Billy gestured to the side like a chauffeur.

Eric climbed from the driver's seat to the passenger side. Billy drove the short distance to the hospital and dropped Eric off at the emergency room.

Billy looked to his friend through the open door. "I'll have my cell on all night. If you need to call me, go ahead. Just remember I'll have it silenced when I'm with John."

Eric nodded and gave a quick wave before closing the car door and walking into the hospital. The fluorescent lights made his tanned friend look comparatively pale.

Billy pulled the rust bucket onto back roads. The clock on the radio was fast, but he'd still be fifteen minutes late. He pulled into the Ocean Front Inn and drove to the rear, and parked next to John's Jeep.

He put the car in park and turned off the lights. John's head popped up in the backseat of his vehicle. He was out of the Jeep with a bag in hand before Billy could open the door.

"You're late." John rifled through the black bag he'd pulled from his Jeep. "Where's Eric?"

Billy closed the door gently and gave it a shove with his hip until it clicked. "I dropped him off at the hospital."

The grumpy look on John's face disappeared. "Is he okay?"

"Yeah, yeah, he's fine. He had some kind of allergy attack or something. He couldn't stop coughing. We almost drove off the road."

John nodded and went back to digging through his bag. "It's better this way. I only invited him because you two are so close. He probably would've tried sneaking in if we told him to stay in the car anyway."

That sounded just like the type of thing Eric would do.

"So we are breaking in then?" Billy put his hands in his pockets to keep from fidgeting.

John nodded.

Billy squinted to see what was in the bag. John's hand came out filled with something black, and he held it toward Billy.

"What's this?" Billy grabbed the pile from John's hand.

"A full-face mask and a pair of leather mechanic's gloves. Put them on, and don't remove them until we're back to the cars."

Billy separated the hat from the gloves and pulled it over his head. "What are we doing here, John?"

"You mean you don't know, Billy?" John's teeth glowed in the moonlight. "We're getting those three plates back and testing that destiny you're always yapping about."

John

John pulled on his mask and leather gloves. One Glock went into his front pants pocket, the other in his ankle holster. Breaking into Jackson Incorporated alone would be safest, but Billy earned his place by John's side. He didn't believe all the destiny crap the kid spouted, but better to let him learn on his own than push him in a specific direction.

John pulled the backpack over his shoulders. He'd scoped the place earlier and found no cameras in sight, but that didn't mean they weren't there. Pretending to be a pizza delivery guy at the wrong address allowed him a better look at the security system. The only security Jackson Incorporated used were deadbolts. Something didn't feel right; they had to have more. John learned to trust his instincts over the years, but not at the expense of his senses, and his eyes told him there were only deadbolts.

Billy adjusted the mask over his face. "How are we going to do this?" .

"I'll do the breaking and entering part. You're here for backup, the eyes and ears. Keep them open and on guard."

They walked toward the brick building, staying to the shadows beneath the trees and close to the buildings.

Billy's shoulders slouched. The kid had spirit, but breaking into a business the first time puts even the strongest wills to the test.

"What am I supposed to do if I see or hear something?"

"It depends on what you see or hear."

Billy's shoulders slouched more.

"Here, take this." John held out a gun.

The kid stopped in his tracks. "I don't know, John. Maybe we shouldn't do this." His voice was an octave higher than normal.

"Come over here a minute." John pulled Billy into a group of cypress shrubs and put his hand on the kid's shoulder. "I know you're nervous, and that's good. That means you have brains, that you're a good person. But think about why we're here, why we're doing this."

"To get the three plates?"

"That's part of it." John nodded. "Think about why we need the plates. They might tell us why Billy Borks exploded. More importantly, they could explain Bryan's death. I *know* it wasn't your fault. You doubt it sometimes, but in your heart, you know it wasn't your fault, that he didn't deserve to die. That's why we're here. Those plates mean something to somebody, and we have to find out what."

With each word, Billy's shoulders pulled further from the slouch. He nodded expectantly at everything John said.

John held the gun toward Billy again. "There's no reason you should have to use this, but take it just in case."

Billy still hesitated.

"Just remember the bow wielding crazies that came after us at the restaurant."

Billy took the gun and turned it over in his hands. "This time, I won't be the one hiding if they shoot at me."

John saw a determined set to the kid's mouth through the hole in the mask. "Good. You remember what I showed you the other day?"

Billy nodded.

Before sending Billy and Eric to spy on Kelly and Amfar, he showed them the basics to using a gun. Billy didn't take long to get the hang of it. He'd shot a .357 with his grandmother in a gun league.

They stayed in the shadows and walked the rest of the way to the back door. John peered through the dark, searching for signs of a camera or security system. Nothing. He didn't have time to think about how odd it was.

John pulled the backpack from his shoulders and placed it on the ground, then pulled out a hacksaw. Under the front of his shirt was a knife. He stepped to the door and slid the tip of the knife into the skinny rubber weather strip around the edge. Working the knife back and forth, the rubber pulled away from the door. John grabbed it with his gloved hand, yanking it off the rest of the way. The deadbolt was visible from the outside. He shoved his knife in, just above the bolt.

"Grab this, Billy."

Billy grabbed the knife and held it in place. "What am I supposed to do?"

"Just hold it for a second." John picked up the hacksaw and put it up to the door, squeezing it in over the bolt. "Use the knife to pry the doors open enough for the saw to fit in. Then hold it in place."

Billy leaned on the knife and the doors came apart, the saw slid into place. John made quick work of the deadbolt. John took the knife back and pressed it into the space just under the deadbolt. This time he used it to push in the latch. The door swung open a few inches.

He looked at Billy just in time to see his eyes bulge. "Pretty cool, huh?"

Billy

Impressive. John cut through the deadbolt and had the door open in less than a minute. Learning more about John would have been a good idea, but he seemed like a nice guy. And he always spoke of his dad being a cop. He couldn't be all that bad.

John put his tools back in the bag, scooped it up, and waved for Billy to follow.

The hallway inside led directly to the front door, with four doors in between, two on each side. Billy's thoughts went to Eric searching the internet for Jackson Incorporated on his new phone, how the building had seven separate businesses in one. He pictured the layout of the building.

John tapped him on the shoulder. "You okay?" he whispered.

"I'm fine. Let's do this."

John moved with silent footfalls. Billy tried the same but his left foot squeaked every step. He must have stepped on something in the cypress bushes.

John stopped quickly before the end of the corridor, his shoulders glided against the wall. Billy followed suit and held his breath. John inched forward and peered around the corner, motionless for a moment, and then stepped around the corner. Billy's lungs began working again. John had just been double-checking the front door before walking into the lobby.

Billy reached down to the pouch at the front of his hoody and felt the weight of the gun. He hoped he didn't have to use it, though he was willing. Anybody that would shoot arrows at him and John deserved to be shot.

John peeked his head around the corner and waved Billy forward. In the lobby, they stood in front of an elevator. John pushed the up button and waited. Moments later, the doors opened to the sea green interior of the Jackson Incorporated elevator. Billy held his hand in front of the doors so they wouldn't close.

"This makes me nervous." John peered inside.

"What?"

"No cameras or security that I can see."

"Isn't that a good thing?"

"It should be." John pulled Billy into the elevator. "It just feels strange. A business with enough money to gain Jarrett's confidence and throw their support into an archaeological dig should have enough to have a damn good security system."

The doors closed.

Billy looked at the numbers running down the wall of the elevator. "How do we know which floor to start?"

"Level six."

Billy's fingers moved toward the six and paused. "How do you know?"

John reached forward and pressed the number for him. "Do you have to question everything?" When Billy didn't answer, he explained. "Fine, kid. I met a couple of Jackson Incorporated employees last night at the Velvet Snail."

"You just happened to meet some of their employees at a strip club?"

"I followed them to the club when they left here last night. I bought them a few drinks and struck up a conversation. What's the big deal?"

Billy shook his head. "It's not a big deal. It's cool. I think you're the only person I know that could pull it off."

"I appreciate the compliment, Billy, but it really wasn't that hard."

"Not hard for you maybe. Imagine being an introvert whose social life consists of getting yelled at in a crappy restaurant and hanging out with a bunch of eighty year olds at a barbeque."

John laughed. "Be ready. We don't know what to expect when this door opens."

Billy's breath caught again. Why did John have to keep throwing things at him like that? He could at least warn him ahead of time, give his body a few seconds to build up the fear.

The elevator dinged, and the doors popped open. They looked down a hallway similar to the one on the top floor, with a large open room at the end.

Billy stood still a moment, listening. The vending machine to the side of the hall clicked. Billy quickly leaned against the elevator wall.

John smiled. "Just the vending machine kid. Calm down."

Billy blinked and gave himself a shake. "Where do we go now?"

John adjusted the bag on his shoulders and stepped into the hallway. "Your guess is as good as mine. Let's start with these side rooms and work our way down the hall."

A small table with three chairs placed around it sat in the first room. Built into the wall were two cutouts. Like the ones for urine samples in the bathroom at the doctor's office. They weren't passing urine back and forth at Jackson Incorporated. He pointed to the cutouts, and John shrugged. The other three rooms were offices, filled with paperwork and file cabinets.

"They must be out in the open area." John nodded to the doorway leading back into the hall.

Billy nodded and turned toward the open door.

"Billy? Wait. Are you okay?"

"I'm fine, why?" His lips were sticky and wet. "What the—"

John's brows furrowed. "You're bleeding."

"Weird." Billy grabbed the bottom of the mask to lift it up.

"Wait." John held Billy's arms down. "You best not do that. I'm not one hundred percent sure there aren't hidden cameras. Let's not take any chances. It's just a bloody nose. It'll go away. Probably from the de-humidifiers they run in places like this. Just hold it like this until it stops." He made a pinching motion in front of his face and leaned forward.

Billy copied the movement. "I thought I was supposed to tilt my head back?" The words came out sounding more like, "E taught woz posed two lilt me head bock."

John's eyebrows scrunched down, then popped back up and he nodded. "If you do it that way the blood will run into your throat and choke you. That's something they do in movies to make it more dramatic or something."

Billy felt dumb for not knowing. John seemed to know everything. Careful to enunciate each word, he said, "How do you know all this stuff?"

They stepped back into the hallway, and John flipped the lights off to the office. "The thing about your nose?"

Billy nodded.

"My father made me take EMT training." He said it like it was something everybody's dad made them do. Not that he would know, since his grandma was the one who raised him. The closest he'd come to EMT training was when Grams's fishing buddy, Bob, taught him how to remove a hook from a fish.

They finished searching the offices and stepped into the open area at the end of the hall. John flipped some of the light switches, splashing fluorescent light across fifty or more desks. Each with a large stand placed in the center, holding yellowish paper between thin layers of glass.

"Are you sure we're on the right floor?" Billy's eyes gazed over the room.

"If not, I'm not looking forward to searching five more."

John

Poor Billy. He's blown up at work, shot at by arrows, caught breaking into the cottage, takes his best friend to the hospital, and now he has a gushing bloody nose. John wasn't superstitious, but Billy's luck made him question that belief.

They searched through each of the pristine desks. The cupboards and tables along the walls were empty, save some old coffee cups. John questioned whether the two young men he'd bought drinks told the truth about level six.

Two rows remained. John didn't voice his doubts they'd find the plates. Straightening from a desk, he lifted his arms overhead and stretched. Working out three times a week didn't make him immune to pain or tightness when bending over continuously for an hour. Tacked up papers and charts covered the outline of a door on the back wall, hard for either to notice. Billy searched bent over, flipping through endless amounts of paper at another desk a few feet away, no longer holding his nose.

John walked to the door and gave the handle a pull. It stuck for a moment then jolted open with a few more pulls. The office looked like the three they already searched. Pictures on the desk and wall were of two children, a boy and a girl. In some, the boy wore a baseball outfit, the girl a cheerleading uniform. The girl looked to be a few years older than the boy, probably siblings. In one picture, the children hugged a woman wearing a researcher's smock, most likely the owner of the desk; beautiful thick brown hair and glowing white teeth.

John wasn't here to look at pictures, but it was hard to look away. The rest of the building had a cold personality behind it, even the dark blue and green paint. This office was the only place where someone had taken the liberty to make it feel like home, a welcome break from the sterile monotony of the building.

"Find anything in there?" Billy called from the other room.

The yell snapped John out of staring at the pictures. "Nothing yet."

The plates wouldn't be sitting out on a desk. He pulled the cupboards open, one by one. Files, more old coffee cups, more files, and a small collection of glass clowns. No plates.

Unless Billy came into the office declaring he'd found the plates, they'd need to search the other levels, and that wasn't safe. They'd taken far too long already. *With the lack of a security system*, John thought, *we should be safe for a little while longer.*

John sighed and leaned onto the back of the black office chair. It bobbed forward under the weight and rolled forward, thumping against something. John paused. He rolled the chair out and looked beneath the desk. A glass chest with thick walls, rubber hinges, and a digital lock sat against the wall; three plates gathered into a neat pile in the center.

"John? Can you come out here please?" The strain was clear in Billy's voice.

"What is it?" John ran into the other room.

Billy backed toward John, the gun held out in front of him. John's eyes followed the direction of the gun, straight to three Dobermans standing in the hallway, blocking their path to the elevator. The lithe and graceful animals sniffed the air as they walked side by side toward where John and Billy waited.

Billy's voice cracked. "What do we do? I don't want to shoot a dog, but I bet they don't care who they eat."

John placed his hand on Billy's shoulder. "Stay calm, Billy. Don't hold the weapon up yet. Your shoulder will tire and it will affect your shot. Be patient and keep your voice low."

"Be patient? Are you serious?"

"Deadly serious." He hoped Billy heard just how serious he was. His father had shown him what a K-9 unit could do to a man. "Never underestimate an opponent, even when that opponent is an animal," he'd said. Jackson Incorporated *did* have a security system, just an old-fashioned one.

"There may be more than three," John went on. "Keep that in mind. Don't waste rounds; only shoot when there is no other option."

Billy's eyes scanned the room. The dogs made their way closer, sniffing the air in front of them.

"I found the plates," John whispered.

Billy's eyes stopped darting and turned toward John. "You found them? Where?"

John's attention never strayed from the dangerous animals. "I said be patient, not be a fool. Keep your eyes on the Dobermans."

Billy spun back toward the dogs and lifted the gun again. He glanced to the weapon in his hands. He lowered the weapon slowly, but his hand bumped the desk in front of him.

All three Doberman heads popped up at once. Seeing their prey, each lowered into a crouch, their stubby tails pointing straight back, black lips pulled back showing their curved canines. A low, vicious growl rumbled from the guard dogs.

"Oh shit." John stepped closer to Billy.

"Oh shit? What do you mean oh shit? I thought you said be patient, stay calm?"

Before Billy finished his sentence, the Dobermans launched toward them. Billy's eyes grew to the size of saucers. John wrapped his arm around the kid's waist and threw him toward the back office. For every step they took, the dogs took three.

We're not going to make it. I can't let Billy get hurt.

John gave Billy a final Herculean shove toward the office and pulled the gun from his front pocket. The scene played out in slow motion; Billy flying backward toward the black office chair, the weapon rising in John's hands as he turned, the angry glare on the face of the first Doberman bouncing in rhythm with John's racing heart.

They were closer than he thought. His hands came up, his stance completed. One squeeze of the trigger and the first dog fell. The second was in the air and latched onto John's left arm before he had a chance to pull the trigger a second time. The momentum pulled John from his feet toward the office where Billy should be hiding with the door closed.

John slid through the doorway on his rear, knowing it meant the two of them were in a tiny office, wielding two guns against two blood-crazed Dobermans. The third Doberman was in mid-leap, teeth searching for flesh to tear.

This isn't going to be pretty.

Billy

John took out the first dog, no problem. The second hooked onto John's arm as they slid backward into the office. Billy had landed in the office chair. His arms popped up in front of him, but he never lost the weapon.

Billy aimed the Glock at the third dog flying through the air toward John's throat. He braced for the recoil and squeezed the trigger. Instead of the loud blast he expected, there was a "snick" sound and a tiny dart with yellow feathers flew from the end of the gun into the Dobermans neck.

The dog's momentum brought it flying through the air over John's head, smashing into Billy's arms and knocking the gun free. Two were down, but John pounded and punched at the Doberman attached to his arm. Billy searched the room for the dropped weapon.

Anger grew inside Billy as before, at Billy Borks. Each heartbeat pumped life through his veins, and his chest heaved with every breath. Both scary and thrilling at the same time.

Billy was on all fours pushing through papers clinging together with John's blood. He pulled himself up with the help of the desk. Anger grew hot in his chest.

I don't deserve this. These dogs need to die. Now!

Billy howled at the Doberman on John's arm. The dog launched through the air toward the room with the manuscripts. John flew partially through the door with the dog, until its teeth let go. The once ferocious beast slammed through two desks before crashing into the wall. Chunks of cement fell down around the animal as it collapsed in a heap, blood dripped from its nose and mouth.

John was on his hands and knees halfway out of the office, not paying attention to his bleeding arm. Instead, he stared at the dog that had pulled a Superman across the room. John's eyes flicked back and forth between the dog piled on the floor, the two desks obliterated in its flight, and his now mangled arm.

Billy wasn't sure what happened. He didn't dare say anything until he knew how John would react.

John's face lost the look of bewilderment, quickly replaced with determination, the look Billy usually saw on the man. John glanced to his maimed arm again and rolled over to his back, pulling the arm to his chest.

"Billy. Bring me the backpack, and hurry."

The backpack must have come off when the Doberman's teeth pulled John from the office. It sat on the floor next to Billy. He snatched the backpack and ran to John's side. He opened it up and placed it within reach. Billy expected John to say something about the flying dog.

"What do you need me to get?"

"The duct tape." John still held his arm to his chest. He rolled to a standing position. With his uninjured hand, he yanked on the collar of his shirt until it tore, then began wrapping it around his bloody mess of an arm. "Hold the shirt right here and hand me the duct tape."

Billy did as he asked. John grabbed a length of tape and tore it with his teeth. He used his free hand to place the tape, repeating the tearing and placing of the tape four more times.

"Is this really going to work?" Billy still held the strip of torn shirt in place.

"You can let go now, kid. It'll be fine. EMT, remember?"

Of course he did. The longer Billy spent with John, the more he felt like he should call him MacGuyver. Grams couldn't get enough of that show.

"Grab the plates, and let's get out of here." John peered through the door behind Billy at the destroyed glass case the plates had been stored in. "Do you mind carrying the backpack? I seem to have had an accident." He held up the ragged and bloody shirt covering his arm.

"Yes, I can carry it, you weirdo. Don't we have to clean up?" Billy eyed the plates as he placed them gently in the backpack.

John surveyed the room. "There's no cleaning this up. Not with the amount of time we have anyway. It's three now, and I'm guessing there will be at least a few early birds getting here at six." He turned to where Billy squatted over the shattered glass case. "On second thought, maybe we should take all of those papers covered in my blood." He reached under the closest undestroyed desk and pulled out a two-liter white jug. "I'm not sure what this has in it, but there are enough chemicals to at least confuse any investigators a while."

John pulled a paper towel from above a sink by one of the coffee makers. The chemicals made short work of the blood on the floor in front of the office. Billy stuffed the blood-covered papers into the backpack and around the plates for support. When neither could find more blood, John poured the remaining contents of the chemical bottle on the floor.

Why hasn't John said anything about the last Doberman yet? Waiting for him to say something drove him insane.

Billy threw the backpack over his shoulders and tightened the straps to fit over his bony shoulders. He stepped back into the room where John surveyed the mess they caused.

"We should leave soon. When the doggy you shot wakes, he'll want revenge." He nudged the tranquilized Doberman with his boot. The dog whined a little, but its eyes didn't open. "If he can still fight with a hang-over, that is."

They did one last search of the office and the end of the room where their small battle took place.

"Let's get out of here." John nodded toward the hallway.

Neither said a word on the elevator. They continued the silence to the ground floor and out to their vehicles.

Why hasn't he said anything yet?

They stood between Eric's old beater and John's Wrangler, silent. After a full minute, Billy opened his mouth to ask John why he wasn't talking, but John held his hand up.

"Just wait, kid."

Billy closed his mouth and nodded.

"We had a pretty wild night. Before we say anything, let's go home and get some rest. After you check on your friend, that is." He looked down at his mangled left arm. "My battle wound could use some peroxide too, as long as the lacerations aren't too deep. You go ahead and keep the backpack for now. I'll want it back, but I think you need it more than I do. Check on Eric and give me a call tomorrow after nine. Any earlier and I'll take it as a personal insult."

Billy wasn't sure what to say, so he just nodded. It had been a stressful evening. He had trouble focusing.

Time and rest would do his mind good. He needed to talk to Eric. Sometimes, just having his friend around cleared his mind. They worked well together.

Billy climbed into the old car and shut the door; a cloud of rust fell to the pavement. If he was right about what the plates could do, he had a lot more to worry about than three crazed Dobermans.

Chapter 14

Amfar

Amfar sat with Kelly on the veranda overlooking the calm waters of the Atlantic, a morning ritual they'd developed. She would make a pot of coffee, and he would step over the railing to her side. They didn't need to talk. They would sip their coffee, read the newspaper, and enjoy the sunrise. After about an hour, they would resume their normal conversations.

Amfar's thoughts wandered to Jarrett's motives behind letting him and Kelly stay at the hotel for weeks while the bones stayed at Jackson Incorporated. He couldn't be worried about being sued. The man's ego wouldn't allow him to be nice just to get out of losing a few bucks. *The man has to have an ulterior motive. He would not let us stay at the beach out of the kindness of his heart.*

The morning's first rays reached toward the sky, the tawny sun about to crest, when Amfar's phone vibrated on the table. Kelly sipped at her coffee and continued reading her celebrity covered magazine. The phone vibrated again, displaying an international number. *Park.*

Amfar hadn't told Kelly about calling Park. She would probably understand why Amfar went behind Jarrett's back, but he wasn't willing to take the chance. Leaving his coffee on the table, he rose and stepped over the railing toward the beach until he was certain Kelly couldn't hear him. He pressed the talk button.

"Are you sitting down, Ammy?"

Amfar looked back to where Kelly sat with her coffee held to the side, wearing her downy white robe she donned after showering. "I can't really sit at the moment,

Park. What is going on? Did Dawson learn something about the manuscript?"

"Learn something? Dawson had the thing cracked in no time. We spent all day yesterday, and a good part of today working on it."

"You have already learned what it says? Tell me, please." Amfar hoped Park didn't hear the desperation in his voice.

"I have to explain something first, Amfar, something you probably remember me explaining in college. You can lose important information through translation. I know you understand, because you know two languages. Dawson and I both believe there's a lot of that going on in the manuscript. Regardless of what's lost, you also know the basic idea is hard to miss."

Why is Park flustered? The little man loved to chatter, but he was good at explaining things, never spent too much time on the details. "I understand, Park. I remember the conversation. You complained about the English language and how much of it can be misconstrued as meaning something other than what is said."

Park sighed. "Now listen, I'm going to tell you what the manuscript says. Keep in mind that people back then were mystical or extremely religious."

"Enough," Amfar snapped. "Are you going to tell me or not?"

"Sorry, Amfar. Wait, you'll probably want to write this down so you can read it out loud, and maybe find other meanings that we missed."

Amfar slapped himself on the forehead. Park was right, but he could have mentioned it a few minutes ago. He stepped through the sand toward the hotel. The confused look on Kelly's face told him she questioned why he broke their morning ritual for a phone call. He smiled and waved.

She returned the smile and went back to her magazine.

Amfar stepped over the railing and into his room, situating himself at his makeshift desk. "Go ahead, Park. I'm listening."

"I'm going to remind you one more time, we're still translating, trying to figure out what the manuscript means in its entirety. Though what I am going to read to you is the whole transcript. Okay, here we go,

'The bearer of these words must guard them with their life. For not only their life depends upon it, but all life. Three disks: the power great. Only can they be used in accordance with their intent or the results will devastate. Harm will harm, safety will save. The voice must encompass the strength of will to use the power it has imagined.'

"That's all of it?"

"It's not exact." Park cleared his throat. "But you get the idea. You should get those plates somewhere safe and find out if there's any truth to what the manuscript says." He paused. "If you sent us this manuscript a few weeks ago, I'd laugh at how quiet you are. After what you told me about the explosion... I'm a little freaked out, man."

"I understand, my friend. I'm sorry to cut this phone call short, but I need to go over these words. I am not sure what to think. I will need time to process this new information."

Amfar hung up and peered at the words staring back from the desk. The wording was strange, not quite right. Why would all life depend on the plates? Does it depend on the use, or the lack of use? Or does it depend on the manuscript?

Regardless of the intended meaning, Park was right. Amfar needed the plates back. They were probably safe at Jackson Incorporated, but when the studies were completed, Tom Jarrett would have control.

"The voice must encompass the strength. The voice must encompass the strength." The more Amfar repeated the lines to himself, the more nervous he became. If by "The voice" the manuscript literally meant anybody speaking in close proximity to the plates, then at any time an employee of Jackson Incorporated, or Jarrett himself, could use whatever power the disks, or plates, contained. Amfar wasn't willing to risk anything on the strength of Jarrett's will, let alone the planet.

John

Billy called John at exactly nine o'clock, complaining of not having slept a wink. John wasn't surprised. When they left Jackson Incorporated the night before Billy's face held confusion and terror. The reason John sent him home. Billy needed the night to relax in his home. Even if he didn't sleep, just to straighten out his thoughts.

John filled his large coffee cup from Mrs. Lancaster's giant carafe on his way to Buster's Breakfast Nook. The kid sat outside on his bike when John pulled up.

"What happened, John? Do you think I did that? Or do you think it was the plates? It could have been either really, me or the plates I mean. Because you didn't do anything. Did you?"

"Wow. Calm down, Billy." He put his hand on the hyper teenager's shoulder. "I know you're excited, I am too. Keep in mind that just because we have these plates doesn't mean we'll learn how to use them. We may never know." John urged Billy toward the door. "What we both need right now is to relax. Let's go inside, drink a few cups of coffee, and chat about the details of last night. If we're lucky, we might figure something out. If we're not, then we won't."

Billy's shoulders sank a little at the last comment. He trudged toward the entrance to Buster's.

They sat in the front corner, as far from Buster's prying ears as possible. The old man was a good guy, and John ate at the nook most mornings since coming to

Myrtle Beach. But the one time there were other customers, Buster acted like a stereotypical schoolgirl. Rumors flew from his mouth faster than a machine gun could fire. He must have the memory of an elephant to remember so many details about his customers.

When they settled in, their coffee cups filled, John leaned forward and said, "I know you're the one who blew up Billy Borks."

Billy

Billy almost dropped the coffee on his lap. 'I know you're the one who blew up Billy Borks.'

For what seemed like an eternity, he stared at John, waiting for him to go on. Waiting for him to say he'd go to the police and that Billy would spend the rest of his life in prison. That he was a freak belonging in an institution.

"My God, Billy." John sat down his cup and leaned forward. "Your already pale face just turned three shades lighter. Are you okay?"

Billy didn't hear him. He concentrated so hard on what John's next words would be that he didn't hear the sounds coming from his mouth. Instead, he pictured himself in handcuffs, in prison, on the cover of magazines.

John slammed his hand on the table, causing Buster to flip an egg almost to the ceiling. The sound snapped Billy out of his dream state.

"What did you say?" Billy managed to get out of his dry throat.

"I asked if you're okay. You look ill."

Billy stared. Buster pretended nothing happened but kept one eye on John while preparing the food.

John's head tilted back and his chest shook as he laughed. "Wow, kid. You need to calm down. I said I knew you did it. I didn't say you did it on purpose."

Billy didn't know what to think. He hadn't slept. He was too busy thinking about the repercussions of what he'd done at Jackson Incorporated. John should think he was crazy or a freak. Instead, the man sat here and laughed at him as if he'd told the funniest joke in the world.

"Okay, Billy, since you're having a tough time functioning, I'll talk first."

Billy nodded.

John held up his hand and counted on his fingers. "We thought the plates had something to do with the explosion but we weren't sure what. You said you felt strange when the whole thing went down. The building actually imploded rather than exploded. There wasn't any soot, which tells me there weren't any flames, something strange for a large explosion."

"I never thought about the soot." The words croaked from Billy's mouth.

"I didn't at first, either. I remember there being something strange about how things looked. With all these details bounding around in my head, when that Doberman flew so fast he pulled me into the room with him, it wasn't that big of a leap to think you had something to do with it. Especially since you made that weird bark sound at exactly the same time the dog went flying."

"Bark sound? I remember growling in frustration. I didn't think I barked."

"A bark isn't exactly the right word. It sounded like a bark, a human bark, but not like you tried to sound like a dog. It sounded too deep for your body, like it came from inside rather than from your mouth."

"That's the same thing Amfar said when he explained it to you in the hospital." Billy took a sip of his coffee. When John didn't respond right away, he looked up. One of John's eyebrows arched.

"You heard Amfar and me talking in the hospital?"

Billy's face flushed. "Yes, but that was before I knew you. I didn't know you were going to be so... so...."

John laughed again. "You're pretty sneaky, Billy. I give you credit for listening in on our conversation, two guys you'd never met before. Daring for your age. Or stupid."

Billy's shoulders straightened. "I was going to say I didn't know you'd be so cool. I didn't want to say cool, because I don't want you to think I'm just some kid, but it's the only word I can think of that fits what I was going to say. You're the first adult I've met that really listens to what I have to say. You appreciate that I have my own opinion, and you let me do things for myself."

John nodded. "I remember when I was your age, that was how I preferred to be treated. That's how my father treated me, when he wasn't training me anyway." He looked away. "Sometimes I wonder if treating me that way was part of his training." He looked back to Billy. "My old man was very deliberate; everything he did was for a reason. Rarely would I find him relaxing."

"Either way, John, thanks for being cool, and thanks for not telling the police about Billy Borks." He turned in his seat to be sure Buster hadn't heard what he said.

"Of course I wouldn't tell them, Billy. As I said, I knew it wasn't your fault. I've come to know you the past few weeks, and I can see you have a golden heart. Somewhat misguided at times, but golden nonetheless." John leaned across the table. "That's going to be our goal today. We're going to find a way for you to use your golden heart."

Bile rose in Billy's throat. "What do you mean?"

John patted him on the shoulder. "Don't you worry about it, Billy. We're just going to head down to the beach. See if we can get those three plates to work at will."

John

"What are we doing here?" Billy shaded his eyes from the bright midday sun.

They sat in front of John's cottage. John was shirtless wearing khaki shorts and flip-flops, leaning back in his lawn chair. He wondered how Billy could stand to wear blue jeans and a dark baseball cap on such a beautiful warm day.

"Are you sure you grew up here?"

"Why do you say that?"

John took one more glance at the dark clothing and pale skin of his new friend. "No reason." He leaned his head back on the chair. John grew up in Michigan; he appreciated days like today. "Just keep an eye out."

"I don't get it. What am I keeping an eye out for?" The brim of his hat sat low on his head, one of his hands over the bill trying to block more sun.

"Something to use the plates on. Falling airplanes, a beached whale, maybe help a girl with a loose strap on her bathing suit."

Billy guffawed.

"I don't know what to expect. I'm as new at this as you. One thing we do know is we have to test the plates out." He glanced behind Billy's chair to check that the backpack holding the plates was still there. "Since that's our only goal at this point, why not do it while enjoying a day at the beach?"

Billy nodded "It's good to see you relax, John. For a few days there, the rings under your eyes made me nervous. Did you ever get a chance to talk with Kelly?"

The kid was more observant than he let on. "About a week ago." He wasn't sure how comfortable he felt discussing his ex-fiancée with a nineteen-year-old. "We kind of just said one last goodbye. She had another chance to tell me I acted like a kid. I had another chance to tell her I was sorry.

"Now that I know more about the three plates and the explosion, I feel better. Not knowing how, or why, Billy Borks blew up, made me nervous. Now that I know it was an accident," he made sure to look Billy in the eyes, "I can relax knowing there isn't anybody around with some new weapon that causes buildings to implode."

"I can see how that would help you sleep better." Billy's shoulders sank a little.

John leaned forward in his chair. "Hey, man. You'll be fine. I'm not going to lie and say this whole situation doesn't scare me because it does. But I'm not going to leave you out to dry either. You've had some crazy stuff thrown at you, and I'm not going to let you go it alone."

"Thanks, John," Billy whispered.

Billy

Billy liked having John by his side. Eric was normally the only one he counted on to be there for him, but he'd been distant lately. *Probably girl problems.*

He didn't know what John expected to accomplish. They had a decent enough conversation going on, but he'd much rather be inside with Grams's air conditioning. Sitting in the recliner in front of his computer and playing a game was more than enough to keep him happy.

"John?" *How do I say this without sounding like an idiot?* "I just, uh… I just wanted to say thanks. For being here with me, I mean. It means a lot."

John kept his focus on the beach. A moment later, he turned and the corners of his mouth barely turned up. "I know, kid." He gave a slight nod and turned back toward the water.

Billy's head snapped up toward the direction of the beach. John's eyes followed. An old man jogging along the beach stumbled. Everything slowed down, the man falling forward, hands starting to rise to catch his fall. Billy's mind went to the plates in the dark backpack beneath his chair.

He focused, his mind traveled to the air in front of the old man. Billy's chest began to vibrate, similar to the way it felt when singing. The plates vibrated too. He imagined the air in front of the man solidifying to force him upward to stand straight. When the picture in his mind was perfect, he let go.

The old man's hands were inches away from the sand. His light blue eyes bulged as he let out a grunt. Instead of standing back upright, he flew through the air, reminiscent of the Doberman the night before, flipping end over end sideways until he landed fifty yards out into the waters of the Atlantic. Billy's stomach sank.

John sprinted off in the direction the man flew. A girl that had been running a few feet behind the old man shook her head and continued running.

I wouldn't believe it either, Billy thought.

Three children next to the water pointed in the direction of the old man, their parents held them back, not sure whether they were in danger or not.

Billy sat with his hands tucked beneath his legs, not knowing what he'd done. John was already halfway to the old man, whose frantic waving arms were hard to see from the beach.

While something amazing had just happened, Billy didn't know how happy he was that it had. *What would've happened if I killed the guy? So much for my destiny. The first person I try to help turns into a Frisbee.*

Minutes later, the old man walked back toward his car with the help of one of the parents. When John had reached him in the water, he was fine, just a little confused as to how he'd flown there in the first place. He was in good shape and made it back to shore with John's help. After double-checking the man was okay, John let him go on his way.

The relaxed look on John's face all morning was gone, light wrinkles appeared between his brows. He walked back to his chair and plopped down next to Billy.

"Okay then." John paused. "Apparently we need to work on subtlety." John turned to Billy, and they both began laughing.

"Seriously though," John continued. "What the hell? Why did you try blowing him over to England? Maybe we should have started with something smaller. When you tossed the Doberman as easy as you did, I assumed it would be easy to do again. What happened?"

"I'm not sure." Billy rubbed his palms on his jeans. "I pictured the air in front of him pushing him back to standing. That was all. I don't know why he went flying like that."

"I'm not sure either, but I prefer not to see any more flying octogenarians. Maybe you need to visualize it happening softer, or slower. It might have had something to do with how fast you responded, like your reaction time or something."

Billy thought for a moment. "I think you're right about imagining it softer. When I saw him stumble, I was scared he'd be hurt. I pictured him going back to standing right away. It's as if the plates responded to my will. Like whatever I saw, happened." He shoved his shaking hands back under his legs.

"If that's the case, you better be careful what your will demands."

Billy waited for John to say more, but he didn't go on. He liked that about the man. When he said something, he expected you to listen. He didn't believe in 'beating around the bush' as Grams called it.

John stood. "I need a break. You want a beer?"

Billy sputtered.

"Take it easy, kid." John laughed. "I didn't ask you to be an alcoholic. It's the right time to have one. I'm willing to bet you drink with your buddy anyway, right?" Billy nodded and followed him into the cottage.

"What was up with Eric last night anyway? He okay?"

"He says he was having problems with hay fever."

"You don't sound so certain." John opened the refrigerator and pulled out a short dark bottle with a red label.

"I'm not. I can't explain it, but Eric and I have always been close. He's been quiet lately, more calm. Usually he has to be the life of the party." Billy shrugged. "Usually there's a girl in the picture when he acts this way. I've never seen him mope about for so long without coming to me about a girl."

John harrumphed and handed Billy some type of Jamaican ale. "I think he'll be just fine then. He's been in good spirits since I met him. Especially when I asked you two to spy for me."

The more they talked about Eric, the more worried Billy became. He told himself it was the lack of sleep and the constant stress causing him to question his friend's behavior. Maybe Eric was distant because Billy was the one being strange. Eric always stood by him, but maybe telling him about the plates had been too much. Maybe their friendship couldn't withstand the strain.

Chapter 15

Amfar

Sitting around drove Amfar stir crazy. His father had made sure to keep him busy at all times. It bothered him as a child, but now he was thankful for the strong work ethic instilled within him. After all, that work ethic was much of the reason he graduated at a young age with a doctorate and been at the top of his class.

Sitting around the hotel while Kelly healed and Jackson Incorporated took their time studying the bones and plates, became too much to handle. He could only watch the local weather and news so many times. Kelly became fast friends with one of the girls working the front desk two days a week. The girl brought her a new book every shift, romance or sometimes a thriller, and Kelly tore through them like a hurricane.

There wasn't much more he could learn from Sheriff Scott's book. He didn't want to learn any more about the local Native American's in Kentucky.

He asked Kelly's friend about a local library, and she pointed him in the right direction, only a mile from their hotel.

At first, he didn't want to go through the hassle of setting up a new account, but if he didn't find something to do soon, he would explode. Kelly was content to read when she could, then would spend the rest of her time resting her eyes while lying in the sun. She took full advantage of their time on the beach, but it didn't work as well for him. The worst part was Tom Jarrett would likely never give them another chance to take as much time off.

Amfar slid his shoes on and stepped to the balcony. Kelly reclined in one of the bright white lawn chairs, her hair pulled back and sunglasses on, reading another fluorescent pink book. *Why are all the romances pink?*

"Hey there, Kelly."

She jumped a little at his voice.

"Sorry about that. I am going to walk to the library. I wondered if you would like to come along. If not, is there anything I can get for you while I am out?"

"No thanks, Amfar. I have three more of these." She wiggled the book in her hand. "Thanks for asking. Getting sick of sitting around? I've noticed your knees bouncing more than usual when we sit down to eat."

He bounced his knees? He would have to pay closer attention to his actions around Kelly.

"I admit, I am getting bugsy. I've never been one to lounge. Even when I had the time, my father didn't allow it."

"Bugsy?" Her head tilted to the side.

"Yes. I dislike spending time in one place for too long. I would like to leave soon. You know, bugsy."

Kelly threw her head back and howled with laughter. "You're so cute, Amfar. The word is 'antsy', not bugsy." She let out another little giggle and pulled the book back in front of her face.

In case she watched him through her dark sunglasses, he gave a quick wave and turned back into his room. He locked the door and left for the library on foot.

He and Kelly became close during the two weeks after her return from the hospital, but now she pulled away. It was good to see her laugh. There were times he thought they might become more than friends. Now he doubted himself. She wasn't mean, or acting different than normal, but he became used to her needing him during her recovery. He hated to admit, but he missed it. He enjoyed her depending on him. Her independence was one of the many things that drew him to her in the beginning. Maybe that was why he liked her needing him; it gave him some type of empowerment. His father had been right; life would be much easier if he left women out of it.

While he walked, he let his mind wander, going over the words of the manuscript. Thoughts of Kelly slipped in as well. Tires crunched over gravel. A dark blue Oldsmobile pulled up beside him. Amfar bent over to see the driver.

"Sheriff Scott?"

"Howdy, Dr. Ditpra. Need a lift?"

It was the same Sheriff Scott, the local sheriff in Morehead, whose book he'd just been thinking about. They'd been cordial with each other when they met to discuss zoning rights and other legal issues for the site. *Why is he in Myrtle Beach?*

"I guess." Amfar nodded. "I am heading to the library this way a few more blocks."

"Hop on in."

Amfar climbed in, his curiosity overcoming his improprieties. "What are you doing in Myrtle Beach, Sheriff Scott?"

"Please, just call me Robert."

Amfar nodded.

"I'm here to see you, Amfar. We need to talk about the three plates."

***

As far as Amfar knew, the only people that knew about the three plates were him and Kelly, Tom Jarrett of course, and any of the people that Jarrett talked to inside the tent the night of the find. Maybe a few people at Jackson Incorporated as well, but Sheriff Scott? Wouldn't Jarrett have told him if the Morehead police were part of the investigation?

They sat in the parked Oldsmobile outside of the Myrtle Beach Library, windows closed and air-conditioner cranked up. The day was hot, even for Myrtle Beach.

"I'm not sure what you want to talk about, Sheriff... I mean, Robert. Mr. Jarrett made it clear the plates were not something I should discuss."

Scott removed his cowboy hat and turned in his seat to face Amfar. "Mr. Jarrett doesn't know I'm here, Amfar, and I prefer to keep it that way."

Amfar nodded.

Scott went on. "I've watched you the past few weeks, and I've judged you as having good character."

Sheriff Scott has been watching me? Amfar shuddered.

"I'm certain this sounds strange to you," Scott continued. "But I don't have time to beat around the bush. First, I'll tell you what I know. Tom Jarrett's team found three plates, a manuscript, and some bones at the dig site on Riley's Ridge. I know he had you and Kelly drop them off at Jackson Incorporated."

"How do you know all this, Robert? And what does it have to do with you? I do not mean to sound rude. I'm just confused." Was he in danger? Amfar glanced to the door handle, then to Sheriff Scott's holstered gun.

"The relics they found in Morehead are part of the Cherokee tribe that lived there five hundred years ago. Part of that tribe is still around, me included. The things in that cave were never meant to be found, and I hope you will heed your friend Park's warning."

The sheriff knows about Park? The guy had some good resources for a small town sheriff.

Amfar leaned away from the Sheriff and placed his hand on the door handle. "I'm not sure what to believe. I've thought the whole thing over for a few weeks. The warning from Park just added to the questions. The day Billy Borks imploded, I knew something wasn't right, though I didn't know what. When Jarrett was so adamant about finding the three plates, I began to wonder if they had something to do with it. He is so hard to pry information from, I pretended that none of it mattered. When Park called with the translation of the manuscript, I knew I would have to learn more."

Scott ran his fingers through his thick black hair. "That's why I watched you, Amfar. Part of my job within the tribe is to judge people, to determine whether they're worthy to partake of the knowledge that's now yours."

Amfar didn't want to think what would happen if Scott had deemed him not worthy.

"Since you've been deemed worthy, and things have begun spinning out of control, we need your help finding the plates. We need to bring them back to Morehead and to entrust them to another tribe member."

Amfar let go of the door handle. "What do you need me for? If you knew Kelly and I dropped them at Jackson Incorporated, then why not just go get them."

The Sheriff shook his head.

"They're not there anymore? What happened?"

"We're not sure. We knew the security system at J.I. was less than stellar, and we planned to remove them. Someone got there before us. By the time we reached the correct floor, someone had already removed them, leaving a storm of broken concrete in their path."

"Broken concrete? What about security cameras?" Amfar tapped his chin with a finger. "They had to have seen something."

Scott sighed. "There are no security cameras, just as there is no security system beyond some viciously trained dogs."

"How can that be?"

"The only thing we can assume is that Jarrett knew about the power of the plates and used that knowledge in conjunction with Jackson Incorporated employees. Rumors say the plates can interfere with electrical equipment."

Amfar looked at the entrance to the library. A small child pulled on his mother's hand. Something was happening in Myrtle Beach, yet people go on living every day as if nothing bad will ever happen. He wished he could be that way, but his father taught him differently. There would be no rest this day, no reading books.

"I need some time to think, Sheriff Scott. Your information has given me new questions to ponder."

Scott looked into Amfar's eyes and spoke in a slow drawl. "Don't wait too long, Dr. Ditpra. Events outpace us, and I don't know how long before we fall too far behind."

Amfar nodded and climbed from the car. Sheriff Scott's car pulled away from the library. The walk back to the hotel wasn't as bright as it had been when leaving. Knowing something grave brewed in Myrtle Beach, and he had no control, made Amfar think twice about the beauty surrounding him.

***

"Hello. This is Dr. Amfar Ditpra. May I speak with Mr. Tom Jarrett?"

"Please hold."

Amfar didn't know what to say, but he didn't think it wise to wait any longer. Park hadn't called back again, but even a fool could understand the words from the manuscript were a warning.

"Go."

"Excuse me?"

"I said go." Tom Jarrett's voice was loud and clipped.

"Oh, um, hello Mr. Jarrett, this is..."

"I know who it is, Amfar, that's why I have a secretary. What do you want?"

He tried not to stutter. Jarrett had the same bearing as Amfar's father. He pictured his dad standing over him. "Quit your stuttering child," he would say. "Think of the shame you bring our name."

"Well, you see, Mr. Jarrett," Amfar managed to get out. "I am calling because I have some information I thought you would be interested to learn. It concerns the three plates."

"What is it, Amfar?" Jarrett said after a long pause.

"I know you told me to go back to the hotel and relax when we were released from the hospital, but I had to do something with my time. I'm not one for relaxing."

"Get to the point."

"Yes, Mr. Jarrett." The conversation was going worse than he had imagined. The man had so little patience, even for one of his employees. How did he become the most successful archaeologist in the world? "I did something you will not be happy about. I sent a copy of the manuscript to a friend in London, a paleographer."

More silence. "You did what?" Jarrett said just above a whisper.

"I sent it to my friend to see if he could determine what the writing said. I didn't know if they had someone working on it at Jackson Incorporated or not, so I took the initiative." Only half a lie.

"And did your friend translate the manuscript, Amfar?"

"Actually, yes he did. He said—"

"I know what it says, you idiot. You think I got where I am because I waited for morons like you to 'take the initiative'?" He said the last three words in a high-pitched imitation of Amfar. "I am where I am because *I* am the one that takes the initiative. Me, the owner, your boss."

Amfar was speechless, mouth agape. *How does Tom Jarrett already know the words to the manuscript?*

"Forgive me, Mr. Jarrett, I didn't know—"

"You're right, you didn't know. You don't know anything that goes on in my office, because I don't let you know. This is the reason why. You stick your nose where it doesn't belong. If you weren't so damn good at your job, I'd can you right now. I'm tempted to anyway."

Jarrett's deep breath echoed through the phone.

"This is what you are going to do," Jarrett continued. "You're going to call your friend in London and tell him to forget he ever heard of the manuscript. It's just a piece of shit we found along with the bones and plates. It wasn't a big find; it was barely a small find. No reason for anybody to know anything about anything, especially some idiot's friend that thinks he's a paleographer. I'll do my best to forget this conversation took place, and it would be in your best interest to do the same."

Jarrett hung up the phone.

Amfar had imagined the conversation in his mind twenty times before making the phone call. Not one had been near what actually happened. He'd assumed Jarrett would be upset Amfar went behind his back, but that he would appreciate the work done on the manuscript. Amfar didn't know if Jarrett would believe Park's translation, but he had to try. What an utter failure. *What am I supposed to do now?*

Since returning from the library, he and Kelly hadn't spoken a word. She would wonder what his lunch plans were. He wanted to tell her about sneaking into John's cottage, taking the plates, meeting Kirkwall, talking with Jarrett, and even Sheriff Scott. So far, there hadn't been the need. It was easier if she didn't know. But they had grown closer. She would know if he kept too many secrets. Besides, after Park's warning and then the confirmation from Sheriff Scott, things really were spinning out of control.

Protecting Kelly was Amfar's priority, more so after Billy Borks. She was an intelligent woman. Maybe with her assistance, she'd help decide their next step and whether that step involved Sheriff Scott.

He knocked at the back door she normally left open during the day. She poked her head around the curtain and opened the door with a smile.

"Hi, Amfar." She waved him in. "Did you find any good books for that big brain of yours to delve into?"

"Not exactly."

She paused reaching for the refrigerator.

"There are some things I need to discuss with you, Kelly."

Her hand pulled back from the fridge, and she crossed her arms. "What kinds of things?"

The way Kelly stood was reminiscent of the way she did when speaking about John. *Crossing her arms must be one of her defensive stances.*

"I have done some things the past couple of weeks that I believe you should be aware of. One of them illegal."

Her arms dropped to her sides, and she took a step toward him. "My God, Amfar. What's going on? What have you been doing?"

"I have been working with Mr. Jarrett."

She took a step back.

"Not like you think." He raised his hands. "Since the explosion, my mind has been on overdrive. Any detail that even remotely has to do with the case, I have been over and over in my mind. There were things that did not make sense, and some that did, but should not. I know this is a lot to take right now, but I need you to believe that everything I've done has been to keep you safe." He couldn't believe the words coming from his mouth. It was as if someone took control of his body.

Amfar pictured Kelly's amazing smile showing on her face as she rushed up and threw her arms around his shoulders, thanking him for protecting her. The smile didn't appear, but she did step closer. Her hand flew from her side to slap him across the face, snapping his head to the side.

"How could you lie to me after everything I told you about John? I thought you were different, Amfar." She took a few steps back and crossed her arms again.

Amfar rubbed at his cheek.

"The one great thing John had going for him was that he never lied to me. Even when he knew I'd leave him, he confessed to sleeping with that girl. You protected me? How? By lying to me and not telling me about things that could hurt me? That doesn't make any sense, Amfar. I'm not a child."

Words wouldn't form in Amfar's mouth. Every time a new thought came into his mind, he realized how stupid it would sound to Kelly.

"I'm sorry," he squeaked, the words sounded like a question.

"And you should be." Kelly's face twisted for just a moment, and Amfar thought he could see tears forming. Instead, she closed her eyes and took a deep breath. When they opened, she pointed to the door.

"Kelly, wait." Amfar took a step toward her. "Can we please talk about this? There are some things that—"

"We don't need to talk. I'm going back to Morehead. You don't need to create anymore lame excuses for protecting me."

"But—"

"Out!" She jabbed her finger toward the door.

Chapter 16

Billy

"I can't believe you're really not drinking tonight." Billy sat in the passenger seat of Eric's rust bucket.

"I told you I wasn't. What's the matter, Billy? You afraid to have a few beers without your buddy?" Eric rolled his eyes.

"I'm not afraid. It's just weird. I don't know that I've ever gone to a party with you when you didn't drink." He paused. Faking a serious voice, he said, "What if you were only fun because of the beer, Eric?"

Eric gave him an open hand smack to the back of the head. "Whatever, man. You should be happy you have a designated driver, a sober one."

Billy nodded. "True. You think Jessica is still mad at me for punching her?"

Eric laughed so hard he struggled to take a breath.

"Knock it off. Or I'll have to take you to the hospital again." Billy laughed a little too. Looking back, the situation was somewhat funny. Except the part about getting beat up afterward. Tonight was the first time Jessica invited them to a party since. For over a week, she'd worn make-up to cover the two black eyes.

In between laughs, Eric forced out a few words. "No. Said she's fine now."

"Well, good. As long as Bull isn't there again, we'll be fine."

An hour later, they sat at Jessica's kitchen table playing cards when Bull walked in. The party was smaller than the one a few weeks before, but it was busy enough Bull didn't notice them right away.

"You have to be kidding me." Billy sighed.

"What?" Eric looked up from the cards in his hand.

Billy nodded toward the front door.

Eric saw Bull, closed his eyes, and shook his head. "I'm not even drunk, and I want to hit the guy."

They were almost finished with the Euchre game. Eric didn't turn on the charm like usual with the two girls they'd just met. Billy hoped to score a phone number or two. He wasn't sure if it was because Eric wasn't drinking, or if it was their recent conversation with John causing his friend to be so reserved. Maybe a combination of the two.

"Well, ladies, looks like this is our last hand." Billy put on his best smile. "Eric and I have a prior engagement we forgot about." He flipped the cards onto the table, dealing their last hand.

"We're only four points behind," said the one named Sherri. "How do you know we won't have a come-back?"

She had short brown hair cut like a boy, but was attractive enough to pull it off. She was quiet most of the night, but loosened up after a few malt beverages, not the type Billy usually went for. Too shy. The girls he usually talked to were willing to make the first move. The second move, and the third, as well. He needed to work on his pick-up abilities, but tonight he did fine.

Billy winked at Sherri. "We only let you win the last two because we felt bad. Now we'll show you how we really play."

Before the last word was out of his mouth, a huge hand slapped the table, causing some of the empty beer bottles to fall over.

"I didn't think I'd see you ladies tonight." Bull leaned on the table, eyes focused on Eric.

Sherri glared at the guy, but didn't say anything. Her friend Mary was the more outgoing of the two.

"That was rude." Mary straightened the fallen bottles. "And who the hell are you anyway? I've never seen you before."

"I wasn't talking to you two." Bull sent a deliberate look in Billy's direction. "I'm talking to the ladies who punched out a girl at the last party."

Billy shrank into his seat. So much for hoping Jessica had enough sense not to let her brother invite Bull back.

"Look, B—man." Billy reminded himself the guy's name wasn't really Bull. "We don't want any trouble. We're leaving anyway."

Sherri had a pained look on her face. Did she really like him? What did it matter, he was going to leave anyway. Being Bull's punching bag again sounded less than pleasant. He and Eric tossed their cards on the table and stood up.

"You want an escort?" Bull leaned back and held his arms out to the side. "I wouldn't want you to get into any trouble on your way out of here."

Other people at the party watched now, knowing about Bull's temper. Things were quieter than a few minutes before.

Neither responded to Bull's question about the escort. They worked their way through the meager crowd and into the parking lot. They pulled on the rust bucket's doors when somebody yelled Billy's name.

Sherri waved just outside the apartment holding Billy's backpack. "Hey, you forgot your backpack."

Bull came up behind her and snatched the bag from her hands. She gave him a dirty look but took a couple steps back.

"This your fanny pack, Billy boy?" Bull held the bag in the air and gave it a shake.

Billy's heart fell through his feet. The backpack held the three plates. John said to keep the plates with him at all times, in case he needed to defend himself from bow and arrow wielding crazy men. Now the giant version of a twenty-year-old held the bag up in front of him, pulling on the zipper.

A thousand questions zipped through Billy's head at once. What would happen if Bull broke the plates? Could they be broken? Could Bull use them? What would happen if he pulled them out? Would everybody make fun of him for bringing plates to a party? He stood there with his mouth open.

"Billy," Eric snapped. "Wake up. Bull has the plates. What do we do?"

The questions stopped. The plates were more important than Billy was. More important than being beat up. No matter what, he couldn't let Bull have them, even for a minute.

Sherri glanced back and forth between Bull and him. She was beautiful. Not the best time to think about her beauty, but he couldn't help himself.

Time slowed, as if his senses increased to the point everything else seemed slow. Eric voiced another complaint about Bull. Bull yanked on one of the zippers but didn't have any luck. Sherri looked at him, pity showing through every inch.

No pity, no remorse. Billy wouldn't deal with it anymore. He'd been entrusted with a power, and he'd use it. He took a step toward Bull. Eric stopped mid-sentence and stared. Sherri's brows moved up, and she took another step back. Bull's mouth turned up at the corners.

Billy felt the familiar burning in his chest, the anger. It was happening again, he'd need control. Wouldn't do him any good to send the jerk flying through a wall.

A picture formed in his mind, a wall of air around his body a foot thick, impenetrable. Bull's fists wouldn't pound on him this night. Billy would throw a single punch and move the air in front of that fist in a quick blow to Bull's temple. Just enough to knock him down. A breath of air. The pictures repeated in his mind. This time, he'd be the victor; nobody would make fun of him anymore. He started toward the backpack.

When Billy was within three feet of Bull, he chanced a look to Sherri. She wore a nervous smile now. Fear lit her eyes. She didn't know about his power. Nobody did except Eric and John. Billy's eyes moved back to Bull who'd given up pulling on the zipper. At least one thing went right. Billy didn't know how close the plates had to be to make them work, but they'd been thirty yards away in Amfar's trunk when Billy Borks imploded.

Now was the time. The backpack dropped from Bull's left hand, and his right shot forward with the quickness Billy remembered so well. He prepared his own fist. When Bull's hand slammed against the impenetrable barrier surrounding Billy, his counterattack would be quick and had to look as natural as possible.

The fist came toward his face, inching closer. He visualized the barrier one more time. His head snapped back and blood spurted from his nostrils when the fist made contact.

***

"I'm guessing that wasn't what you had planned?" Eric glanced at Billy.

Billy sat in the passenger side of the rust bucket leaning forward as John taught him, holding his nose to keep blood from pouring out.

"Real funny." The garbled words came out sounding like, 'Wheel fuddy.'

Eric let out a laugh and cringed, tucking his right arm to his side.

"You said Bull didn't get you very good." Billy forgot about his nose for a moment. "Were you lying?"

A smile grew on Eric's face; the one Billy expected. "Maybe a little. I didn't want to take away from your glory."

"What glory?" Billy let out a long breath, blood spilled down his fingers onto his T-shirt. "Did you see the way Sherri looked at me?"

"The brunette? Yeah, she looked sad. I'm surprised."

"Why surprised?"

"I'm surprised she even talked to you. Look how ugly you are." Eric glanced over to Billy again and they glared at each other until both began laughing.

Billy's laughs came out more like honks. "I hate to admit this, but I guess you're still fun even when you're not drunk."

Every heartbeat brought renewed pain. The crooked nose bulging toward Billy in the rearview mirror convinced him Eric made the right choice driving to the emergency room. The fight, if you could call it that, didn't last long. The first punch laid Billy out, and he smacked his head on the cement. The next thing he remembered was Eric pulling him toward the car. Other partygoers had come out to watch. Bull, showing off, held his arms in the air and chanted like a pro-wrestler. He kicked at Billy and Eric a few times, mostly for show, but threw in a couple extra fists, too. Eric took a few hits while dragging Billy to safety. Eric may say he's fine, but the cringe moments ago told Billy otherwise.

The woman working the emergency room front desk recognized Eric from before.

"Hey, kiddo. I thought I told you to keep your butt out of here." She ran her hand through her graying hair. Billy guessed her to be fifty or so, but the warming smile dropped years off. Scared visitors to the hospital probably found it comforting.

"Hi, Nancy." Eric pointed his thumb over his shoulder. "We're not here for me tonight."

Billy waved with his free hand, nose held between the fingers of his other. Nancy lost some of her joviality when she saw blood covering Billy's hands and face.

She stood and waddled over to Billy, placing her arm around his shoulders. "Oh, sweetheart. Let's get you in here. There isn't anybody else in the ER tonight, we'll get you right in. Doctor Faust can take a look straight away."

Her arm draped around Billy's shoulders, she guided him toward the ER room and pushed the handicap button to the side. The door swung open, and she directed him into the first room on their left, reassuring him everything would be fine. Billy eased himself into a chair near the door.

"There you go, sweetheart. Now you just keep holding your nose like that, and I'll get Doctor Faust. Nurse Stinson will be here shortly too."

Billy waited for Eric to follow and sit in one of the other chairs. He prepared for Eric's smartass comments after seeing Billy manhandled by a woman almost old enough to be his grandma.

Billy ignored Nancy's nattering and put his hand on her shoulder, nudging her to the side, peering behind her. "Where's Eric?"

She looked behind and leaned into the hall, looking both ways. "Well, I don't know, sweetie." She turned back toward Billy with her smile still planted firmly in place. "I'm sure he just went to the john. You just calm down now. Your nose looks like it stopped bleeding, but we should still take a look at it."

Ice formed in the pit of his stomach.

"Eric wouldn't have gone to the bathroom without saying something first," he mumbled to himself stepping around Nancy, no longer holding his nose. He looked both ways down the fluorescent-lit hallways.

"Why don't you just sit down for a second, honey? I'm sure he'll be right back." She grabbed Billy's arm and pulled him toward the chair.

He yanked his arm away.

Putting hands on her hips, she lowered her brows in a practiced glare. "You listen here, son. Don't you go treating me like that. I've been nothing but—"

Billy ignored her and stepped into the hallway, calling Eric's name. No answer. He pushed open the heavy door to the waiting area, searching for his friend. Still nobody else in the waiting area. He turned back to Nancy. Maybe she was right after all.

As he turned, he caught a glimpse of something dark against the white tiles of the waiting room. Eric's shoes.

Billy let the door swing shut behind him and ran around the front desk. Eric lay on the ground in a heap, blood trickled from his mouth and a wound on the back of his head.

"Nancy! Get Doctor Faust now." Billy sat next to Eric and cradled his head. *The blood on his head is probably from the fall, but what is the blood from his mouth?* Did Bull hit him that hard?

Nancy poked her head from the hallway, eyes bulging. She turned without a word.

If Eric were hit that hard, he wouldn't have been able to stand or drive for that matter.

"It's okay, man." Billy rocked back and forth. "Everything is going to be fine. You there? Wake up, man."

Eric mumbled something. Billy couldn't hear what, he was just happy his friend was coherent enough to say something.

Chapter 17

Amfar

"I didn't peg you as the drinking type, Doctor Ditpra." The bar stool wobbled as Sheriff Scott took a seat next to Amfar. He waved the bartender over and ordered a summer ale.

Amfar sipped his dark liquor. "My father always blamed my mother for his drinking. I finally understand why."

"Dr. Pierce?"

Amfar nodded and took another sip.

"Interesting. I didn't realize you two were an item."

Amfar studied the array of liquor bottles in front of the mirrored wall.

"So you've taken my advice and thought more about the three plates?"

"I did, and you are right." Amfar turned to Scott. "If there is any truth to the legends about these plates, we must find them. And I might know where they can be found."

Billy

"What do you mean you're on the way to New York? What happened?"

The urgency in John's voice made Billy feel even worse for leaving. He probably thought Billy was such a wimp.

"I know it sounds crazy, John, but it's what I have to do."

"Calm down, kid. Tell me what I can do to help. Did you leave already?"

Billy's chest shook from holding in his sobs. "Yes, I already left. I'm on the road right now. Some things have happened the past couple days, and I needed to get away." He paused. "In my dreams, something always happens in a big city anyway. I think it's New York where they take place, where I'm supposed to be."

"You went to New York because of some dream you had?" John huffed. "Billy, you should've talked to me. I live in New York, remember? At least tell me where you're headed so I can meet you there."

"You don't need to do that, John." He calmed down enough that his voice didn't quiver anymore. "I know where I need to be, and I might know what I have to do. Thanks for being so kind the past few weeks. When I know for sure what I'm going to do, and where I'm going, I'll contact you."

He heard John take a deep breath. "One of the things my old man always told me was to prepare people the best you could, and let them make their own mistakes. Either they'll learn from them, or they won't. You're a smart kid, Billy, and you're my friend. I'm not going to lie and say I'm not afraid for you. But none of that matters. You do what you feel like you have to. I'll be here."

John continued to surprise Billy; an enigma. One of the most intelligent and responsible men he'd ever met. Yet, at the same time, he constantly put himself on the line for Billy. He was either an amazing judge of character or a very bad one.

Billy liked to think he was a good person, and if he was, then he was doing the right thing. The gift given him didn't work the way he thought at the party, and it scared him. From the beginning, he thought the dreams had something to do with the plates. There was some clue he'd learn in New York, a key to his understanding.

"John?"

"Yes, Billy?"

"Thanks for being a friend."

"Just make sure you make it back to Myrtle Beach, kid. I don't think your story with the plates is over yet."

They hung up. Billy looked out the window. Dark hills moved by, interrupted every so often by a glowing billboard sign. He'd used Grams's credit card to rent a long distance taxi service to drive him across state lines. After what happened with Eric at the hospital, he wouldn't have been able to drive even if he owned a car. His chest heaved as he fought back the tears. He wasn't the crying type. If anything, he didn't cry enough, but today he couldn't help himself. He closed his eyes as last night's events rolled through his mind.

He and Nancy had found Eric on the floor of the emergency room in a heap. While he cradled Eric's head, Nancy went for help. She came back with Doctor Faust and three nurses. They lifted Eric onto a stretcher. Nancy held Billy back while they carted his friend away, the nurses yapping at each other and hooking things to Eric's body.

Billy had calmed enough to sit in the waiting room. Nancy joined him. At first, her constant prattling annoyed him, but he realized it calmed him more. She talked about everything. The six brothers she grew up with in Kentucky and how they taught her to play baseball. Her father was a small town preacher but a "God's man, through and through" she told him at least a dozen times.

Nobody told him how his friend was doing. The whole time he listened to Nancy, he imagined all the things that could be wrong with his best friend, from having an aneurism, to a heart attack.

When Doctor Faust returned two hours later, Nancy was reciting her favorite slow-cooked pot roast recipe.

"You can see him now if you would like." The doctor had dark rings under his eyes, yet smiled. That had to be a good sign, didn't it?

"He's okay? I mean, he's..." The words wouldn't come, so he hopped up and followed Faust.

Eric lay in a room slightly larger than the one they visited earlier. The rings around his eyes were darker than Doctor Faust's. He looked as if he were asleep. The heart monitor beeping was a welcome sound.

Doctor Faust turned to walk out and paused. He turned to Billy. "Before you leave this morning, be sure to get that nose checked out. It looks like it's broken."

He'd forgotten about his nose.

Eric opened his eyes when Billy put his hand on the bed.

"If you even try touching me, I will make sure every girl in Myrtle Beach knows you're a switch hitter."

Billy's first reaction was to hit his friend in the shoulder, but he stopped himself short.

Eric let out the breath he held in anticipation of the hit. "Thanks for not hitting me. The pain killers are awesome, but I don't want to test them."

"What happened? They won't tell me anything." The words poured from his mouth. "I tried calling your parents. Your dad is still on his run from Idaho, and your sister wants me to call her back when I find something out."

Eric closed his eyes again and took a long drawn out breath. When they opened, he looked into Billy's. "You've been my best friend for as long as I can remember, Billy. I need to tell you something, but before I do, you have to promise me something."

"Anything."

"Promise me that you will still treat me as the same Eric you always have."

"Of course I will, why wouldn't I?" He regretted the words once out of his mouth.

Eric took another of the deep breaths. A smile came to his lips, the same smile Billy had seen his friend wear thousands of times. This time it didn't reach his eyes. "Billy, I have stage four stomach cancer. They diagnosed me a month ago. The doctors say I'll be lucky to see another Christmas."

John

John sat on the cheap couch in his rented cottage, pondering his decisions over the last month. He left New York in the hopes Kelly would give him another chance. Instead, he learned she'd almost been killed and still wants nothing to do with him. In a way, it was calming to know that he didn't have to worry about making her happy anymore, that he could go back to doing whatever he wanted to do, even go back to Elite Bodyguarding full-time. A strange feeling; he didn't think he'd ever feel that way for someone. He still didn't know why he'd slept with Ashley, besides the obvious reasons. Was he so weak that he'd turn down the possibility of a lifetime filled with happiness for a one-night romp?

He stared at the stains on the drop ceiling, listening to the air conditioner hum. It was early in the morning, and he'd already polished off three cups of coffee. Now a beer sounded like a good addition to his woeful thoughts. He wasn't used to feeling sorry for himself.

He walked to the kitchen and pulled a Corona from the fridge. He popped the top onto the flimsy kitchen table. The bitter taste the beer left in his mouth was fitting.

Two shadows crossed in front of his bedroom window. This early in the morning, there would only be shadows if someone stood within feet of the cottage.

With his left hand, he checked the gun taped to the bottom of the kitchen table. With his right, he removed the one he'd hidden in the breadbasket on top of the refrigerator. He stepped backward, ready to make a run for it if he had to, or to dive behind the recliner in the living room if that was what the situation called for.

The two shadows were at his front door and knocked. *Knocked?* He let go of the breath he'd been holding. He was more on edge than he realized. At least he was sleeping again; the two weeks Kelly had been in the hospital were hell on his body.

"What can I do for you?" he called toward the door.

"John? It's Amfar. I would like to talk to you, please."

He slid the gun into his rear waistband. There wasn't any reason not to trust Amfar, but with the way things were going, one never knew. He unlocked the door and pulled it open a few inches. He hoped the second shadow wasn't Kelly. The way he felt, he'd probably say something he would regret.

Amfar peeked his head around the edge of the door and squinted, eyes not adjusted to the darkness in John's cottage. He kept the shades closed; the darkness fit his mood.

"John? Are you in there?"

"Come on in, Amfar. Who's your friend?" Amfar jumped a little.

The door swung open the rest of the way, letting in the early morning light and humidity.

"This is Sheriff Scott. He is the Sheriff in Morehead, Kentucky, where we were stationed for the dig."

The slender man behind Amfar was in his mid-forties and had a jaw as strong as his character. Ed Reeves drilled John about paying attention to how a man held himself, and this man held himself with pride. It was a strange combination seeing this man with Amfar, who held himself in almost the opposite manner and looked worse today than normal. Maybe the pressure of the last few weeks weighed on his shoulders too.

Amfar was arguably the most intelligent person John had ever met, except for Rachel. The man put tremendous pressure on himself to perform, and it showed in the way he carried himself, as if there was always some unseen weight pulling him down.

"Come on in." John waved them into the kitchen.

Amfar and Sheriff Scott stepped in, eyes open wide.

John stepped to the shades and pulled them up. "Sorry about that, I just woke up."

The Sheriff's eyes went to the Corona bottle sitting on the table. "You have an interesting way of preparing yourself for the day, Mr. Reeves."

Apparently, he was quick too. It made sense. A Sheriff would have to be intelligent and quick on his feet.

John let out a small laugh and pointed at the beer bottle. "That there is the perfect way to start your morning when on vacation and enjoying the amazing weather Myrtle Beach has to offer."

John wished they'd hurry with the pleasantries. Having Amfar and the unknown man in his living room was uncomfortable, not to mention it was hard to work his way around the cottage keeping his back turned away from them. It wouldn't do any of them good if they saw the gun stored in his pants.

"So what's going on today, gentlemen? I'm assuming you didn't come here to discuss my drinking habits."

Scott pulled out a chair from the table and sat, leaning back as if he didn't have a care in the world.

John looked to Amfar and swore he saw a dark look pass over his face. But it was so out of place, he must have imagined it. Amfar's hands opened and closed repeatedly. Maybe John didn't imagine the dark look.

Sheriff Scott glanced to Amfar. He shook his head and opened his mouth.

Before he could get any words out, Amfar spoke. "Where are the plates, John? We know you have them." A vein bulged on the side of Amfar's head.

John sensed Scott's muscles tense as the cop leaned forward in the kitchen chair. John felt the hair on his neck rise.

Billy

Billy's cab drove through the night and dropped him off downtown near Central Park. Now, he sat on a park bench, eyes closed, letting the warm late summer rain pour over his face and soak through his clothes. Not many people passed by. Some braved the weather with umbrellas and a runner splashed by every so often.

Billy's eyes opened. The steady beat of the rain and the thick grass swaying in the wind relaxed him, but he still held some tension inside. After making the old man fly at Myrtle Beach, he wasn't sure what to expect.

Flashes of the dream worked their way through his mind. He compared his current surroundings to what he remembered. It rained in the dream, but just a light drizzle. Not the heavy kind falling today. The smells were similar; the exhaust from too many vehicles mixed with the fresh scent of the soil. The appealing scent from the vendors a few hundred yards away wafted through the rain and made his mouth water. At the same time, the thought of food, or putting anything in his stomach, nauseated him.

His thoughts drifted to his friend as they had the entire ride to New York. Eric, usually strong and carefree, sat in a hospital bed, skin pallid. The recent changes in personality made sense now. He wondered if there were other signs he'd missed.

Less than a year to live? What would he do without his best friend? Eric was the only person who understood the way he thought about life and women, the only one who could comprehend his sense of humor. He was the only one who didn't let him feel sorry for himself when his parents died. Instead of telling him he was crazy for researching his parent's crash, Eric asked how he could help. When he asked Eric why he helped, he'd replied with a simple, 'You're my best friend, Billy,' and that had been it. In a life where people were lucky if they even had a friend, Billy was losing the best kind to some disease.

His anger rose, growing in his chest the way it did before he unleashed his newfound power. The plates sat under the bench in the backpack. He sensed them vibrating with energy, not a vibration felt with the hands, but with the soul. His anger, his ambitions, and his thoughts reverberated within the plates.

He closed his eyes to the world and drew soothing breaths; the humid summer air filled his lungs. Some anger subsided, but the anger of having his friend taken away would never subside completely.

A thunderous boom echoed through the park. Billy dove to the ground beneath the bench, remembering how his dreams sometimes ended with him shot. He searched the park for assailants. He held the bag under his chin as the rain dripped down around him. An old couple walked by muttering to themselves while they watched him under the bench. Hadn't they heard the gunshot?

Bang.

Two-hundred yards in front of him, a car backfired as it pulled into a parking lot. He shook his head. *What an idiot.* He stood up and wiped at the chunks of mud and grass that stuck to his pants.

He sat back down on the bench and waited. Something would happen. He had no idea what, or when, but it would. It had to. The dreams were the reason he came. Some time during one of his conversations with Dr. Flanagan, he deduced the chase took place in Central Park.

The dreams were so realistic, and he'd been in the big city, carrying the same backpack he had now. It rained, people chased him, terror filled him... something wasn't right. *What feels different?* Whatever chased him in the dream wasn't there now. He felt no fear, except that he'd be alone when Eric died.

John

John thought about Billy describing how time slowed when using the plates. Maybe it was different for Billy, but the surge of adrenaline running through John's bloodstream made him think otherwise.

The anger on Amfar's face distorted his normally calm demeanor. His chest heaved, brows lowered, teeth set in a rictus snarl. Scott's head leaned around Amfar, eyes on John and every muscle tense. *Why is Amfar so angry? Is he willing to fight if he thinks I have the plates?*

John's hand had automatically drawn itself back toward the gun in his waistband. Not noticing at first. Thankful for his natural response, he studied Scott's eyes. They followed his hand. Smart man, he knew what was about to happen.

The muscles in Scott's neck flexed as his arm started toward the weapon waiting in his shoulder holster.

John was faster. "Wait!" John lifted his left hand up. The right held the Glock aimed between Scott's eyes.

Amfar stared at the gun in John's hand, eyes wide. Scott's hand remained partially hidden behind his dark brown sheriff's jacket.

"What are you doing, John?" Amfar's voice cracked. "Why would you pull a gun on us?"

John nodded his head toward the man at his kitchen table. "Not on you, Amfar. On your pal, Scott."

Amfar glanced over his shoulder and saw the sheriff; hand paused on its way toward his gun.

"Sheriff Scott, what are you doing? Take your hand out of your jacket." He turned back toward John. "And you, John, put that gun away right now. Please! Both of you calm down. There is no reason for either of you to have your weapons drawn."

John still focused on Sheriff Scott's eyes. Scott's muscles relaxed and he released a small breath, pulling his hand from his jacket and raising them both in surrender.

John shoved the Glock back into his waistband and raised his hands like Scott. He lowered himself onto the arm of the couch, a second pistol hidden in a stack of magazines nearby.

Amfar walked to the other end of the couch and plopped down. He rubbed the palms of his hands across his eyes, looking considerably more tired than minutes before.

"John, why did you pull a gun on Scott? You don't even know him. And what are you doing with a gun anyway? I thought you said you were on vacation."

"I am on vacation. My gun goes where I go."

"A lesson learned from your police officer father I assume?"

"Good assumption." John smiled.

"You never answered my first question. Why pull it now?" Amfar shook his head.

John barked a laugh to calm everybody down. The effect didn't take. "Sorry about that, Amfar. I didn't tell you about the first time I visited Billy Borks. You remember the boy, Billy Hitchings?"

Amfar nodded.

"He happened to be there at the same time. We made the decision to keep searching, regardless of what the other was there for, and we were shot at."

"Somebody shot at you? Did you call the police?"

"No, and that was my fault. The situation was a little strange though. We weren't shot at with bullets; we were shot at with arrows."

"Arrows? As in bow and arrows?" Amfar sat forward on the couch.

"That's the kind." John tried to look calm, but glanced to Sheriff Scott.

"You still should have called the police."

"I agree, but there were some things I didn't understand. Looking back now, I'm glad I didn't. I think our buddy Jarrett has a few local officers in his pocket."

Amfar looked away.

John's eyes went to the man on his couch. "I'm right. Aren't I?"

Amfar hid something. Did John make a mistake confiding in Amfar? Maybe the Scott guy with him was really one of Jarrett's goons.

Amfar sighed and rubbed at his eyes again. "Some things have happened over the past couple of weeks that you should be aware of. One of them is that I haven't been completely honest with you."

"Only one way I know to remedy that, Amfar." John's hand slid into the bundle of magazines and gripped his pistol. "But first, let's talk about having your friend remove his hand from my pistol."

Amfar

"What do you mean?" Amfar looked confused again, his eyes going to Scott at the kitchen table.

John nodded to the Sheriff. Scott sat with his right hand on the table, the other beneath it. His face flushed as he smiled at John and stood. He lifted both hands up for the second time.

"Okay, John Reeves. I surrendered my weapon. Now it's time for you, too."

Amfar's head whipped toward John on the couch. He watched as John removed his hand from the bundle of magazines with slow precision, then raised them the same as Scott.

Amfar sputtered, head swiveling back and forth between the two men. He closed his eyes. With a heavy sigh, he opened them again. "This is not the Wild West, Sheriff Scott," Amfar said between them. "The same goes for you, John. Now that we have seen who has the bigger gun, can you two calm your testosterone for a few moments so that we may have an adult conversation?"

They nodded.

Amfar couldn't believe he was stuck between two gun-slinging idiots. The fate of the world might be in their hands, and the only people he had to work with were concerned more about who could shoot the fastest than how the world might end.

"Why don't we all take a seat at the table?" Amfar gestured toward the kitchen. "If you don't mind, I will get us all a drink, John. I know I could use one."

John and the Sheriff sat down at the rickety kitchen table. John took the seat Scott had been in the moment before. He slid his hand under the table and with a ripping sound, tore the gun loose, and sat it in the middle of the table.

Amfar finally understood John's threat toward Scott. The Sheriff must have had his hand on the gun under the table, and John must have had another weapon hidden near the end of the couch. He'd been furious at the day he had, especially when Kelly left, but shooting someone never crossed his mind.

Amfar pulled three Coronas from the fridge. He took one for himself and sat the other two on the table.

"I have limes in there if either of you want one." John pointed toward the refrigerator.

"This will be fine, Mr. Reeves, thank you." Amfar stood at the head of the table. "Before we go any further, I need you both to understand something."

The two men looked at one another, then back to Amfar and nodded.

"The three of us must be absolutely honest with one another. Holding anything back could have devastating effects. There are forces at work we know nothing about, save Sheriff Scott. And the information he has is based on legend and hearsay."

The Sheriff and John sat quietly at the table. He became conscious of the way they looked at him, as if he was in the spotlight. He spoke again but continued to stutter.

Sheriff Scott rose and placed his hand on Amfar's shoulder. "Why don't you have a seat, Amfar. Take a drink. I'll come clean first since I'm the newest member in this triad."

Amfar sat with a nod and took a drink of the ice-cold Corona.

"John Reeves, I'm sorry about our little gun show. This is a very serious situation, and I wasn't sure, yet, if I could trust you."

"And you are now?" John flashed a devious smile.

Scott smiled. "Yes, of course. I don't have time for much detail, but I'm sure Amfar will fill you in when he has the time. Let just say that I'm a good judge of character. Though you are a little rough around the edges for my liking, you would do the right thing if forced to make a moral decision."

"Really?" John huffed. "Then I shouldn't mention that the reason I'm in Myrtle Beach to begin with is I cheated on my fiancée. I came here to talk to her, maybe get another shot."

Amfar snorted.

Scott looked at Amfar for a moment then turned back to John. "Kelly was your fiancée I presume?"

John nodded.

"What matters now, is that we tell each other everything we know about the three plates, and that starts now.

"The three plates are part of a Cherokee legend. For right now, I'll only give details I believe pertinent. About four hundred years ago, two of our tribesmen were on a hunt when an explosion took place. The two went to investigate.

"This is the part nobody can agree upon. The hunters claim they saw part of the forest cleared and trees and brush pressed flat to the ground. When the two tribesmen came back from their hunt, they told of the strange clearing and a meeting with a man wearing peculiar clothes. He gave them the plates and with them a warning. Only one pure of heart should use the plates, for if they found their way to another, the world would be in peril. The people of the tribe didn't believe the hunters, but they had seen the explosion so went to investigate themselves. Many searched for hours, including the two original hunters. They never found a thing.

"Believing the brothers were up to some elaborate hoax, the elders reprimanded them and said never to speak of the incident again. Strange things began to happen. Two-headed dogs spotted on more than one occasion, large amounts of stillbirths, and tribal members were disappearing. One of the elders claimed he had a vision that the three plates were a curse, and that the brothers were the cause of the strange occurrences. Most of the tribe took his word as truth and shunned the two brothers, a punishment worse than most in our society.

"However, some didn't believe the elder. These few helped the brothers when they could but still wouldn't look them in the eye. They set out food for them at night, traded with them in the winter for clothing or blankets. But only when their needs were great. As time passed, only one came to the city to trade, then neither. They believed Riley's Ridge was where they lived, the same place Jarrett's dig site now sits.

"The story is one of many passed on to our children. Until recently I thought of them as a way to remind our children to listen to the elders so they may never be shunned as the two brothers were." Scott leaned forward and picked up the beer from the table, took a long swig, and sat it down. "As it pertains to the three plates, that's what I can tell you both."

Neither Amfar, nor John, had taken a drink of Corona the entire time Sheriff Scott spoke. Amfar didn't know why John hadn't, but he'd been intent on Scott's every word. He'd heard most of the story already, but Sheriff Scott added more details during this telling. With Amfar's scientific mind reeling over the past few weeks, he tried to absorb everything. To gain a better grasp on what happened with the three plates.

John stood and walked to Scott's side, holding out his hand. "I'm sorry about the whole gun thing too. If you haven't noticed, things have been a little crazy around here. I've seen some things I never thought I would. I've seen imploding buildings with no soot marks, a magical nineteen-year-old, a flying octogenarian, and did I mention I've been shot at with arrows?"

Scott took his hand. John shook it and turned back toward his seat.

"Sorry about the arrows, John," Scott murmured.

John paused, unmoving. "What was that, Sheriff?"

Scott cleared his throat. "Sorry about the arrows. We hoped they'd deter you and that boy from investigating any further. We had no idea the two of you were so bull-headed."

Chapter 18

Billy

Rays from the sun beat down on the sidewalk in front of Billy, the trees shimmered like a mirage. Park sprinklers completed their morning work, making the air thick and muggy.

Three days he'd spent on the same park bench. Most of the first night as well until a police officer asked if he needed a place to stay. Hailing a cab was easy enough. The driver took him to a cheap motel, cheap being two hundred dollars a night. An ATM machine sat located in the main lobby. Cash only. Grams's credit card filled up fast.

Guilt rolled over him at the thought of Grams. She'd been nothing but wonderful to him. She took him in when his parents passed, her love for him impregnable. Now he'd stolen her credit card, spent her money without restraint, and all without telling her why.

A clown strolled by carrying a bundle of floating balloons. He should join the clown. The past month he'd made enough mistakes to be one without the makeup. Today was no different. He came to New York because of a dream about running through a park with a backpack. Now his backpack sat back at the motel. He didn't notice it missing until he'd sat on the park bench for over an hour. Running back to the hotel for the plates tempted him, but at this point, he didn't feel like doing much of anything. His anger simmered, but without the now familiar buzz in his chest when near the plates.

He stretched his arms high overhead. Sitting on a park bench for hours is hard on the body, especially when he spent his nights on a lumpy mattress only as thick as the clothes on his back.

"Billy?"

He jumped, his heart thudded in his chest. The man calling his name should be able to hear it.

"Billy Hitchings?" the man called again. He was tall, almost as tall as Billy, but heavier.

Most of the stress Billy felt upon his arrival in New York ebbed away over the last three days. Every person walking by wasn't a bad guy, but this one knew his name. He looked nice enough, and wore a disarming smile, but butterflies flitted around in Billy's stomach again.

"Who's asking?" Billy leaned forward and placed his hands at his sides on the bench.

The man's smile grew, and he put his hands up. "Hey, kid. I'm glad we found you. My name is Sergeant Kirkwall. I work for the Myrtle Beach Police Department."

"What are you doing in New York?" Billy should treat a police officer with more respect, but his over-taxed senses wouldn't allow it.

Kirkwall dropped his arms to his side as his smile withered. "We're here to find you, Billy. Your grandmother is very upset. She asked us to find you. She was worried when you left so unexpectedly."

"How did you find me?"

"Do you always ask so many questions when someone tries to help you?"

When Billy didn't respond, Kirkwall let out a deep sigh and kept talking.

"Think about it, kid. How did you get here? Where'd you get your money?"

The credit card.

"You tracked a credit card to find an adult for an old woman, and then came to New York to find me?" Before the words were out of his mouth, he knew he shouldn't have voiced his thoughts aloud. This cop came to New York to find him, and it wasn't for Grams.

Billy's eyes darted behind the officer, to his left, to his right. The man repeatedly said 'we' but Billy didn't see anybody else. There were few places to hide, none close enough to stop him from running.

Kirkwall's eyes followed Billy's. The officer took a step forward.

Billy leaped from the bench and dashed toward the closest public place he could think of, the parking lot where the car backfired days before. The officer's shoes clapped on the pavement behind him.

Mind racing as fast as his body, Billy urged his body to move faster. He couldn't hope to defend himself against a man outweighing him by fifty pounds and trained in hand-to-hand combat. The closest Billy came to learning hand-to-hand combat was on a martial arts video game.

Amfar

Amfar and Scott accepted another cold beer from John and stepped outside onto his porch. Now that the initial testosterone filled trials were in the past, things went much smoother. Sheriff Scott and John seemed to get along.

His scientist's mind relished the information it was fed. The strange happenings in and around Myrtle Beach came together.

The plastic seats were almost too hot to sit on, another hot and humid day. Amfar was used to the heat now, but it slowed his thinking. The ice-cold beer went down well today. "So? What do you think of Mr. Reeves?"

The Sheriff smiled and glanced toward the cottage where John was inside grabbing more drinks. "I like him. As I said before, rough around the edges but likeable."

"I think so as well." He wasn't sure what Scott meant by rough around the edges but assumed he spoke of John's coarse personality.

Sheriff Scott leaned back in his chair, hands clasped behind his head. Amfar didn't imagine the Sheriff had much time to vacation.

"You made the right decision bringing me to John." Scott's light blue eyes went to the shoreline. "He's a good person to have on our side."

"Our side? It sounds like you discuss a movie, the good guys and the bad guys."

"I know it's never that black and white, Amfar. But in this case, it has to be. Either they're with us, or they're against us. If we take any chances, things could end very badly."

"I have to admit I do not understand that completely either." Amfar clasped his hands. "You say the plates have great power, which only certain individuals can use them, but you never explained just what they could do."

"Because I don't really know." The smile left Scott's face. "What I do know is they *can* be dangerous," he paused, "and there are rules."

"Rules?"

John walked around the corner of the cottage, a silver bucket filled with ice in hand. Condensation dripped from the sides. He sat between Amfar and Scott and pulled another beer from under the ice.

"I tell you what, gentlemen. This is the life. When this is all done, I just may have Rachel rent this cottage for the rest of the year."

"Rachel McCall," Scott said.

John paused with the beer to his lips, some dribbling down his chin. "Okay, Rob. I can call you Rob, right?"

The Sheriff nodded.

"I just started to like you. Before I lose it, will you explain how you could know about Rachel? That's the third, or fourth, time since we've met that you come out and state some random comment there is no way you should know anything about."

Scott popped the top from his beer and tossed it into the silver bucket. He tilted his head back and took a long drink.

"Like the arrows." John shook his head. "Why arrows, anyway? Why not shout, 'Hey guys! Stay away so we can save the world'?"

"I guess I can't keep it secret from you two any longer."

Though spending time with Sheriff Scott and John Reeves relaxed Amfar, half the time it felt like they spoke another language. Amfar had no idea who this Rachel friend was.

Scott continued. "Even though the folklore surrounding the three plates is believed to be just that, folklore, there's a contingency plan. The elders of our tribe, depending on our skills, or in my case, standing in society, choose individuals for this contingency. We keep watch on Riley's Ridge, and the plates if located. A few train in the old ways, with the bow and arrow, for example. I never saw the use for it, but try telling the others."

"That was why you were so vehement at the town meeting." Amfar finally understood. "You didn't want Jarrett's group on Riley's Ridge because you didn't want us to find the plates." Guilt flowed through Amfar. He had spoken for Jarrett, along with others, to talk the city into granting a temporary permit for digging on the ridge. His argument had been the scientific finds could put Morehead on the map. He didn't realize how true that was.

"Exactly." Scott nodded, his hand wiping at the condensation on his drink. "But to be honest, we didn't believe you'd find anything. Groups have come and gone over the years, hunters new to the area go up there too. They never find anything. Until now. About ten years ago, we put together a group of our own to search the area. There were those of us wanting to learn whether what we'd protected really needed protection. We didn't find one clue."

"I am not surprised, Sheriff Scott," Amfar said. "The small cave where we spent most of our time caved in on occasion over the years. I remember telling Kelly the area looked as if its exposure to nature happened only recently. The way the rock wasn't worn as expected if open to the environment."

Amfar thought he saw tears in the Sheriff's eyes. Before he knew for sure, Scott rose and looked toward the ocean. Though Amfar hadn't known it at the time, he had been digging into somebody's secrets, a place nobody was ever supposed to go. "I hope you can forgive us, Sheriff Scott."

The dark-skinned man nodded, a half-smile appeared. "I told you before, Dr. Ditpra. If I didn't believe you were a good person, I wouldn't be here. You wouldn't have done anything to hurt us on purpose. That was one of the arguments when Jarrett came to Morehead. Some thought if we were to tell you about the legend, maybe you'd be willing to walk away."

"There is no way Jarrett would have left that site without a fight." Amfar sighed. *And would I even if I'd known?*

"That was the argument that eventually won out. We knew he was a power-hungry man, that if we dug in our heels, he'd only push harder. We just never thought he would find anything, at least not like this."

"And your secret bow wielding vigilantes?" John said.

Scott's eyes turned from the water and focused on John. "Amfar isn't the only one who needs to apologize today. I'm sorry if our antics scared you in any way, Mr. Reeves. Let me assure you, though. You were never in any danger."

"Never in any danger, huh? Well I guess if you say it's so, then it must be." The sarcasm in John's voice made them all laugh, and the sadness left Scott's eyes.

People on the beach stared at the three laughing men. Maybe it was the alcohol that made them laugh, but it didn't matter to Amfar.

Billy

Billy's lungs burned even though he couldn't have run more than a mile. The tall cop didn't catch up, but he didn't fall back either. When the chase began, he thought maybe his dream was finally coming true, that maybe rain would begin to fall as others joined Kirkwall in the chase. None of that happened. The air was just as thick as when he'd awoke, thicker now that he'd left the park and ran through the city streets.

He didn't run as much as he made his way through all the people. The streets weren't as busy as he remembered from movies, but close. He stopped saying 'excuse me' after the first five people he ran into. Every few seconds, he'd chance a look behind him, to see if he'd lost Kirkwall.

This time, he saw Kirkwall's puffing red face. Billy kept his eyes open for any of the "we" Kirkwall mentioned minutes before. The cop's friends might be hiding, or in plain sight, but Billy wouldn't know until they were upon him. He stayed away from every male wearing a suit looking even a little like the one Kirkwall wore.

The crowd in front of him thickened as they waited for a crosswalk. He turned to his right and sprinted down a side street. The crowd in his path would have slowed him. He didn't know what Kirkwall wanted, and he didn't care to find out.

The clear side street allowed him to pick up the pace. His face was probably as red as the man following him. He imagined Eric making fun of him for being out of shape. The thought of his friend caused him to stumble a few steps. He straightened himself, but not before twisting his ankle on a shoe on the sidewalk.

Billy cursed again for not having the plates. He had this great and powerful weapon at his disposal, yet they might catch him because some schmuck left a shoe on the sidewalk in downtown New York.

He limped around another corner back to the main street, keeping close to the buildings. The slip had sprained his ankle. He felt the swelling. Hiding in one of the buildings would have to suffice. Kirkwall was still thirty or forty yards behind. He'd try to make it one more block before hiding.

Billy bumped into a woman carrying a small dog under her arm. She cussed at him while he ran for his life. The last street he needed to cross before picking a building to hide in was only yards away.

He chanced another look behind just in time to see Kirkwall run into the lady with the dog and send them both sprawling onto the pavement, fur and credit cards filled the air. Billy smiled; this was his chance.

When he turned back, two men stood in the middle of the foot traffic on the other side of the street wearing suits like Kirkwall. The suits weren't only *like* Kirkwall's, they were exactly the same.

Billy reluctantly slowed, knowing once he did, he wouldn't be able to speed back up. His ankle swelled, making it difficult to continue.

The end of the sidewalk was five feet away when he saw a white car speeding from his right. It headed straight for him. No way for him to stop in time, his painful ankle saw to that.

He slowed as much as he was able; lifting his arms up in front of him in what he knew to be a useless act. He closed his eyes. Tires screeched. It was over.

He waited with his hands up and eyes closed. Nothing happened.

"Get in, Billy," an unfamiliar voice said.

Billy opened his eyes. The car idled in front of him, and he looked at the face of the driver. Some red-haired guy, a long scar drawing down his jaw line.

"Hurry up. Those two don't look happy."

Billy looked to the men across the street. The driver was right, they weren't happy. Their faces were as red from anger as Kirkwall's from running. He looked toward where Kirkwall fell. The cop was just standing up.

"Look, Billy. Last chance. John says, 'don't try to pull a flying octogenarian' on these guys. His words, not mine."

Billy yanked the back door open and dove in. The red-haired man had the car moving down the street before Billy stopped bouncing in the back seat.

Chapter 19

John

John's father described it as having a 'deadly grace'.

"You were born with it," Ed Reeves had explained. "You have to learn from my training if you're going to live as long as me. Others with the same 'deadly grace' will sense it about you. They will sense it and kill you."

At the time, John thought his dad was crazy. Until he met two others with the unexplainable grace. One, a bank robber gunned down outside of his bank in downtown New York. The other, a librarian.

Sheriff Scott possessed the same grace. Whether it was innate, or developed over time, John didn't know. Either way, he was happy to have Scott on his side. After they were past the 'gun show' as they'd dubbed it, he felt as comfortable with the man as he had his own father.

"What was that?" John realized he'd been daydreaming.

"I asked if you were still with us, John. You stared at the table like a wolf eyeing a freshly won carcass," Scott said.

Amfar nodded.

"Never mind that," John said. "I wondered why you two thought to come to me with this information." He looked to Amfar. "I mean, you barely know me. I've only talked to you like three times, and on two of those, Kelly was about to kick me in the eye. Not the greatest of impressions, I'm guessing." He turned back to Sheriff Scott. "And you, Sheriff, I've never met. I'm sure I'd remember."

Amfar spoke. "There are a few reasons, John." He ran his fingers through his hair. "My reasoning is based on logic. I chose to speak with you because I know you are somehow involved with the three plates. This is the part I should have told you earlier." He looked into John's eyes. "Tom Jarrett called me a few weeks ago to tell me the three plates were in your possession. He told me where to find you, when you were gone, and how to get in to your cottage to get them. I didn't ask questions, though I know I should have. He was my boss, and I was upset that you messed around where I did not feel you belonged."

"Trust me." John laughed. "It was a big surprise to me, too. I have to admit, I've seen you in a new light since I found out you were the one who took them."

"You knew?" Amfar's face flushed.

John loved it when he had that effect on people. "Of course I knew. My dad was a detective; he taught me every detail he learned."

Amfar looked shaken, but went on. "On a personal note, Kelly didn't know anything about the plates. I'm sure you are aware; she is much smarter than she lets on. She questioned me, and three days ago I came forward with everything going on with Jarrett."

So that's why she left Myrtle Beach without saying goodbye. He'd thought maybe something came up at home, or that Jarrett called her back to Morehead, some significant reason. She'd left because she was upset with Amfar. John had hoped he was part of the reason. "And that was why she left Myrtle Beach?" he asked with one last shred of hope.

"It is, John. She packed and left within the hour."

It was final. The only woman he'd been able to love, and it was over. She moved on, and it hurt. He nodded and put on his best smile.

Amfar continued. "I can see that you still have feelings for her. The pain in your eyes gives you away. Sometimes I do not understand the intricacies of the English language, but what I am about to say, I believe you would call it a cliché. But if it is any conciliation, she loved you very much, John. She spoke very highly of you."

"Thank you, Amfar. It means a lot." He needed to change the subject. "So, I get your reasoning behind all this, Amfar," he looked to Scott, "and you have an obvious interest in the subject. But how did you two meet? I'm trying to put all the pieces together." The pieces of the story, and his emotional stability. "Wait. Let's grab a few more barley pops."

Billy

The door Billy dived through slammed into his feet every time the little white car hit a bump. There were few instances he cursed his height, but this was one of them. He curled his legs beneath him and rolled to his side. The next bump closed the door the rest of the way.

Sweat dripped from the red-haired man's face despite the air-conditioner on full blast. "You okay back there?"

"I think so." Billy pulled up his pant leg. Dark blotches covered his ankle, and the swelling was noticeable. "Mostly anyway."

"You scared me for a second. Those guys didn't look real pleasant." The man looked at Billy huddling in the back seat. "I'll pull off up here in a second. You're a tad too tall to sit in the backseat of a Ford Focus."

Minutes later, they turned in to a corner parking lot and Billy hobbled from the back of the car to the front. The red-haired man took off again, checking his rearview mirror often.

"You're a friend of John's?" Billy rubbed at his ankle.

"Oh yeah, sorry." He kept one hand on the wheel and his eyes on the road, but offered a hand to Billy. "My name is Joel Rowe. I work with John."

"You work with John? You mean at the publishing place?"

"That's the place."

"You must be a good friend of John's to do all this."

Joel checked the mirrors again as a drop of sweat fell from his nose. "You would think. Don't get me wrong, John's a great friend, but he didn't say anything like this would happen."

"What did he tell you would happen?"

"He called me a few days ago and asked me to take some time off. Asked me if I would watch a friend of his. He gave me your name, and your description, then told me to go to Central Park."

"He knew I was in Central Park?" Billy laughed.

"Yeah, why?"

"I never told him where I'd be." John surprised him yet again.

Joel let out a laugh. "John can be like that. He has an uncanny way of learning things you don't want him to. Anyway, he said you'd be there, and I should keep an eye on you. He's always working with problem children here in New York, so I assumed you were a runaway or something. Then today, as I pull into the parking lot on the east side of the park, you blaze by me. That red-faced guy following."

"That would be Kirkwall. He's a cop."

The car swerved a few feet before Joel took control again.

"Look, Joel. I know you're doing John a favor, but you don't need to anymore. You got me away from those guys. You can let me off up here somewhere."

Joel puffed his chest out. "No way, Billy. You don't understand. John has helped me out more times than I can count. And he doesn't even do it on purpose. That's the funny part. It's as if he can sense what you need, and then it comes to him how to fix it. Kind of like today for example. If not for Johnny, you'd be on the losing side of a boxing match with those thugs... or police officers, or whatever they are."

"A little of both, I'm guessing." Billy sighed and pulled down his pant leg. "No matter what happens, thank you for your help."

The music playing on the radio quieted and a voice said in a robotic voice, "Call from John Reeves."

Joel pushed a button on his steering wheel. "Hey, John. How's your day going?"

"Good, Joel. Drinking some cold ones with my new friends. Anything new happening with Billy?"

Joel winked at Billy. "I guess you could say that."

"What? What happened?" John's voice had lost its carefree sound, quickly replaced with urgency.

"Calm down, Johnny. I have it taken care of. He's sitting right here."

John didn't respond.

"You there?" Joel tapped the volume control on his steering wheel.

"Yeah, I'm just a little taken aback. Can he hear me?"

"Sure can," Billy said. "Your friend has great timing."

"That so? Good to hear you did your job, Joel. Although, I did tell you not to let him see you. I guess I'll have to pay you half-rate for the three days you took off."

Joel sputtered.

"I'm just kidding, buddy. You went above and beyond. I think you deserve a bonus. I'll double it."

"He deserves it for sure" Billy smiled. "I sprained my ankle, and I was stuck between some a-hole named Kirkwall and his two thugs. Joel came busting out of nowhere and gave me your secret message. That was cute by the way."

John didn't laugh. "Kirkwall you said?"

"That was it. You know him?"

"You could say that. Looks like I made a mistake. Nothing I can do about it now. You two are okay?"

Joel responded. "We're good, John. Nobody is following, though I bet they saw my license plate."

"That's what I was thinking too. Maybe you should call in for another week or so, drive down to Myrtle Beach until this whole thing blows over."

Joel rolled his eyes. "Oh, man, Brenda's going to be so pissed."

"Not as pissed as I'll be if you get yourself hurt up there because you didn't listen to me." His voice became serious again. "And, Joel, thank you. I mean it. I didn't want to get you involved, but I was worried something like this might happen. You may have saved Billy's life. Either way, I owe you one."

Joel's already red face flushed even more. "Don't get all squishy on me; you would have done the same thing in my place. Besides, I think I owe you about twenty. This one was on the house."

"What about the plates?" John said.

"Back at the motel," Billy chimed in.

"Good to hear. Hopefully Kirkwall and his men assumed you had the plates on you. Well, I'm afraid I have to let you go. I need to get this beer out to the porch. Help Billy with whatever he needs and you guys get down here. Maybe I can show you around the town a little, Joel. You're coming back. Right, Billy?"

He didn't realize he'd made the decision until John said it. "Yeah, I'm coming home. I made a mistake coming here."

John laughed. "If we didn't make mistakes, we wouldn't be human. Let's just try to keep them to a minimum until we get this stuff figured out. One last thing, you might want to fill Joel in on everything on the way home. He's a good friend. You can trust him."

John

"Just ask Billy. He knows how to get to Lizards. You'll like it. It's a small burger joint, but they're damn good," John said into his phone.

Joel and Billy were almost to Myrtle Beach. He hadn't been there for his friends in New York. Buying dinner at Lizard's was the least he could do.

"Billy says we'll be there in five minutes or so," Joel said. "Although that king size bed you promised me sounds pretty good right now."

"Isn't that why you stayed up in New York last night? To get your rest? You said something about going out on the town when you got here, too."

"Okay, you're right. I was wrong. I'm getting older than I'm willing to admit. You don't have to tease me about it."

John laughed. The two-year-old at the table next to John jumped. The child's parents shot him a dirty look.

"Sorry, bud. I just know a long ride can take a lot out of you. I'll be waiting here for you. I haven't ordered yet, but it looks to be pretty slow."

Joel and Billy had retrieved the plates and headed out of the city within an hour of John's call. They'd stayed at a cheap hotel close to the freeway, paying in cash. They were on the road by nine the next morning, but with the traffic, it took them almost twelve hours to get to Myrtle Beach.

The Focus pulled into the Lizard's parking lot. Joel stepped from the car and to Billy's side, throwing the kid's arm over his shoulder. A funny sight; his five foot eight friend with Billy's long arms and six foot five frame, leaning over him. The kid must have a nasty ankle sprain for him to ask for help. He wasn't the type to bother anybody if he could help it.

John could tell from one of their phone calls on the way home that Billy worried how his grandma would respond. John hatched a plan, without Billy's knowledge, to pay back the kid's grandma.

He walked to the door and helped them both to the table. The few people in the restaurant must think the sight of his tiny friend helping the lanky boy was funny as well; a few stared, and some giggled.

They fell into their seats and let out matching sighs. John sat down between them.

"How's that ankle holding up, kid?"

Billy smiled. "Much better than it looks. I iced it on the way down. Not to mention your friend here has some kick-ass pain meds."

Joel shushed him. "I told you not to tell anybody. I could get in big trouble for giving you those."

"Giving pain meds to a nineteen-year-old should be the least of your problems at the moment," John said.

They all laughed. Just how dire of a situation they were in even after Sheriff Scott's explanation, he didn't know.

The plates's power could throw a dog halfway through a brick wall and an eighty something man fifty yards; yet, being dangerous for the whole world didn't make sense.

"When the meds kick in, I'll be fine." Billy picked up a menu and licked his lips. "The long ride made it tighten up a little, that's all. The few times we stopped to get gas, it loosened right up."

"Glad to hear it." John turned to Joel. "What's your excuse, old man? I saw you limping up here. Did you get chased by some goons, too?"

"You have the old man part right. I sprained my ankle last year, and now it's hurting just from the drive. I might take you up on that gym membership when we get back."

John didn't respond but smiled instead. Joel didn't know Brenda fired him weeks earlier. Once his two weeks of vacation were up, he called to ask for more time, but she said some corporate higher-ups had tied her hands.

"Like I said on the phone," John slapped them both on the shoulders, "nothing a good Lizard burger won't fix."

He called the waitress over, and they all ordered. Billy ordered enough for two men. They ate in silence, enjoying the smoky grilled taste of the burgers.

John forgot what it was like to be nineteen. At one time, he'd probably eaten just as much as the chips and cheese appetizer, the two quarter-pound burgers, and a piece of cherry pie the kid finished up.

John leaned back in his chair holding his stomach. Joel sat in a similar manner, except that he stared at Billy.

"How can you drink that much soda?" Joel shook his head.

Billy polished off another glass, the straw gurgling in the bottom of the empty cup. He gave a 'who me' look to Joel and laughed. "This is only my fourth. You should see me on a good night."

John liked to see Billy in such high spirits. Last time they spoke on the phone had been another story. He was distraught he'd misinterpreted his dream. Billy said he felt deep down that he did the right thing. Hard to explain to a nineteen-year-old that sometimes no matter how right something feels, that doesn't make it so. Billy had taken a liking to him, and he to the kid, so he'd done his best not to sound too preachy. It wasn't the same as the kinship he felt with Sheriff Scott, but he saw much of himself in Billy.

"Speaking of drinking too much, I need to take a wiz." Billy slid his chair out and stood.

John pointed toward the hallway leading to the restroom.

Chapter 20

Billy

Billy's thoughts wandered to Eric again. They hadn't spoken since Billy left for New York, though he didn't know what he'd say given the chance. Eric should have told him about the cancer sooner. The feelings were selfish and a little childish as well, but he couldn't help but feel the way he did.

The door to the Lizard's bathroom sat open at the end of a short hallway toward the back. Billy shifted the backpack higher on his shoulder. The plates never left his sight after the incident with Kirkwall. Mistakes are great learning experiences.

Billy finished in the restroom and stopped in the hallway to check on the plates before entering the main dining area. The zipper slid open and he looked inside. The three colored plates sat on some chapstick and a pencil jammed in the bottom of the pack; leftovers from school. He zipped up the backpack and tossed it over his shoulder.

His heart stopped, his senses shifted into overdrive. Standing just outside the glass doors on the other side of the restaurant was Kirkwall and his two thugs. Their eyes met. The officer's lips curled into a sneer.

John and Joel sat at the table still, so far away. They'd helped him in more ways than they knew. John would hold his own, but Joel could get hurt. This was his fight.

In a split-second decision, he turned and slammed the handle down on the glass door to his left, running into the parking lot, swollen ankle barely slowing him.

This time he would go it alone, but not completely alone. This time he had the three plates.

John

"You were right, Johnny. It didn't matter how tired I was. The burger did the trick." Joel looked around the dining room. "I need to talk to a manager. I wonder if they would share the recipe."

"Good luck with that one." John laughed. "I've been trying for a month."

The door on the west side of Lizards opened with a loud clang; people sitting close by jumped at the loud noise. Three men wearing black suits pushed their way through people standing in line at the front counter, one of them a tall man with a receding hairline... Kirkwall.

John's eyes went to the other exit, knowing what he would see. Through the fading light, Billy sprinted between two buildings on the backside of the parking lot. Coming from the other direction were two more men in suits. His friend was in trouble again, and he'd been right here. *Why did he run?* John couldn't protect him if he ran.

Joel stared at John. He lost the look of contentment and spun around in his chair just in time to see the three men leaving through the east door. "Billy," he whispered. He turned back to John. "We have to help him. What do we do?"

John's friend had a golden heart, but no training; he looked like a scared puppy.

"We don't have much time, Joel. Do exactly as I say."

Joel nodded.

"I don't know how many Myrtle Beach officers Jarrett has under his thumb, so we can't trust any of them. There might be more in the parking lot, watching."

His friend fought to stay calm, but the whites of his eyes showed as he looked from side to side.

"Stay calm. I'll leave the money on the table. We'll stand together and walk to your car. *Walk,* I said. Understand?"

Joel's head bobbed up and down.

John sensed his friend's frustration. Joel's feet shuffled across the floor, eyes darting back and forth like a wild animal. John faked a stretch while walking behind his friend and used the motion to slide his hand into his jacket and unclasp the weapon in his shoulder holster. He hoped there was no need for the weapon.

The fading light made it hard for John to see the parking lot as well as he'd like. When they reached the Focus, Joel looked at him with questions in his eyes.

"Get in," John said with a fake smile.

Joel's hands shook as he slid the keys from his pocket and clicked on the unlock button. The locks clicked open, and Joel climbed in. John opened the passenger door and leaned forward. He pulled his pistol from the shoulder holster and sat it on the floor. Joel's eyes traced his every movement.

"I hope you don't need that, Joel. But you should be prepared."

"What about Billy?" The words barely came through Joel's tightlipped smile.

"He's a smart kid. He'll be fine, for now. I'll take care of him, but you need to stay calm and listen. Go to the police, but not the locals. We don't know who we can trust. Use your GPS and find the city of Konig. It's small, but they have their own police force. I didn't want to involve the police, but things just spun out of control. Explain to them that police officers are chasing Billy. Don't mention the plates. Call 911 just before you get there too, maybe they'll send the county police as well."

"Where do I tell them to go?"

"I'm not sure, Joel, but I have a feeling it won't be hard to figure out when they get here."

Amfar

"Exactly how many people from your tribe are in Myrtle Beach right now?" Amfar added a creamer to his coffee.

"Twenty-two."

"That is amazing. It impresses me they are able to follow people like they do, and nobody notices them. Very impressive. Something a person would not usually see unless on television."

Sheriff Scott took a sip of his coffee. "It's not that big of a step to go from hunting animals to stalking humans if you think about it, Amfar. The animals are a little bigger, more cunning, and the surroundings are different. Yet the hunters still follow something that may or may not wish to be found."

"I guess." Amfar had never been hunting, though what Scott said made sense. "You make it sound so simple. It is still impressive. Your tribe is lucky to have such skilled members."

"We truly are." Scott took another sip. He nodded toward his cup. "What brand is this? The flavor is great."

"I'm not sure. I would have to check. I never thought about it. The hotel puts the new bags right in the coffee maker for us every day." Amfar looked at his watch. "Billy should be back by now. I'm not sure I can wait until tomorrow morning to speak with him."

"I'm sure John has things under control, Amfar. He doesn't strike me as the type to leave things to chance."

"Regardless, if what John says is true, then the boy can truly use the plates. If that is so, then we should get him to safety sooner than later."

Scott's cell phone vibrated on the table between them. Amfar looked out to the Atlantic. The sunsets in Myrtle Beach were picturesque, but not as breathtaking as when it rose each morning, though he no longer shared it with Kelly.

Scott wasn't saying anything into the phone. Amfar looked at him. The Sheriff's brows furrowed more by the second.

Finally, he spoke. "We'll be there in five minutes, John. Don't wait for us. You must protect Billy."

Amfar's heart tried pounding through his chest. The look on Sheriff Scott's face had let loose a surge of adrenaline. "What happened?"

"Jarrett's men are after Billy. We must go. You have two minutes to do whatever you need. Then I'm leaving."

Scott's demeanor changed. Seconds before, he was relaxed, sipping on a weak cup of coffee as they discussed past relationships. Now, the man's shoulders and face turned to steel. He wasn't Robert Scott the local sheriff now, he was Robert Scott the Cherokee tribal member, and he looked fierce.

Amfar scrambled into the hotel room, sending his coffee to the floor. He spun in a circle in the center of the room and realized he had no idea what to do. Scott stood on the veranda and spoke into his cell, his movements animated.

He must be speaking with the other tribal members. He wasn't sure how much help he'd be if he went along, or if he would get in the way, but it didn't matter. John and the Sheriff were his friends. If they were in trouble, he would help in any way he could.

Billy

The combination of painkillers and Billy's adrenaline made his ankle painless. The swelling was still there, but it didn't slow him. He ran like the wind. A zigzagging wind. He'd been able to get a jump on Kirkwall and his men, leading them away from Joel and into the back neighborhoods where he could hide. One quick phone call and John would've been all over these guys. Only one problem. His cell phone still sat on Joel's dash.

The sun completed its descent, but the moon and stars led his way through the clear night. They would lead Kirkwall's way as well.

He took a quick turn and stopped behind the edge of a shed. Controlling his breathing was near impossible. If they couldn't see him, they'd probably hear him. He edged around the end of the shed, peering around the corner. Kirkwall's two men searched with flashlights. They'd looked upset in New York. Now the shadows on their faces made them appear livid.

Backing away from the corner, he took a deep breath. He took off in the opposite direction, staying behind the nearby house to block the sound of his footfalls. Adrenaline drove him now, the weariness from the long trip forgotten.

Running away felt different this time than in New York, probably because of the plates. The plates allowed him a way to fight back, even if he didn't understand how. He wouldn't be able to run forever. Kirkwall had at least four other men helping with the search. Eventually, they'd catch up, and Billy would make a stand.

But where do I make that stand? The sooner he made the decision, the better. If he were to face off against the police officers, he would do so on his terms.

He'd worked his way further inland, but not on purpose. More to hide behind in that direction. The years of playing online games popped into his head. How would he do this if it were a game? If he faced at least five-to-one odds, what would be the best way to gain an advantage? Take out one at a time. That was it. One officer at a time.

So far, he'd seen two groups of two, plus Kirkwall. Separating them wouldn't be easy. A small stand of trees stood behind a mobile home. He slowed and slid behind one of the palm trees, turning to face the direction he'd come from. The officer's lights were barely discernible, over a hundred yards behind, moving through a yard he'd passed through moments before. He had a lead and he wasn't about to lose it.

He needed to find someplace he knew better than the officers, a place where he'd gain the advantage. *Grams's neighborhood.* He knew details the officers wouldn't. The weekend cookouts with Grams had allowed him to exercise his imagination and plan escapes from each yard. Little did he know that someday he'd put those plans to use.

Kirkwall wouldn't know about the rabbits Lori Matz always had running around her backyard. He wouldn't know the Goodwin's had a shed used for smoking venison. He also wouldn't know about the secret entrance George Lovelace used to sneak out of his house for a few drinks while his wife slept. Kirkwall was in for a surprise. Billy wouldn't go down easily.

John

John paced in the cottage parking lot while he waited for Sheriff Scott and Amfar to arrive. Hopefully, Joel was almost to Konig. He hoped the officers there were willing to listen to his story. Billy should be okay, but John didn't know just how crazy Jarrett was, or this Kirkwall guy.

John hoped Scott's men were half as good as he said. They were good enough to know he and Billy had the plates, and good enough to shoot arrows three inches from his head without grazing him. They should be able to help get Billy back. Too many hopes for one day.

The tires on Sheriff Scott's Ranger squealed as he turned into the parking lot, Amfar in the passenger's seat.

"Get in," Scott said through the open window.

John hopped into the back of the truck with barely enough time to grab hold of the roll bar before Scott took off.

Amfar opened the sliding window. "Scott wants me to tell you that a few of his men are already on the trail.

They should be able to find him within five to ten minutes."

"Is he headed toward his Grandma's?" John shouted.

"Yes, you were right. Scott thinks he'll try to force a confrontation there."

"Scott's right." He hoped to God he was wrong, but hoping never did anybody any good. *There I go hoping again.* "Tell him not to let his men talk to Billy. He doesn't know them, and he's scared right now. He might try to hurt them. Tell them to wait for me."

***

Moments later, they pulled into the darkened parking lot of a par three golf course. John leapt from the back of the Ranger before it finished moving. Robert and Amfar were out almost as fast.

"What are we doing here?" John checked the three Glocks stashed on his body.

Robert checked two of his own. Amfar looked scared to death, his face pale in the moonlight. Sheriff Scott just looked determined.

"I have six men right behind Kirkwall's, and they are right behind Billy. They think he'll pass through this golf course on his way to his neighborhood. If he went around, it would take a lot of time. They followed his trail from Lizard's and said he zigzagged at first, but started in a straight line toward his Grandmother's house, and hasn't changed directions since."

"They know to protect Billy if the men get too close, right?"

Scott looked at him with a small smile. "Of course they do, John. They're good men. I have six more ahead of Billy, letting me know which direction they believe he'll go. Ten also surround his grandmother's house in case he makes it that far."

Headlights glowed on the other side of the course on one of the holes farthest from the city lights: three vehicles, probably trucks. They pulled onto the course and cut their lights.

"Those your men?" John squinted as if it would help.

"Mine are all on foot. I don't know who they are. I doubt the Konig police department drives unmarked police trucks."

The only explanation was that Tom Jarrett called in more men, but why would he bring in more than the five he already had for a single boy? Unless he knew about the power of the plates, and that Billy could use them. Then he'd know even twenty more men might not be enough.

If they were Jarrett's men, he didn't know Billy didn't have complete control of the plates. He'd thrown an eighty-year-old man fifty yards when he tried to help him stand, yet, he wasn't able to protect himself when fighting a single man. John hoped Billy learned more about his power during his short stay in New York.

"We need to get out to the center. Right there." Scott pointed toward a small stand of trees in the middle of the course. "Two of my men are there now and say it's the most likely place for him to cross."

"Let's go." John took two steps and stopped. He felt as if he'd swallowed a porcupine. "Wait!" he shouted.

Amfar and Robert slid to a stop on the pavement and faced him.

"What is it, John? We don't have much time," Scott said.

"I know how they work."

"How who works?"

"Not who, what. The plates. I know why they didn't work for Billy. We have to hurry."

Billy

Billy leaned against a thin wooden fence in the last yard before he'd have to cross the road to the par three golf course between him and Grams's house. Blood dripped from his arms where rose thorns had torn at his skin. *Abe Reyes's house*, he growled. Grams always bragged about Abe's roses. *Damn things.* Just one more thing to piss him off.

There were a few narrow escapes between Lizard's and here. When his jacket had caught on the prong of a metal fence, the sproing sound echoed through the neighborhood. Moments later, he'd crossed an open yard to hide next to, or in, a willow tree the neighborhood kids loved to climb. Yards away, he'd seen movement in the willow's foliage. The surprise made him turn sharp to dive behind a shed, and his ankle twisted again. Not as bad before, but the painkillers wore off. He hadn't been able to tell if the movement was Kirkwall's men or just a cat, but he wasn't willing to take the chance.

Each time danger lingered, he'd feel the anger well up within him, searching for a release. The plates hummed in anticipation. He forced down the anger. Not hard to do when he was scared half the time and exhausted the rest.

He closed his eyes and took deep breaths, part relaxation, part rest. There were no signs of any of the men for the past three or four blocks, and this was his last chance to make it to Grams's house. He hoped Joel and John noticed his failure to return. Maybe they'd call in everybody they knew, though he didn't know how many friends two guys from New York would have in Myrtle Beach.

He took another deep breath and stepped to leave the shelter of Mr. Reyes's yard when a raindrop splashed on the tip of his nose. He stood still a moment, listening. Raindrops splashed around him; he would be safe. The only reason they'd been able to follow him this far was because the night was silent. If the rain kept up for just a few more minutes, he'd make it to safety. At least he hoped it was safety. John knew where Grams lived. He hoped Joel's insight about John having an uncanny ability to figure things out was true. He hoped and prayed that Grams's house would somehow save him from the men following. Too many hopes.

He counted to ten, waited for the rain to pick up, and took off across the street in a low crouch.

He imagined what would happen when he arrived at Grams's house. The men would probably break down her door and take him from there, maybe hurt Grams in the process. A bubble of anger almost burst from his chest; he stumbled the last few feet across the road and tripped into the ditch next to the golf course. He lay in four inches of stinky muck and water. He pulled himself up the other side of the ditch and underneath some bushes. He peered toward the side of the road where he'd just been, but didn't see anybody.

If anybody hurt Grams, he'd... *what would I do?* He didn't know if he was willing to use the plates to hurt anybody, but he wouldn't just stand around and do nothing either. Rage burned inside him with nowhere to direct his angst.

A gust of wind blew against the bushes and drops of water cascaded around him. It felt like one of the tropical storms that came ashore every year. If so, the winds would pick up even more. He smiled. *One more way to hide my path.*

He froze, not sure what to do. At first, his fear drove him to take each step, but now that fear was gone. Standing and fighting was his only option. He didn't want to involve Grams. She'd gone through enough in her life. Besides, she'd taken care of him for so long. What a way to repay her, by having her home ransacked and destroyed by some rogue police officers.

The decision was made. He'd fight. He'd been led to the plates, or they to him, for a reason. He was the only one who could use them. *Why not use them to destroy those who seek to take them from me?* Now he just had to decide where to attack from.

"Shit," he heard someone say.

He didn't move; someone was behind him in Abe's yard.

"You could have told me there were rose bushes here."

"You didn't ask."

Kirkwall's men were right behind him, talking loud enough he heard them through the rain. If he was going to move, he had to do it now. He slid from beneath the bushes and pushed himself up. His ankle protested with a sharp pain that shot up his leg. He stooped down again, trying to stay low.

"There!" one of them yelled.

Billy's heart raced. *Now we'll see just what these plates can do.*

Amfar

Did John just say he knew how the three plates worked? Amfar wondered how a man with a police officer for a father, with no expertise, could know. He considered himself a scholar, and yet he had no clue, and neither did Sheriff Scott. Park Huang and Dawson, among the best paleographers Amfar had ever met, had only been able to glean the barest of information from the manuscripts stored with the plates. He preferred to have proof before he said or did anything definitive, but John didn't have the same training. Amfar just hoped he wouldn't do something stupid.

Rain began to fall as they crouched low behind a tree line, working toward the center of the course where Scott's men said Billy would probably go. His new dress shoes squeaked on the wet grass. He hadn't thought to change them before leaving. Of course, he didn't think he'd chase some kid with the keys to ancient Cherokee folklore either.

Scott led the way, John right behind.

John stopped. "What the hell is that noise your shoes are making?"

"I'm not sure what to do." Amfar spoke quietly, not used to the sneaking as his two new friends were. "What should I do?" He thought he saw John smile.

"Take them off. You'll run faster."

John and Scott took off again. They moved so fast he barely kept up. He pulled his shoes from his feet while he ran.

They made it to the copse of trees in the center of the course. The rain poured down around them. He didn't see the two men crouching behind the trees until they were almost upon them. He jumped a few inches and almost let out a yelp. At least John jumped as well.

The two men must be Sheriff Scott's relation. One was squat with a crooked smile; the other had long dark black hair pulled back in a ponytail like the one Scott wore.

"You should stay low," the short one said. "He'll be here in less than two minutes, though with the rain it's hard to tell."

Scott nodded. "Either of you know who the men are that just pulled in?"

"We're not sure," the one on the right said. "Jett said they have Kentucky plates."

"We don't have much time." Scott turned in the direction Billy came from. "Find out who they are, and let me know when you can."

The two young men nodded and dropped close to the ground as they took off in the direction they'd seen the headlights minutes before.

Scott grabbed John and Amfar by the shoulders and pulled them toward the ground. "You have little more than ninety seconds to share your epiphany with us, John.

Make it quick." He watched John with an expectant look in his eyes.

They squatted behind the trees. Scott peered around the thickest of them, searching for any sign of Billy or Kirkwall's men. John muttered something hard to hear with the rain splashing around them.

"What did you say, John?" Amfar leaned toward him.

"I said this is horse shit. Nevermind that now. Just listen. The first time Billy used his power was at Billy Borks, but I think that time was an aberration, a mistake, maybe him learning how to use the plates. But every time after that, it worked just the way he planned. For the most part anyway."

"What about what you said about that party he went to? You said him and Eric were pounded on by that guy."

"He tried to use them as a weapon." John shook his head. "Either that or in his own defense, either way, that didn't work. What did work was when he defended someone else. He protected me from the dog, and the old man from falling and hurting himself. It's the only thing that makes sense. His power will only work in the defense of another."

Though John was not a scientist, and had no training as such, his argument was logical. Variables were missing, and it didn't follow the scientific method, but it made sense. It would have to do.

"What do we do then? If Kirkwall's men get scared, they could hurt him. They could shoot him. Plus, we do not know who those other guys are. What if they try to hurt him?" Amfar searched John's eyes for answers.

Scott watched John too.

"Why are you two looking at me?" John snapped.

Amfar wasn't sure why, but it seemed right.

Scott shrugged and looked around the large tree again.

John sighed. "You don't need me to tell you. Billy has a special talent that if harnessed could be amazing. We must protect him."

"I hear something." Sheriff Scott peered around the tree.

John crouched low and leaned forward, as if doing so helped him hear better through the heavy rain. Amfar almost laughed when he realized he did the same thing.

A cascade of lights appeared around them, flashing bright through the wet, dark night and accompanied by a high pitch whining, loud enough to pierce the rain.

Billy

Billy saw where he'd make his stand. High ground. His games always said to get to high ground. Forty yards in front of him sat a green situated high on a hill surrounded on three sides by sand traps. The small group of trees about twenty yards behind the green would be his weak point. One large tree rose up between five or six smaller, filled with broad green leaves. *A fine place to hide.*

Lightning flashed, fixing the vision of the green in his mind. The lighting had saved him from the two men that caught up to him minutes before. He'd been rounding an outbuilding when the first flash struck, giving him just enough light to avoid the pile of rocks in front of him. He leapt to the side just in time, but the two men following hadn't been so lucky. They crashed into the night-hidden stones and into each other. He'd glanced back to see two men wearing dark suits rolling across the ground and down a small hill toward a pond.

Billy cycled through the targets in his mind. At least three different men, plus Kirkwall. Possibly more.

Billy closed his eyes and inhaled the warm, damp air. The scent of fresh pine tar seeped from the trees around him. Each part of his body had a new or old ache, and his injured ankle was the size of a softball with the other not far behind. The torrential rain drowned the sound of his movement and eased the pain of salty sweat searing the gouges left from Abe's rose bushes.

He tightened the backpack straps, reassuring himself the plates were secure. His eyes still closed, pictures flashed through his mind, visions of how the fight would go. And it wouldn't be pretty for Kirkwall or his men.

The pain gave him purpose. His will grew within the plates, his anger, his need. They hummed softly in his mind, a beautiful sound, a song of retribution. He was tired of running, tired of not understanding. *Tired of not doing what I'm meant to do.*

Another flash.

He shot toward the green, limping with every step. Red and blue lights appeared to his left and right, accompanied by the familiar sound of sirens. Shouting came from every direction at once, too many voices to be only Kirkwall's men.

Flash.

Two men about the same age as Billy rose from a bunker to his left, but didn't pursue; only watched. From the stand of trees on the backside of the green, eyes reflected the flashing lights. *Only my imagination.*

Flash.

Three sets of eyes. Not his imagination. The men chasing him hadn't been in groups larger than two all night.

With a tremendous push from both legs, he leapt over a sand trap and landed on the green. Flashing lights from the police cars came closer. He heard their engines; they cut across the course straight toward him.

Pain exploded in his already sprained ankle as he felt a crack. He turned as he fell and landed on his rear, facing the group of pines he'd just come from. His toes had caught in the cup of the green. The plates hummed violently in his mind.

Flash.

The high ground; he could see in every direction except through the stand of trees now behind him. Nobody was close, though the yelling voices still surrounded him.

He unlatched the backpack and pulled it from his shoulders and onto the ground in front of him.

Flash.

A new group of men rushed toward him no more than fifty yards to his left, opposite of the young men who still watched from the sand bunker. The quick flash of light showed Billy the men in the new group wore black, not like the suits Kirkwall and his men wore. More casual.

The plates sat in place at the bottom of the bag. His long fingers wrapped around the edges and pulled them free.

Flash.

Eyes surrounded the green where he sat. Many more than the four with Kirkwall. Flashing lights from the police cars bounced from the plates into Billy's eyes.

Anger flooded over him; anger at his physical pain, anger about his best friend's cancer, and the not knowing whether the plates would save him. Anger about his friends leaving him to his fate. Most of all, anger that his parents had been taken from him, that they weren't here to give him direction, to guide him.

The will to stand almost eluded him, but he pushed with the last remaining strength in his legs.

Flash.

Some of the men held their arms up, as if they aimed weapons. Billy rose the rest of the way to his feet and lifted the plates over his head, anger thrumming from within. He visualized the destruction he'd cause to anybody who meant him harm. Billy thought about his friends. *I hope none of you are out there in the dark.*

Two police cars crested a small rise to his right and another three cruisers from his left. Billy winced away from the lights that caused partial blindness but allowed him to see men surrounding the green. Some held guns.

The strange growling from his throat began with a low hum, growing with each beat of his heart. Soon, he'd release the harnessed power.

The police cars slid across the golf course, stopping just beyond the men watching him. More came over the ridge. Their lights shined on the men in black suits, Kirkwall, his men, and the young men he'd seen earlier. Their tanned skin made it almost impossible to see them in the dark.

Billy no longer heard the yelling. He saw the men he needed to hurt, but he needed to direct the power carefully. He didn't want to hurt any of the officers. They were probably out of range, but he didn't want to take the chance.

He lifted his head to look at the plates held overhead. Water slipped from their edges onto his face. He reached for the power. Brought it forth. Visualized his wants, his needs.

"Billy!" someone yelled behind him.

Still holding the plates overhead, prepared to release the power if whoever yelled came too close, he turned slowly to the side and looked over his shoulder. The red and blue lights spinning across the face of the man running toward him almost made him too hard to recognize.

"John?" The name came out as a whisper, barely audible over the growl growing in his throat.

"Wait!" John sprinted toward him.

The word sounded like another language through the gushing rain and almost constant thunder, mixed with the adrenaline racing through Billy's system. He turned his body the rest of the way to face John. Only feet away now, John held up one hand as if hailing a taxi.

John had said wait. Too late, the power needed a release, or Billy would explode. John was almost to him. One last time, he pictured where to direct the power, lashing out at each individual not an officer, or John. It would shove them the way he'd shoved the eighty-year-old man at the beach. Flying that far and landing on the wet grass would hurt them more than the water had the old man.

The power exploded from Billy's body as John reached him.

Instead of taking the brunt of John's force to the stomach, something bit Billy's left shoulder and his right calf. John spun in a half circle before falling at Billy's feet.

Billy lowered his eyes to his friend lying on the grass in front of him. Two stout arrows with white fletching stuck out from the center of his chest. John's hands grasped the shafts, his face twisted with pain.

Blood spattered on John's face. It fell from somewhere. Billy looked to his own chest and watched as blood poured from the bullet hole.

Falling to his knees, he dropped the plates beside John. The bites had been bullets. He glanced behind to his right leg; two holes pierced his jeans where his calf was. There was another flash of light to his right, not lightning, more compact, and his body spun in a circle. Landing on his back, he stared into the night sky. Raindrops pelted his face. The voices resumed their desperate yells.

An inferno flew in the sky over their heads, a twisting and roiling ball of flame. It didn't make sense. It shouldn't be there. More lights flashed around him, not the lightning, but just as bright. The screams he'd heard faded. John's breathing slowed with the shouts.

Flash.

Still surrounded. Some of the men held their guns in front of them. Some ran. Some laid still.

A soft laugh escaped Billy's lips; his ankle didn't hurt anymore.

Chapter 21

Billy

Flashing lights swirled in disarray, every color of the rainbow floated through the sunny cloud-filled sky. Silence. The scent of fresh cooked apple pies wafted by. He floated, bobbing up and down through the clouds. A soft sound echoed in the distance. *Singing*, Billy thought.

The clouds coalesced into ceiling tiles, still moving and twirling above him. The floating spiraled into dizziness. The smell of apple pie was replaced with the scent of industrial strength sanitizers. The kind used in a hospital. He blinked. *The hospital?*

Memories from the golf course accosted his mind, adrenaline renewed. He sat up but only made it a few inches before falling back down onto the hard hospital bed. Pain exploded in his chest and shoulder, and sweat dampened his brow. He blinked his eyes to clear them of the crusty goop. He must've been sleeping awhile.

The heart rate monitor beeped in unison with the rapid pounding of his heart. Only splintered, nonsensical pieces of his memory remained in his mind at any one time. Dizziness spun the room. He swallowed the rising bile from his empty stomach. He squeezed his eyes against the spell.

"Pleasant dream?"

Billy opened his eyes. He didn't recognize the voice, probably his nurse checking on his heart monitor.

"How long have I been here?" Speaking made his dry throat ache.

"Three days." The owner of the voice didn't come any closer. He was an outline against the white walls of the room.

Billy continued blinking, vision becoming clearer with each blink. "Are you my nurse? My doctor?" He lifted his head from the pillow a few inches and squinted.

"Probably a little of both, Billy Hitchings."

A chill ran down Billy's spine. The tone in the man's voice didn't sound right. It was too... cold.

"I have a police officer outside your door. You might know him. Sergeant Kirkwall?"

Dizziness threatened Billy again, adrenaline surging, now from fear.

"I see you do. His orders are to shoot to kill."

"Who are you?" His voice sounded so weak. He could see the man in front of him now, wearing blue jeans and a green polo shirt with a vest. Thirty or forty pounds overweight, most of it in his belly. He couldn't make out the man's face.

"Who am I? I guess that depends on how much you're willing to work with me, Billy." When the man said Billy's name, it came out like a curse; short and blunt.

"Jarrett?"

"Bingo, kid. If you haven't noticed, I have pull in this city. If you work with me, I'll get you cleared of all charges. But only if you do as I say. More is at stake here than just your puny little life, so think carefully before you make any decisions."

Billy's eyes cleared. The man looked as haggard as Billy felt; dark rings circled his eyes, shoulders slouched. The creases on his forehead told of immense stress. *Probably from being an asshole*, Billy thought.

"What do you want me for? Obviously I can't use the plates, or I wouldn't be here."

The man studied him with the focus of an artist, his head moved in a slight nod. "You're right about that, Billy. You can't use the plates. But you did something, though I'm betting it wasn't what you planned."

Billy's breath caught. "What do you mean?" He was afraid of the answer; in his mind, he saw the old man flying toward the ocean.

"You don't know? Well that's too bad. You seem like a nice kid." Sarcasm dripped from the man's every word. "Maybe I should just show you."

Jarrett stepped closer, and Billy's arms jumped with an involuntary twitch.

The man stopped and looked at him. "What? You think I was going to smack you or something?" The man let out a raucous laugh and picked up the television remote from the stand next to Billy.

Jarrett stepped to the end of Billy's bed and pointed the control at the television in the corner. The screen flashed on, and the volume blared.

Jarrett spoke over the sound of the television. "Let's see here. Shouldn't be too hard to find." The screen flashed a few times, stopping on a news channel. "There you go. Have a good look at what you did, Billy. What you caused. I'll be sure to leave you in here for a few hours, let you soak it all in." He tossed the control at Billy's feet.

Billy's eyes followed Jarrett as he walked from the room and closed the door behind. The sounds blasting from the television were too much to ignore. He turned to the screen. Destruction and chaos threatened to crush his soul, desolation filled every crevice within his mind. When the reporters showed the forlorn wail of a mother as she fell to her knees, Billy began to weep.

***

An eternity later, the sound from the television cut out. Billy didn't care. How could he? He wanted only to sleep. More painkillers, and to sleep.

The sudden pain in his leg brought him out of the dream state. Jarrett loomed over him, hand squeezing the two bullet holes under the bandages on Billy's calf. The pain was excruciating, though dwarfed by the pain in his soul.

"What do you want from me?" he moaned.

Jarrett let go. "You fool! Snap out of it. There isn't anything you can do now, except help me. Maybe by helping me you can relieve some of that guilt."

The visions from the screen still tore through his mind; the fire, the screams, the chaos.

"You hear me?"

"I don't care." Billy could feel the warm tears running down his face. "I just want out of here. Please, no more." He sounded pathetic.

"For the life of me, I can't figure out how you got away from Kirkwall for so long. They said you were strong. How strong can you be if you can't even accept what you did?" Jarrett harrumphed and stalked from the room, his shoes echoed across the linoleum floor.

Billy hated Jarrett, especially after what he pulled with the television, but his last words struck a chord. *If you don't accept blame for your mistakes, how can you move on to repair the wrongs?* One of the few things he remembered his father always saying before he passed.

With the television turned down low, Billy heard Jarrett talking quietly with someone in the hallway. The gruff man didn't look like he knew how to whisper. The man's presence had a physical bearing of its own. Billy turned his head toward the hallway, trying to see who he whispered to. Jarrett paused and looked in his direction.

Billy assumed what he hoped looked like a drug-induced stare; his eyes crossing, tongue lolling from his mouth. It must have worked because Jarrett resumed the whispering.

"I don't think he'll be any use to us. I don't think he even knows how he did it. His brain short circuited when I showed him the plane crash on the news."

The other voice came from a female, speaking just as soft as Jarrett. "Tom, I know you don't think he can help, but do you know for sure? Would you be willing to lose the chance if we had one? We've both said from the beginning, if there were anything in our power to help

Crystal, no matter how remote, we'd do it. That's the only reason we've come this far."

"I know, sweetheart."

Sweetheart? The man had a heart of stone.

"You're right," Jarrett continued. "I'm not sure what help he'll be, but we have to try. I just pray someday Crystal will forgive me for everything I've done."

Billy could only see Jarrett standing in the hallway, leaning on the nurse's desk. The person Jarrett spoke with lifted a hand to his cheek, and wiped away a tear.

"She's your daughter, Tom. She'll always love you, no matter what."

John

"Your fever is getting worse, John. If we go back to Morehead, I can get you some anti-biotics. If we stay here, you'll only get worse."

Sweat beaded on John's forehead though they were in an air-conditioned hotel room. Several of the men the Sheriff brought to Myrtle Beach were still there, but most returned home in case someone connected them to the plane crash. His stomach turned. Three days had passed, but authorities said it would take weeks to pull the rest of the wreckage from the Atlantic.

John mustered a smile. "You know, I wouldn't have a fever if your pals hadn't shot me."

Scott dabbed at the edges of John's wounds with an alcohol swab. "Don't try to turn this around on me. You're the one that figured out what could happen if he used the plates incorrectly. You knew how dangerous it would be."

"That's true, but I didn't tell you to shoot him."

Scott let out a deep sigh. "Apples and oranges, John. We needed to stop him, and a couple arrows were the fastest way to do that. How could my men know you'd jump in the way? Those arrows were both headed toward his shoulder." He let out a small laugh. "You're just lucky you passed out when you did. You didn't want to see what that doctor's so called office looked like anyway."

"Thanks for that, too. I pass out, so you send me to some work-from-home doctor. Don't you ever watch movies? Things never turn out the way they're supposed to when someone goes to a doctor at his house."

"Lucky for you, this isn't a movie," Sheriff Scott chuckled.

"You think Billy knows about the crash yet?"

"Hard to say. Kirkwall stands outside his door almost the entire day. When he leaves, two more officers take his place. It's going to destroy Billy when he does find out." John cringed at the touch of alcohol. "He's a strong kid, but knowing he caused something like that... He'll be changed forever. I don't think Jarrett will let him go, but that just means we'll have to make him."

"You mean I'm going to make him let go. You're not going anywhere, John. The doctor said those stitches holding you together could come apart easily. Nothing over twenty-five pounds, remember?"

"I remember, Mother. And my Glock is only two and a half pounds." One of Scott's men laughed. "I'll make you a deal. Let's get him out of there, but we'll be sneaky. I'll just be your backup. You and two of your boys could come up with a sham to get those officers away from the door." John moaned at the touch of alcohol again. "Long enough for us to get in and get out."

"I'm sure we could. But within forty-eight hours you won't be able to stand; even then, you might bleed to death from the inside out if you're not careful. Know when to walk away, John, even if it's only temporary. Billy is on his own now. Leave getting the plates to me and my men. And if we get the chance, we'll get him away from Jarrett." He paused. "You should think about going home. I'm sure the police will be looking for the man that had two arrows stuck in his chest."

"I'm just glad you're in such good shape. I don't know that I'd have been able to carry you back to the truck if you were the one that was shot." Scott could stop him from going after Billy with ease if he chose to. "You just said I wouldn't be able to walk in forty-eight hours right?"

Sheriff Scott nodded reluctantly.

"So we have that much time to figure something out and get Billy out of there. I can't leave him there, Robert. Not if he knows about the crash. He'll go crazy. Tell me that you'll help me."

Scott looked at him for a long time. His head moved in a slow nod.

"I'll help you, John Reeves. If for no other reason than there's something about you. My father called it the hunter's spirit."

Billy

Jarrett did this for his daughter? What does he mean he hopes she'll forgive him? What did he do? Billy was happy the painkillers were still in his system. His tongue lolled from the side of his mouth as he concentrated. When Jarrett glanced back to the room, Billy didn't have to pretend to be out of it. He already looked the part.

Jarrett looked back to the woman he whispered to and smiled. "I hope you're right, Lisa. The stress of the last two months is getting to me. Being so close, and then almost losing everything. It almost destroyed me. Seeing Crystal like that. It kills me. I want her pain to stop." Another tear escaped down his cheek.

The woman leaned in and hugged Jarrett, her head settled on his shoulder. Another burst of adrenaline ran through Billy's body, making his toes tingle and breathing grow louder. The woman Jarrett now hugged was the same one whose office he and John had taken the plates from. They had a daughter together?

The woman heard his heavy breathing and lifted her head. She whispered to Tom. "He's still drugged right? He can't hear what we're saying?"

"He's as high as a kite. Look at the way he's slobbering."

Lisa nodded and gave Tom a quick kiss on the cheek and wiped away another tear. "Okay, sweetheart. I'm going to check in on Crystal before I go home. Are you going to be there tonight?"

"I'm not sure. Depends on Billy boy there." He nodded in Billy's direction. "With or without the drugs, if he doesn't start talking soon, I may have to make him."

"I don't want to hear about that. I'll see you tomorrow then."

They gave each other another hug and parted ways, leaving Kirkwall to watch his door.

"Have a good night, Dr. Gibbons," said a new voice.

Billy couldn't see who it was, but Lisa, or Dr. Gibbons, nodded and walked away.

Jarrett pulled his shoulders back a little and straightened himself. His voice took on the rough edge he used when speaking to Billy.

"Dr. Pierce." Jarrett nodded to the newcomer.

The woman stepped into view and Billy's heart sank. Kelly Pierce, John's fiancée, or at least she used to be. *What the hell is she doing here?*

"I trust you've taken care of things like we discussed?" Jarrett's forehead wrinkled as he lifted his brow.

"Everything is taken care of, Mr. Jarrett. The plates and the manuscript are both returned to Jackson Incorporated and under constant supervision."

"Good." Jarrett sighed. "No more mistakes. I still don't know how your boyfriend, or whatever he is, figured everything out."

"I don't know either, Mr. Jarrett, but I prefer not to talk about it." Kelly's face didn't betray any emotion.

Jarrett nodded. "I'll see you back at Morehead by the end of the week then."

It was Kelly's turn to nod as she looked toward Billy's room. He squinted, pretending to sleep. Jarrett's eyes followed Kelly's.

"What is it, Kelly? You have a thing for drugged out nineteen-year-olds with a broken spirit?"

Jarrett smiled, but Kelly didn't. She continued looking toward the room.

"I thought maybe I could try to talk to him." Her voice came out a whisper.

"You have some insight into kids his age that I don't know about?"

"I have a brother his age." She looked back to Jarrett. She reminded Billy of a puppy begging for food. The outer half of her brows lowered, and the edges of her mouth turned in a slight pout.

Jarrett watched her for a moment and then nodded. "Do whatever you want. He's fallen, Kelly. He's broken. When he saw what happened, he shut down."

"I feel like I should try." Kelly looked back toward the room.

Jarrett nodded again and held out his hand toward the room, as if he introduced her to some grand show.

Kelly took her time walking in. Billy had his eyes closed the rest of the way. Her slow footsteps echoed through the small room until they stopped at the end of his bed.

"Billy Hitchings," he heard her say.

He didn't dare open his eyes to see if Jarrett still watched.

"I've never met anyone who brought so much pain to so many people. It's disgusting."

Her every word bit into his soul. John said he loved this woman. *How could he love something so evil?*

"Jarrett says you're broken, that you've given up. Is that true?"

Billy opened his eyes. He wasn't sure if he'd done it on purpose or not, but he didn't want to pretend anymore.

"I'm not sure you can comprehend this or not, but the pain you caused is nothing compared to what Jarrett is going to do to you."

I don't care. He's right. I am broken. There's nothing he can do to my body worse than what's been done to my spirit...

Kelly took two quick steps and lurched across Billy's chest, her hands holding down his arms. She gritted her teeth while she spoke just above a whisper. "Billy, pay attention to me."

Billy's heart rate monitor beeped faster.

"I only have a moment before Jarrett figures out something is going on. He knows you used the plates. He knows something went wrong. They know more about the plates than anybody does. Him and his wife, or whatever she is." The whole time she kept her face only inches from his. "John says you're strong, Billy. And he's not wrong about much. Quit your sulking, quit feeling sorry for yourself, and get your ass out of here."

The heart rate monitor beeped so fast Billy couldn't believe there weren't nurses rushing in to save him.

"Wait, did John send you?" The words croaked from Billy's mouth.

Kelly smiled. "Nobody sent me. I work alone." She pushed herself up and stalked toward Jarrett still in the hallway.

"Well?" Jarrett asked.

"You're right. I don't know what I was thinking. He wouldn't even talk when I got in his face. He just mumbled."

"Maybe it's better he didn't know how to use the plates." Jarrett looked toward Billy's room and shook his head. "See you in Morehead, Dr. Pierce."

***

Billy didn't know what it was like to be in shock, but was certain he felt it right then. He'd caused a passenger jet to crash into the Atlantic a half-mile from the beach. Lisa and Jarrett knew something about the plates. Maybe what they knew could have stopped him from pulling apart the jet and killing almost two hundred passengers. Maybe whatever Jarrett did that he needed forgiveness for was the very thing that had caused Billy to lose control of the plates.

Familiar anger grew in the pit of his stomach, different than it had with the plates, but similar. He couldn't feel the thrumming of the plates, or the vibration in his throat, but the pure rage running through his veins was exactly the same. A lot of good it did to have the anger without the plates. Whatever drugs had been in his system were gone, driven out by his adrenaline. His thoughts were crisp again, as pure as his anger.

He still faced in the direction of his door. A portly nurse rounded the desk carrying a cup of coffee held in both hands. His nurse. The one checking his IV line and painkillers on a regular basis. *Jarrett probably bought her out too.* Billy didn't think so, though. Every time she checked on him, she'd give him a new detail about her grandchildren, reminding him of the way Grams talked about him.

The laces on her left shoe were untied, one floating through the wind generated by her steps. As it landed on the linoleum with her next step, Billy already knew what would happen. Her other foot followed and stepped directly onto the untied lace sitting on the floor, her weight transferring to that foot. The foot with the untied lace began to lift from the floor and stopped after a few inches. The nurse's eyes opened wide, as did her mouth. Her hands moved toward the floor when the momentum threw the cup forward, hot coffee pouring from the top as it flew. Straight toward Kirkwall.

Kirkwall raised his hand, as if it would stop the coffee. The cup's momentum carried it into his hand as if he'd been the one carrying it the whole time, black coffee splashed onto his chest. Meanwhile, the tripping nurse had somehow caught herself before landing face first on the hard linoleum and been strong enough to push herself back to standing before the cup landed in the officer's hand. She stumbled into Kirkwall. The coffee continued its trek down his jacket and onto her hands.

She shrieked. Nurse Lindberg was her name. Nurse Lindberg shrieked and hurried into Billy's room to the sink. She held her hands in front, blisters already appearing. Kirkwall followed her into the room, cussing. She ran cold water over her fingers, her face red from pain.

"What the hell was that!" Kirkwall yelled. "This is an $800 suit your clumsy ass just spilled coffee on."

"I'm sorry, sir. If you would just hold on for a moment I'll be happy to help you." She looked over her shoulder at the tall police officer. "Are you okay? Other than your suit I mean?"

"No, I'm not okay. Are you going to pay for this? Who the hell makes coffee that hot anyway?"

The water still ran over the Nurse Lindberg's fingers, but the red in her cheeks receded.

What just happened? Did I cause the nurse to fall? Or did I cause her to keep from falling the rest of the way? Or neither? Billy felt horrible for Nurse Lindberg. The few times she'd spoken with him in his stupor, she'd only shown him kindness. A kind soul. She didn't deserve the burn, and she certainly didn't deserve Kirkwall yelling at her.

Billy wished the plates were there so he could use them to hurt Kirkwall. *No!* Every time he used them to help, he only caused pain. *What good are the plates if I can't even stop Kirkwall from yelling at this nice woman?*

"Oh." Nurse Lindberg turned off the water. "Isn't that odd?"

"You not helping me, or you whispering to yourself over there?" Kirkwall wiped at the stains growing on his suit.

The nurse turned toward Kirkwall, hands held out in front of her as she turned them over. "I guess they weren't as bad as I thought." Her hands were a little red, but the blisters Billy saw forming were gone. "Why don't you come with me, Mr. Kirkwall. I'll find somebody to take you down to the cafeteria. A little soda water and that coffee will come right out."

"Soda water? Are you serious?"

Nurse Lindberg nodded.

"I guess it wouldn't hurt to try. Not like I even need to be here. The kid is so out of it over there in his slobber. He didn't even move when we came in."

"Let's get that jacket off you." Nurse Lindberg urged Kirkwall toward the door. "You're right. I've been giving Billy his medication myself. He isn't going anywhere."

Kirkwall nodded and followed her through the door and down the hallway.

The corners of Billy's mouth curled to form a smile. *Time to visit my friend.*

***

Nurse Nancy Klapper, the same nurse who admitted Eric the night he passed out, had been working the front desk of the emergency room when Billy walked by. Her happiness in seeing him seemed genuine enough, but he didn't care either way because she'd given him Eric's room number. She explained that he'd left the intensive care unit the night before, and was under heavy sedation. She told him too, that he wasn't in very good shape, that they pumped him full of painkillers, 'trying to ease his passage' she said.

When he'd been able to speak again, he thanked her and went in search of his friend's room. Now he waited outside the door to room 315, barely able to breathe. His best friend was behind this door, and it may be the last time Billy saw him. He hoped he'd be awake enough to at least allow Billy to say his goodbyes.

The dark green metal door opened with a light grinding sound. Billy peeked in, but couldn't see in the dark room. He slipped in and closed the door as quiet as he could, then pressed the locking mechanism down. If he was going to say goodbye to his friend. He was going to say it on his terms.

He flipped the switch to turn on two small corner lamps, just enough to illuminate the room. Two steps toward the bed where Eric laid, and he stopped, almost getting sick. It was Eric, but it didn't look like him. The circles under his eyes were almost black. His face so gaunt Billy thought he could see the bones beneath. Where he'd been feeling anger a few minutes before, he now felt sorrow. As deep as the day he'd learned his parents passed. This was his last chance to say goodbye to his friend, nothing would get in his way.

Eric's eyes popped open and he sat straight up, staring at Billy.

"Eric?"

"Billy? What are you doing here? I thought you were in the emergency room."

"Sit back, Eric. You don't look so well. You need your rest."

Eric's face flushed. He leaned back, placing one elbow on the pillow and propping his head up on his hand.

"You don't look so well, yourself. They told me you were shot like four times."

"I was, and it still hurts pretty damn bad." Eric always made him smile, and he was so happy at seeing his friend, this time was no different. When he began to laugh, pain shot through his shoulder and up into his neck. He leaned forward onto Eric's bed, catching himself.

"I can see that." He scooted over to one side of the bed and gestured toward the free half. "Not much room, but if you need to sit down for a minute, feel free."

Eric was on his deathbed, and yet he was the one offering Billy a place to sit.

"Didn't you have surgery yesterday?" Billy sat gently on the free space offered by Eric. "Nurse Klapper said you were out of it."

"I was... I think. I don't remember much of yesterday, except the pain. They were going to remove part of my large intestine" He felt at his stomach with his free hand. "Honestly, it doesn't hurt all that bad, barely noticeable."

"She said you'd be drugged up pretty good, too." His poor friend had so many drugs in his system he couldn't even tell he'd had surgery the day before. *At least he won't feel pain when he passes.* "I came to say goodbye, Eric."

"Goodbye? Where you going?"

How embarrassing, he almost lost it and cried in front of his friend. The noise that had escaped from his mouth sounded like a large hiccup so he played it off as one. "Sorry about that, um..."

"You said you were going somewhere." Eric looked at him expectantly, brows raised.

"Yeah. I'm leaving, Eric, and I don't know when I'll be able to come back... if ever. I've done something horrible, something I'm not sure even you could forgive me for. Anyway, I've been given a second chance, and I have to leave before they catch up with me."

"Oh come on, Billy. It couldn't be that bad..."

Billy didn't say anything.

"Could it? You know what? I don't care. It doesn't matter what you did. I know you, and I know if you did something horrible, it was an accident." Eric frowned and looked at his stomach, his right hand rubbed it again.

"Are you okay?" Billy leaned back.

"Actually, yeah. I feel good. They must have changed my drugs again; I hardly feel any pain at all."

Billy rose, staring at his friend.

"Why are you looking at me like that? Do I have a booger on me or something?" He wiped his hand over his nose.

This time Billy did cry. He sobbed, and he didn't care if his friend saw the tears. He leaned forward and hugged his friend where he laid. At first, Eric didn't move. A moment later, he returned a tentative hug, then tighter.

"You'll always be my best friend, Eric. I hope you know that." He let go and stepped back, wiping tears from his eyes with his shirt. Eric wiped some away too. "I have to go, but I'll see you again."

"You must not be going very far if you're going to see me again. We already talked about this. Doc said I'm not going to make it through next week, man. I may be okay now, but that's just the meds."

"I've never said this before, but have faith my friend." Billy leaned forward, placing his hand on Eric's shoulder. "Have faith. I'll see my best friend again, and it will be after next week, after Christmas." He lifted his hand and took a few steps toward the door.

"Wait. I don't know if you're still on pain meds yourself or what, but you don't make any sense. Either way, thanks for coming to see me again. I was afraid I wouldn't have the chance to say goodbye."

And now you don't have to.

"I have one more stop to make before I leave town. Thanks for always being there, Eric. I'll see you soon." He gave his friend a wave and left the room. He needed to speak with nurse Klapper one more time.

John

"Your boys in place?"

"They are." Sheriff Scott flipped on the blinker and turned the corner. "Remember, those *boys* saved your life a few nights ago. I would call any of them a man sooner than most adults I know."

"I'm sorry." John raised a hand and continued looking out the window of the Oldsmobile. "You're right. It's just the way I talk, Sheriff. You won't hear me call them boys again."

"Ethan and Joel are in place. They're waiting for my call." The car came to a stop. Scott put the car in park and turned it off.

John hurt more than he let Sheriff Scott know. He'd coughed up blood earlier too, and the fever burned him up from the inside. They'd have to make this fast. He put his hand on the door handle, and his phone vibrated across the dashboard.

"Don't answer it." Scott shook his head. "We don't have much time. Call them back when we're done."

John pulled on the handle and pushed the door open a few inches. The phone vibrated again. He shook his head and picked it up. Amfar's name flashed on the small blue screen.

"It's Amfar." John flipped the phone open. "This isn't the best time, Amfar."

"John, wait! Stay on the phone."

Amfar had left for Morehead the morning after John became a pincushion for arrows. They'd decided it best if they weren't in contact for a while.

"I'm here. What is it?"

"Are you near a television?"

Scott opened his door and climbed from the vehicle.

"Not really. We're at the hospital. We're going to get Billy from Jarrett."

"You need to get to a television first. Watch channel eight. Please. There is something going on... wait, you're at the hospital in Myrtle Beach?"

"Yes." John was losing his patience and his willpower.

"Enter on the west side then. That is what I wanted you to see anyway."

"Is that all?"

"It is. Be well."

John looked in the rearview mirror to see Scott leaning against the back of the car. "Amfar?"

"Yes, John?"

He let out a deep sigh. "Take care of Kelly. Okay?"

Amfar paused. "I'm not sure what you mean."

"Don't make me slap ya next time I see you, Amfar."

Amfar sputtered a moment. He cleared his throat. "I will always treat Kelly with the utmost respect."

John sighed again. "That's all I ask."

John tossed the phone back on the dashboard, and pushed the door of the Oldsmobile open the rest of the way. Sheriff Scott came around to the passenger side of the car and helped him out.

"What did he want?"

John groaned. Without Scott helping, pulling himself from the car would've been near impossible.

"He said we need to enter on the west side."

"Why?"

"No clue. Doesn't really matter though, does it?"

Before long, he'd have to lean on the Sheriff just to walk. He hoped to get out of there before it came to that. On their way to the west side of the building, a couple hospital employees walked by on the way to the parking lot. He did his best to act and walk normally. It wouldn't do him or Billy any good if one of the nurses forced him to the emergency room.

John concentrated on the pain in his chest with every vibration of his step. Sweat fell from his nose to the pavement.

He ran into Scott. He hadn't seen him stop. "Why would you stop like that? Why would—" He couldn't finish his thought.

There were no less than ten news crews grouped in front of the west side of the hospital. Surrounding them were hospital patients, at least they looked like patients. They wore the open backed gowns, yet walked amongst the crews. Other people were there too, perhaps family members of the patients. Everywhere John looked, people cried, hugged, and shook hands.

"What the hell is going on here?" John's words came out as a whisper.

"I'm not sure." Scott's mouth fell open as far as John's must have been. "Those look like patients, but why would they be running around outside like this?"

"I don't know. Let's get in closer to one of the news crews."

Now, he did use Scott as a crutch. They hobbled forward, standing behind a group of four or five men, probably in their eighties, laughing and chatting together as if old friends. John concentrated on the reporter behind.

"...and now they are all outside, some having been bedridden for months. Hospital officials aren't commenting yet, but say there will be a conference in one hour to dispense whatever details they are able at that time." A small, pale girl, about twelve years old wandered by the reporter. "Hi there, sweetheart." The reporter placed a hand on the girl's petite shoulder. "Can you tell us what happened?"

"Me?" The girl shied away from the reporter, but kept her shoulders squared.

Tough little one, John thought.

"Of course, honey. You can be on television. We won't take long. What happened? Did somebody release something in the hospital? Did the Doctor's give you some kind of new drug? How is it that every person on the oncology floor is suddenly cured?"

John fell to his butt, and Scott let him fall.

"I'm not really sure," she said quietly, just loud enough for John to hear over the buzz from the crowd. "My mommy tucked me in so she could go to our house to go to sleep. Then I saw a skinny man walk into our hallway. I remember him really good because he made me happy."

"He made you happy?" The reporter's brow furrowed.

"Yeah. I don't know how to tell it better. He made everybody happy, all of my friends. He walked into our room and gave me the biggest hug."

"Did he say anything?"

"Yeah... he said, I didn't need to be scared anymore. He told me that my parents loved me very much, and they would be coming to take me home."

The reporter stared at the girl. She must have been as awestruck as John because she didn't ask any more questions. She rubbed her hand on the girl's back and smiled. As the girl walked away, tears poured from the reporter's eyes, much as they were from John's own.

His eyes followed the poor thing, white as a ghost as she worked her way through the crowd. John's heart stopped when he saw Tom Jarrett walking toward them. The man looked scared to death. His head swiveled back and forth as his eyes went to the girl. His hands flew to his mouth, and he began to shake. Tears welled in his eyes.

The girl wandered for a few seconds before she saw Jarrett. She stopped where she stood. She threw her hands in the air and yelled, "Daddy!" Moments later, a woman with dark brown hair joined them in a beautiful embrace.

"By all that is holy in this world, what's happened here, John?"

"I'm not sure, Sheriff." He fought back more tears. "But I have a feeling Billy won't need us to save *him*."

The End

Thank you so much for taking the time to delve into Billy's world. Feel free to leave a quick comment on the Fall of Billy Hitchings page at Amazon or other online retailers. I look forward to hearing what you think!

Kirkus MacGowan

Don't miss the next John Reeves novel from Kirkus MacGowan

Wrath

Available Now!

1. The Phone Call

"Can you start from the beginning again, Doug? I need to make sure nothing was missed." Alan leafed through the pages of the report. Questioning a close friend like Douglas Fincham was never easy, one of the disadvantages of working as a small-town police officer.

Doug lifted his dusty cowboy hat and ran his fingers through his fringe of gray hair. "Again? How many times you boys need me to go over it? I already told them everything I remember." Doug gestured to the other officers around the police department, typing away or chatting on the phone.

"I'm sure you did, but we need to make sure we don't make any mistakes. You disappeared for over a week with no memory of it. Not an everyday occurrence. You're a friend, Doug. Heck, you're more than a friend. I'm doing everything I can to make sure something like this doesn't happen again. Besides, you told *them*, not me."

Doug sighed and replaced his hat. "Last thing I recollect is loading Johnny's food in the back of the old Dodge." Doug had named his yellow lab after his brother, saying they were both too loud for their own good. "I remember, because my back was hurting real bad that day."

"From when you fell off the barn?"

The broad shouldered man and his wife invited Alan over for dinner at least once a month. He'd been there the day Doug tumbled from the barn roof. An occasional sore back was lucky considering how far he'd fallen.

"That's right. Always tightens up at the worst times." Doug shifted in his seat. "Anyway, I'm throwing the dog food in the truck, and I get a real bad pain in my back. Worse than normal. Next thing I know, I'm lying in the ditch over by Hailey's farm and getting rained on." His face flushed. "I woke up bare as the day I was born, laying there on my side like I was sleeping."

Calming Doug's wife had been virtually impossible. The case was as crazy as any Alan had heard in his ten years on the Clarkbridge police force. He spent most of his time scheduling shifts, writing speeding tickets, or handing out report and repairs. He'd moved back to his hometown to take it easy, live the life of a small-town officer. Clarkbridge wasn't as small as it used to be, but it was much smaller than Detroit where he'd begun his career.

Alan looked at the stack of papers on his desk and adjusted his loosened tie. Cooper Forbes, a fellow officer, had written the report the previous day when they'd found Doug. "Do you remember the name of the woman who found you?"

"Of course I do. Doesn't it say so in your report?" Doug pointed to the pile.

"It does. Just double checking."

"Fine, fine. I'll play along. Natasha Green. Leslie plays spades with her on Thursdays." He laughed. "I'm not a shy man, Alan, but you should've seen the look on her face when I came up out of that ditch. She slammed on her brakes and almost hit me. You would have thought I was wiggling my willy when she climbed out. Her face was as red as a firehouse. Didn't know a face could turn that red."

Natasha was a regular at Doug and Leslie's for dinner. To say she was reserved was an understatement. "I can only imagine." Alan let out his own laugh.

Sergeant Shaw shushed him, and Gibbs just shook his head—two of the three officers assigned to the next shift.

Alan continued. "She brought you straight to the station?"

"Sure did."

Alan hoped Doug's disappearance wasn't some kind of episode. He'd heard it happened on occasion with people getting on in years. The old farmer seemed to be made of tougher stuff than most, but one never knew.

"One last question, Doug. I don't want you to get upset."

"What's that, Alan?" Doug leaned forward.

"Dr. Howard said he'll get the tox report back to us tomorrow. Will we find anything you haven't told us about?"

The other officers had been too nervous to ask the large man if he'd taken any drugs. They'd asked Alan to do it because of their friendship.

"Tox report?"

Alan adjusted his tie again and smoothed the front of his starched dark-brown shirt. "It's short for toxicology report. That's why we drew blood yesterday. It measures any chemicals you may have in your system, like alcohol or... drugs."

Doug leaned back in his seat and lowered his bushy eyebrows. "Why would you even ask?" His voice took on a menacing tone. "You know I don't do none of that stuff." He crossed his arms and looked away.

I shouldn't have let the chief talk me into taking this case. "I know you don't do drugs. Could you have had a drink or two? It measures things like high levels of allergy meds or pain-killers, too."

"Oh, well, why didn't you say that? I wasn't doing any drinking, but I take them horse pills Doc Howard gave me. Helps with the back pain. I only take them every few weeks or so, when the ache gets real bad. Like I told you, it was extra tight that day, so I'd taken a couple in the morning."

"Do you remember the name of the horse pills?"

Doug drew his brows down, rubbing his fingers through his trimmed white beard. "Valium? No, not Valium. That was Leslie's sister." He stared at the floor a moment. "Vicotron... or Vitridun..."

"Vicodin?"

"That's the stuff. Doc knows how to prescribe them, doesn't he? First time I took one, I slept fourteen hours."

A grin grew on Alan's face. "How many do you usually take?"

"Usually just one. Sometimes two if it gets real bad."

Alan penned a note about the Vicodin into the report. "Well, that should be it unless you think of anything else."

"I don't think so. You boys have almost run me dry with all your questions."

They stood. Alan offered his hand. Alan was larger than most men, but Doug's hand dwarfed his own when they shook.

"You have my number," Alan said. "Call me if you think of anything, even if you don't think it's a big deal. It might give us a clue as to what happened."

"Will do." Doug pulled the faded tan jacket over his thick shoulders and turned to leave.

Alan sat in his swivel chair, wondering if he'd missed something. *This doesn't make sense. What were you doing in a ditch, Doug? Why don't you remember anything?*

Doug was almost to the front entrance when he stopped. He strode back to Alan's desk.

Alan raised his chin. "Remember something?"

"Kind of. You said to tell you if there was anything else, even if it wasn't a big deal."

"That's right."

"Well... you mentioned the pain killers and it got me thinking. My back doesn't hurt at all. To be honest, it feels better than it has in years. Like I could go out dancing." He held his arms to the side and tapped his feet in a small jig.

"Really? You think you were kidnapped by a chiropractor?"

Doug let out a raucous laugh. "Wouldn't that be a story to tell? Anyway, that's it. My back feels right dandy."

Alan's phone rang. "I should get this." He tossed the report on his desk and reached for the handset. "You stay out of trouble, Doug. Tell Leslie we're still on for her lasagna this weekend."

Doug waved and headed toward the door.

The man on the phone asked for Douglas Fincham. Alan placed his palm over the receiver. "Hey, Doug. It's for you." He held the phone out.

"For me? Only one knows I'm here is Leslie, and she knows I'll be coming home when I'm done. Maybe she wants me to stop at the store. She's always forgetting something."

"It's not Leslie. It's a man. You want me to ask who it is?"

Doug shook his head, taking the phone. "This is Doug." A short pause. "What was that?" The old man's face went slack. He slowly lowered the phone to the desk.

"Is everything okay?" Alan put the phone to his ear. A busy signal. He sat the phone on the cradle.

Doug's blank gaze lowered.

"Doug? What's going on?"

The old farmer's eyes met Alan's. They peered through him, seeing something a hundred miles away. His skin paled further. He crumpled, sitting down right where he stood. Alan shot around the desk to catch his friend before he went the rest of the way down.

"Talk to me, Doug. What happened?"

No response. Bubbling white foam dribbled from Doug's mouth. His face pinched into a snarl and his body shook, eyes bulging. He reached for his own neck with both hands.

"Shit. Somebody get Doc Howard on the phone." Alan gave Doug's shoulders a violent shake. *God, don't take Doug from me too*, Alan prayed.

Cooper ran to Alan's side and paused; his mouth moved, but no words came out. His buggy eyes flitted back and forth. Sergeant Shaw pounded the numbers on her phone.

Doug's face slowly turned purple. Alan laid him back on the floor. He pried open the man's mouth and peered down his throat, hoping to remove whatever choked him.

Empty.

Even if Alan couldn't see an obstruction, the old man gagged on something. Alan slid behind Doug and lifted his shoulders, wrapping his long arms around his stomach. They barely fit around the man's girth. The Heimlich maneuver was near impossible.

"I got dispatch," Shaw called "We got a bus on the way."

"Call Doc Howard, Coop," Alan groaned.

Cooper nodded and turned to use Alan's phone. Sergeant Gibbs kneeled beside Alan, grabbing Doug's shoulders to help sit him upright.

Doug's body convulsed. He slapped at his arms as if they burned, grunting with each smack. Blood vessels popped in Doug's eyes, turning them red. His skin was purple from the neck up.

"This isn't working." Alan clambered up. Doug's leg jerked, knocking Alan from his feet. Sergeant Gibbs reached to catch him, but missed. Alan's head banged on the corner of his desk. He rolled to his back and put his hand to his temple. Sticky blood covered his fingers. Cooper bent to help him up.

"Not me, Coop. Help Doug." Alan pointed to his friend.

Cooper turned back to the old man. Red stained Doug's tan coat sleeves as blood soaked through. "What the hell is happening?" Cooper took a step toward the man on the floor.

Alan held his hand tight over the gash on his brow. Doug flailed and then went stiff. He collapsed unmoving, releasing what little breath he had left in him.

Cooper put his trembling fingers to Doug's neck. They came away bloody. "I can't get a pulse, too much blood."

"Try the wrist," Alan said, as Gibb's helped him to his feet.

Cooper slid Doug's jacket sleeve to the elbow. Long gashes ran up his arm. Dark red lifeblood seeped from each cut. He put his fingers to the old man's wrist. "He's dead, Alan."

Gibbs and Shaw watched in silence, their faces pale. The nightmare had taken less than a minute.

"No way he's dead." Alan let go of his own wound and scrambled onto the large man's abdomen. He pumped with both hands. Red droplets cascaded to Doug's chest with each pump. "Where is the God damn ambulance?" He continued pumping, not waiting for an answer. He counted to thirty and tilted Doug's head back. He tried to breathe life into him. A gurgling noise came from his friend.

"My God," Cooper whispered.

Sergeant Shaw's hand shot to her mouth. She turned away. Alan sat back. Frothy blood bubbled from Doug's throat. Every ounce of air Alan forced in came back out through a gash running almost ear to ear across Doug's neck, as if someone had slit his throat.

Alan trembled with his bloody hands held out before him. "There's no way. I was right here with him the whole time. No way this just happened."

About the Author

Kirkus MacGowan wrote his first book at age eight about traveling to Mars to find the cure for cancer. He put his writing dreams on hold for twenty-five years and focused his energies on playing baseball. The day he found playing softball with friends more satisfying than baseball, he quit and never looked back.

Since then, he graduated with a B.S. in Psychology, married a woman too good to be true, and moved back to his hometown. He gave up an amazing career waiting tables and now stays at home with his two crazy children. He spends his time writing thrillers and fantasy, playing softball with friends, enjoying the occasional computer game, and wrestling with his kids.

Learn more at:

www.kirkusmacgowan.info